T0271699

Rainy Season

JOSÉ EDUARDO AGUALUSA was born in Huambo in 1960 and is one of the leading literary voices from Angola, and from the Portuguese language today. *Creole* was awarded the Portuguese Grand Prize for Literature, *The Book of Chameleons* won the Independent Foreign Fiction Prize 2007, and *My Father's Wives* was longlisted for the same prize in 2009. Agualusa divides his time between Angola and Portugal.

DANIEL HAHN is a writer of non-fiction, the editor of reference books for adults and children, and a translator. His translations include José Eduardo Agualusa's novels *Creole*, *The Book of Chameleons* (winner of the Independent Foreign Fiction Prize 2007), *My Father's Wives*, and the autobiography of Brazilian footballer Pelé.

JOSÉ EDUARDO AGUALUSA

Rainy Season

Translated from the Portuguese
by Daniel Hahn

First published in the Portuguese language as Estação das Chuvas
by Publicações Dom Quixote, Lisbon, in 1996
First published in Great Britainin 2009 by

Arcadia Books
An imprint of Quercus Editions Limited
Carmelite House
50 Victoria Embankment
London EC4Y 0DZ

An Hachette UK company

Copyright © José Eduardo Agualusa 1996
English translation and Translator's Diarycopyright © Daniel Hahn 2009

The moral right of José Eduardo Agualusa to be
identified as the author of this work has been
asserted in accordance with the Copyright,
Designs and Patents Act, 1988.

Daniel Hahn asserts his moral right
to be identified as the translator of the work.

All rights reserved. No part of this publication
may be reproduced or transmitted in any form
or by any means, electronic or mechanical,
including photocopy, recording, or any
information storage and retrieval system,
without permission in writing from the publisher.

A CIP catalogue record for this book is available
from the British Library.

ISBN(TPB)978 1 90641 320 0

This book is a work of fiction. Names, characters,
organisations, places and events are
either the product of the author's imagination
or are used fictitiously. Any resemblance to
actual persons, living or dead, events or
particular places is entirely coincidental.

10 9 8 7 6 5 4 3 2

Typeset in Minion by MacGuru Ltd
Printed and bound in Great Britain by Clays Ltd, Elcograf S.p.A.

Papers used by Quercus Books are from well-managed forests and other responsible sources.

In memory of Mário Pinto de Andrade

Contents

The Beginning   1
Poetry   15
The Search   41
Exile   55
The Eternal Day   77
Euphoria   113
Fear   127
Fury   145
The End   171

References   193
Glossary of Acronyms   194
Translator's Diary   197

THE BEGINNING

'In the name of the people of Angola, the Central Committee of the Popular Movement for the Liberation of Angola, the MPLA, solemnly proclaims, before Africa and the world, the independence of Angola. At this time the people of Angola and the MPLA Central Committee shall observe a minute's silence and determine that the heroes who fell for the cause of Angola's independence shall live forever.'

Agostinho Neto, in Luanda, at 00:20 on 11 November 1975

Chapter 1

That night Lídia dreamt of the sea. It was a deep sea, dark and full of slow creatures that seemed to be made of that same sad light you see at dusk. Lídia didn't know where she was, but she knew that they were jellyfish. As she awoke she could still make them out moving across the walls, and it was then that she remembered her grandmother, Dona Josephine do Carmo Ferreira, aka Nga Fina Diá Makulussu, a famous interpreter of dreams. According to the old lady, to dream about the sea was to dream about death.

She opened her eyes and saw the great pendulum clock hanging on the wall. It was twenty minutes past midnight. Angola was already independent. She thought about this, and wondered at her being there, lying in that bed, in the old house of the Ingombotas. What was she doing in that country? A useless question, that tormented her every day.

But at that moment it had another meaning: what was she doing there?

She was lucid and felt nothing, neither the bitterness of the defeated nor the euphoria of the victors (it was both at once that night). 'It's the night of the praying mantis,' she thought. And she saw herself, newborn, with a large praying mantis resting on her chest.

When she was small, old Jacinto had talked to her about it: 'Not long after you were born your mother looked over at you and saw a huge praying mantis on your chest.' Much later, Grandmother Fina had retold the episode. She had said to her, 'Life will swallow you up.'

Grandmother Fina had turned 105 that month, but remained a practical, solid woman, just as she had always been. Lídia believed in everything she said, including her premonitions. She considered waking her grandmother to tell her of the dream, but she didn't move. She had no strength. She inhaled the *quicombo*-wood-perfumed air deeply, and felt lighter. A distant, round rumbling drifted to her ears; she couldn't separate the different sounds but knew that they were gunshots, explosions, cries of pain, of fury, of delight. Almost all were sounds of rage, but there must have been some groans of love too, the barking of dogs, the deep sound of beating hearts. Lídia thought about Viriato da Cruz, she thought about death, she thought that beyond her closed bedroom windows life was carrying on. She sat up in bed, reached her hand out and took from her nightstand a little black-covered notebook, one of those long notebooks that grocers use to pencil down the day's accounts.

'Life is happening out there,' she wrote. She crossed the line out and wrote again: 'Out there life was happening / In all its brutal splendour.'

Then she put a circle round the two lines and added the date: '11th of November 1975'.

Chapter 2

On Mayday Square, the President was addressing the crowd. Shortly before he stepped up onto the rostrum a young officer got out of a jeep to give him a message from Commander Jacob Caetano, better known as The Immortal Beast. The situation was critical: the South African columns had advanced some eight hundred kilometres, pulverising the southern and central fronts. Now they were preparing to take the small city of Novo Redondo. In Quifangondo, at such a small distance away that when the wind blew more strongly the square filled with the nervous coughing of machine guns, Cuban soldiers were fighting alongside the FAPLA against the old Portuguese commandos, regular Zairean forces and the guerrilla fighters of Daniel Chipenda and Holden Roberto.

Coloured bullets grazed the night and no one could say whether they were part of the festivities or of the machinery of war. The city's skies had been transformed into an immense trap. Luanda's destiny was so uncertain that many of the delegations invited to attend the ceremony – including the one from the Soviet Union – had chosen not to show up.

The President spoke for forty minutes. When he finished, there was a moment of wonder throughout the square. The President was very upright in the blue suit, with the unshining eyes behind thick lenses, the sad smile – or ironic smile? – with which we always saw him. The same that he would be wearing when they would have to embalm him four years later.

So there was the tiniest moment of wonder through the whole square. At least, that is how I imagine the scene (I wasn't there). The slim figure of the President in the middle of the platform and all around him a dark mass of soldiers, invited guests and high-ranking dignitaries from the regime. In front of him, in that moment of silence, the anonymous populace.

And then the crowd burst into shouts and in an explosion of joy hurled themselves forward, just as the cavalry advanced to protect the rostrum. Lying face-down on her *quicombo*-wood bed, Lídia Ferreira felt the air of her room fill with a violent uproar, and felt herself touched again by the embrace of the sea.

Chapter 3

Lídia do Carmo Ferreira was born in 1928, in Chela, in a decrepit and isolated little farm, half hidden between two big green hills. When she was two years old, her paternal great-grandfather came to take her to Luanda. This was why Lídia didn't retain an image in her memory of the place where she was born, only sensations, the sense of something green and powerful.

In 1988 I went to Lubango. I left Luanda in an army plane, a Casa, with wooden benches along the fuselage and little round windows almost at floor level. We flew along the coast towards the South, and shortly before reaching Namibe turned inland. Crouching down, my face stuck to the window, I could see how the ground suddenly gave a huge leap up and the whole landscape changed colour.

On my first night in Lubango I had dinner with representatives of the party's youth. To my right sat a young man with a broad face and stiff, copper-coloured hair. He introduced himself: his name was Barbosa and he was native to Chela. I asked him then whether he knew Lídia Ferreira's family. Barbosa stopped eating and looked at me with distrust:

'She's my aunt,' he said. 'But I don't even know her. Actually I'm not even interested in meeting her.'

His reaction didn't surprise me. In those days there were a lot of people who would have preferred never to have heard of her. After dinner this heavy-gestured fellow came to hover round me. He began by talking about the weather, wanted to know how I was putting up with the night-time cold, but quickly changed the subject.

'A little while back,' he said, 'I heard you talking to Barbosa about the family of Lídia Ferreira.'

Now that did surprise me, I thought I'd got myself into some trouble. I looked straight at the softly-spoken man and told him I barely knew Lídia Ferreira, apart from as a poet, but that I'd heard she'd been born in the area. The guy nodded yes:

'Yes, indeed she was,' he said. 'My mother was a good friend of her mother's.'

Lídia had never spoken to me about her mother. She did however refer often to her grandmother, a woman of Congolese origins, and especially to her grandfather – in reality her great-grandfather – Jacinto do Carmo Ferreira. In 1954, a few months before his death, she had even dedicated a short poem to him:

Untidy long white whiskers
Hands on his chest, like startled birds.
This is how I recall you, my white grandfather,
Incurably dead.

You know, you really miss that old
Cork helmet and your kingly staff…

Chapter 4

This is the story of a desperate love. It all started in 1926, the year a priest from São Tomé arrived in Luanda. His name was Isaú da Conceição and he was a thin, melancholy young man, given to meditation and poetry. He liked capacious, nocturnal words, and his long sermons invariably examined the transience of life. A brilliant speaker, with a warm, deep voice, he soon became an indispensable presence at the long evenings with the local bourgeoisie. And if the fact that he was black closed some doors to him, by virtue of his being the parish priest others would open.

It was at one of these evenings that Isaú da Conceição met Francisca Barbosa, and allowed himself to be seduced deep into the abyss of her eyes. The grandmother to the softly-spoken man, Dona Assunção, a vast woman, big as a house, quick to laugh, recited one of Isaú's favourite poems to me: 'The moon rides high in the mansion of death,' she said, trying to reproduce the deep voice of the man from São Tomé. It was 'The Engagement of the Sepulchre', by Soares de Passos. 'Already midnight sounded, leisurely,' I added in the same tone, and she looked at me with real amazement. I explained to her that I too had had a grandmother, and my words seemed to amuse her greatly.

Dona Assunção was a friend of Francisca Barbosa. 'Poor thing,' she said to me, 'she was still just a child when misfortune beat her down.'

This is the story she told me: Francisca was living in Chão de Chela, in a big house worn down by time and inhabited only by women. Or rather, by generations of women. The two oldest were dark black women, not related to one another except that both were widows of a Madeiran called Barbosa, an old primary-school teacher and later a businessman and finally a farmer, deported to Africa for the crime of rape. This man became almost a legend across the whole Huíla plateau, and even beyond, because, it was rumoured, he prevented his women and his three mulatta daughters from leaving the house and did to them things that – Dona Assunção said – a man should do only with his wife. And he didn't just do it with one of them at a time, but rather with all of them at once. And having had grand-daughters of his own seed, one by each daughter, he moved on to do the same with them and likewise had offspring by these too. And then he died.

In August 1907 three exhausted, ragged men arrived at Chela. They were deserters from the Portuguese column that had gone to avenge the shameful Vau de Pembe military disaster that had taken place three years earlier when the Cuamatos surrounded Captain Pinto de Almeida, killing him, the sixteen officers who were accompanying him and another three hundred and something soldiers.

None of the men wanted to explain too clearly his reasons for flight. At last one of them, a *mestizo* lieutenant, who said he was called César Augusto and that he came from Luanda, spoke for the other two; he explained that they were very tired, terribly thirsty and hungry and that they would have to remain at the farm until they were completely restored. He added that they had a bounty on their heads for having betrayed their country, but that they didn't recognise the country they'd betrayed as theirs. 'Angola is our country,' the mulatto had said.

The two older women were indifferent, the mulattas and the quadroon girls terrified and the three youngest, very pale, languid, blonde girls – of a blondeness so blonde it worried you to look at it – they started dancing as they sang in a language they had invented themselves, replacing the vowels with musical notes, in such a way that the same word could have different meanings.

At the end of a week the two soldiers left, but César Augusto did not want to follow them: he was in love with the Madeiran's three great-granddaughters. They considered each other cousins, but the truth was that with the exception of the two black women all the women in that house were cousins of one another's, and also sisters. The youngest, poor things, were weighed down by the disgrace of being at once the daughters, granddaughters and great-granddaughters of old Barbosa.

So César Augusto set about restoring the little farm, and as he was young, strong and determined he soon returned the orange groves to their old splendour, he brought water over from distant streams and planted corn and sorghum grain at the foot of the hills.

One day, however, Leda, Dejanira and Polixena – those were the ungainly names of the three cousins – discovered that they were pregnant. Delighted, already forgetting the condemnation that was weighing him down, César Augusto decided to go to Luanda to ask his father for help with rebuilding the farm. He left one foggy day and never came back.

Months later the cousins, fulfilling what seemed to be a secret family destiny, gave birth to three beautiful girls. The last to be born, Dejanira's daughter, was named Francisca, and soon showed herself to be the most beautiful of them all. Dona Assunção remembers her as an adolescent with an absorbed air who spent hours and hours sitting very peacefully floating in the fresh half-light of the bedrooms. Nobody ever understood how Francisca came to know a man, so rarely did she leave the house to go into town, and always surrounded by her sisters and aunts and grandmothers. When her period didn't come, and then came the vomiting and the dizzy spells and her belly began to swell, Dejanira thought her daughter must be suffering from some unknown illness, or that it was an adolescent's whimsical spirits. When they consulted the oldest of the great-great-grandmothers, Nga Samba, a slave Barbosa had brought from Catete and who seemed to have limitless learning on matters of sorcery and household remedies, this lady asked them to bring her a boiled egg and then leave her alone with the girl. The examination was quick and conclusive: Francisca had indeed been deflowered, and carried a soul in her belly. A 'dikulundundu', specified the old woman, 'an ancestral spirit.'

Dejanira, who with the disappearance of César Augusto had become a bitter, abrupt woman, closed herself and her daughter in one of the bedrooms, stripped her and began to beat her with a hippo-hide whip that had belonged to old Barbosa. The screaming of her mother, her nieces and sisters, her aunts and grandmothers, only increased her fury. When she finally opened the door, pale as a ghost, she already knew the name of the seducer: 'It was the little priest,' she said with a voice of astonishment.

Ifigénia, the daughter of Polixena, made the most of the chaos that reigned the rest of the day, escaping from the maternal watchful eye to go and see Maria da Assunção who lived some five kilometres away:

'Ifigénia brought me a letter from Francisca, for me to get it to the priest,' Dona Assunção laughed, opening her large, almost toothless mouth, as she recalled the scene. 'But I could see right away that there was all sorts of confusion going on and I turned the errand down.'

However Ifigénia insisted so much, crying and tearing her hair, that Maria da Assunção ended up agreeing and took the letter to the priest.

'I shouldn't have done it. The priest read the letter in front of me and was left speechless.'

He stuttered something, turned his back on Maria da Assunção and went into the church. It was evening. Early the next morning he threw himself into the mouth of the Tundavala.

When they gave her the news, Francisca went mad with pain. In spite of her pregnancy she refused to eat for several days, till she was so thin that the slightest sliver of light passed right through her and you could see the little foetus within her, swimming calmly in its lunar waters. It took the powerful science of Nga Samba, with her herbs and little powders, to restore her will to live. But not for long. As soon as the child was born – it was a girl – Francisca stopped feeding herself again, submerged in a state of total apathy. One night she soaked a cambric blanket with water, rolled herself up in it and went to sleep. The next morning she awoke with a slight cough, and continued to cough, and to sigh rather than breathing, until her body had lost all its substance and they had to close the windows and tie her with a piece of string to the foot of the bed lest she be carried away by a summer breeze.

When she died she was already so deprived of existence, that it was necessary to dress her in her most solid clothes, to perfume her whole body, paint her hair and her fingernails and toenails with nervous colours just to make it seem credible that she was once of this world.

Before dying Francisca gave her daughter a name: Lídia. Months later, Lieutenant César Augusto's father, Jacinto do Carmo Ferreira, appeared at Chela with news of his death. He said that César Augusto had been killed in Luanda eighteen years earlier, following a chaotic nationalist conspiracy. He said that his son was a hero. Dona Assunção remembered him well:

'A big old man, upright in spite of his age. He could have been a missionary, but he spoke like one of us.'

Jacinto do Carmo Ferreira explained that he had come to collect his granddaughters. He was old, he had made his money, but he felt very alone, and so had decided to gather all his descendents around him. Antónia and Ifigénia, the daughters of Leda and Polixena, were thrilled. To them Luanda was the twenty-first century, the origin of the world. But neither Leda nor Polixena nor the other women liked the idea. Jacinto do Carmo Ferreira tried to argue with them, saying that in the capital the girls would receive the best education, and that apart from this they would be able to visit their family in Chela from time to time. He added that he was prepared to pay to support the women and to restore the little farm at his own cost. It was all useless. The women retorted that they were perfectly capable of educating the children themselves, and of supporting themselves. Jacinto do Carmo Ferreira raged, threatened. Finally an agreement was reached: Antónia and Ifigénia would stay at Chela, but the little orphan girl could go with him.

That was how Lídia left for Luanda.

POETRY

'I firmly believe that it is through poetry that everything will begin.'

António Jacinto, in a letter to Mário Pinto de Andrade, written in Luanda,
1 February 1952

'In some of this poetry, by various writers, there was some insidious matter that frightened power. Not because it confirmed or illustrated the ideological stakes, but because it confirmed a terrible suspicion: that beyond an Angolan will, taken to its extreme consequences with an armed uprising, there was an Angolan soul. And there was nothing to be done to defend against this. For those that feared it, it was defeat announced in verse.'

Ruy Duarte de Carvalho, 'We Are Together in the Country that We Have',
Lavra e Oficina magazine, no. 56. Luanda, May 1991

Chapter 1

Luanda in the thirties was a little city in the suburbs of the world, in the desolate outskirts of time. There was the hill, its solid, solemn fortress, the light rows of houses in the lower town, the upper town skirting the slopes of red earth. Everywhere the air felt charged with torpor and tiredness. On the Island, linked to the continent by a decrepit bridge of wooden planks on cement pillars, a fresh casuarina breeze blew in the evenings, and this was the loveliest time of the day.

Jacinto do Carmo Ferreira lived in Ingombotas, in a white mansion with an ogival entranceway framed by large palm trees. It was the biggest house in Ingombotas. Lídia, at least, always believed this, and for years would always imagine it like this, the most beautiful and largest of any in Ingombotas, until 1974 when she returned to Luanda after twenty-one years in exile and was unable to identify it among the proud dwellings of the new colonial bourgeoisie. It had an enormous back yard, closed in by broad adobe walls. Mango trees, guava trees, medlar-fruit trees, papaya trees, pomegranate trees, soursop trees and Surinam cherry trees grew there, and bougainvillea, rose bushes, sweetpeas and snapdragons.

Old Fina kept chickens, the world was good and simple, and Lídia was happy with their happiness: 'The chickens made nests in the sand and a luminous dust floated around them. Peace for me today is a chicken in the sun.' Lídia wrote this, or something like this, in one of the many notes we exchanged in the São Paulo Prison.

In the Ingombotas mansion the girl found herself once more among women: old Fina, aka Dona Josephine, an ancient slave brought from the Congo by a German bush-trader, later the concubine of a rich mulatto businessman, and finally the legitimate wife of Carmo Ferreira. Carlota, César Augusto's sister, a widow, always dressed in black mourning-cloth, and two of her as yet unmarried daughters, Angelica and Maria do Carmo, who received Lídia as though welcoming a younger sister. On Sundays Carlota's three other children would appear too, three sons with their wives and respective offspring, and then the house would fill with a tumult of voices. Grandmother Fina would prepare a dried-meat *funge*, sometimes a *mufete* with beans in palm oil and a lot of *gindungo* pepper, German beer for the grown-ups and fizzy drinks for the younger ones, and lunch would stretch right through the afternoon. At the head of the table old Carmo Ferreira would recount anecdotes, laugh thunderously, recall old stories of memorable hunting trips or parties and *rebita* dances no longer seen.

One of Carlota's sons, Tito, who was studying law in Coimbra and was married to a Portuguese woman, used to bring along a guitar and would sing in Spanish the popular boleros of the day, *maxixes* and rumbas. Changing language and accent he would then sing *fados*, shameless little sambas and tunes from the Luanda carnivals.

Lídia showed me a photo from those days. It was taken on a Sunday, without doubt, you could tell that at once.

Perhaps Easter Sunday, as Dona Fina is dressed in lilac fabrics as was traditional. For the New Year *bessangana* women wore white fabrics, for Easter lilac, on August 15th a cloth called 'butter-bar', white with pink or blue stripes.

At the centre of the photograph, sitting in a wicker chair, is Jacinto do Carmo Ferreira. He is a little fatter than I'd imagined, but nonetheless he is impressive. He has a colonial helmet on his lap, thick white hair that mixes into his beard. On the floor, sitting on a mat, is Lídia, a fragile girl with little pointed plaits. In one of her hands she is holding a cat, with the other she is gripping the arm of a boy a little older than her, with light skin and blonde-tufted hair. Artur, Tito's son. He died in 1967. He was a commander from the Popular Army for the Liberation of Angola who fell into an FNLA ambush and was tortured for three weeks. They pulled out his hair and his beard, burned his chest with cigarettes and finally impaled him with a red-hot poker.

Standing to Carmo Ferreira's right is Dona Funa, with a tall perfumed hairdo. Although she didn't need to, since Carmo Ferreira was still a rich man who owned businesses in the slums and a coffee plantation in Porto Amboim, Dona Fina still ran a successful sweet shop. Her sweet-sellers crossed the whole town with a board slung over their shoulders crying the virtues of their wares: candies made from coconut, and guava, and papaya, caramels, *micondo* rings, sweetmeats wrapped in silk paper, each taste in its own colour.

In the photograph Carlota is at her father's left hand, in her heavy mourning. Her three sons are so alike you would think them triplets, all of them dark, small and solid, their curly hair plastered with pomade and parted in the centre. One of them is wearing dark glasses and carrying a small guitar. That is Tito. In the left-hand corner of the photograph are Angelina and Maria do Carmo. Angelina is very beautiful, with firm breasts standing out under a white lace blouse, a long gazelle neck. She studied at the English College in Moçâmedes where she learned the language of Shakespeare, and to embroider and play the piano. On the day she turned thirty-four she ran away with a Dutch adventurer and was never heard from again. Maria do Carmo has transparent eyes, a sidelong, enigmatic smile.

Chapter 2

Did you have many friends as a child?

Lídia: Artur was my first friend. I also had a dog, a gigantic pointer, who was a bit crazy, who my grandfather named after the Portuguese governor of the day, Eduardo Ferreira Viana. We had another dog, but he was old and avoided children. He was called Salazar.

When was the first time you left Luanda?

Lídia: The first trip I remember taking was to Canhoca, a stop on the Malange railroad. My grandfather went to visit a friend and took me with him. The train scared me. It seemed very large, stormy, smoky. We occupied a compartment in the first class carriage, and I sat at the window. It was early in the morning, the air was wet and smelled of ripe fruit. I looked out and saw the *quitandeiras*, the street-seller women, selling large green oranges. A blue-uniformed man unrolled a little flag and went past us, trotting towards the locomotive. He was shouting: ALLL-ABOOOOOOAARD.

(Interview with Lídia do Carmo Ferreira, Luanda, 23 May 1990)

Chapter 3

The train shuddered and began to move. Lídia squeezed her grand-father's hand tight. At Canhoca everyone got out. Beside the station was a small restaurant and the train remained stopped a few minutes for the passengers who were headed for Malange to have their lunch. They paid up-front and only then got their food. They used to say that the owner of the restaurant would serve up soup that was very hot so that no one would have time to finish their meal.

Carmo Ferreira's friend was waiting for them at the station: a thin, tiny old man, lame in one leg. Even in this heat he wore a dark suit and felt hat. His beard and curly hair were completely white, his eyes large and gentle. Lídia thought he looked like Father Christmas. They went to his house and the whole afternoon the two friends didn't exchange a word, sitting there playing chess.

The girl got bored and went out to the back yard to bother the locusts. In Luanda she and little Artur organised locust fights, between two locusts, or between a locust and a praying mantis – in this latter case the praying mantis always won. They were like little treacherous gods. They would attack the locusts' backs and eat out their eyes. Lídia would watch them do this mute with horror (with fascination). Then Artur would go and find a stone and kill the praying mantis.

When Lídia returned, at the end of the evening, the two old men were still sitting opposite one another, in absolute silence. A little later a lady dressed in black fabrics came in; she put an embroidered tablecloth on the table, and brought a saucepan with rice and meat in from the kitchen. Lídia had trouble eating. The meat was opaline, sweet and soft, like she'd never tasted before, and it occurred to her that perhaps it might be a giant praying mantis. She wanted to ask her grandfather about this but he was chewing in silence, his eyes on his plate and yet seeming to be somehow apart from the meal. The girl kept quiet.

That night they put her to sleep on her own in an enormous room, in a bed in which she felt lost, and Lídia had difficulty falling asleep. She could hear life beating out there, in a dense web made of whispers, sudden barks, the rhythmic percussive scraping of the cicadas. Noises of night-time in the bush. A distant dragging of bodies, a soft approach of footsteps. The moonlight, straining through the chinks in the window, stirred shadows on the bedroom walls. And again the sound of footsteps. Laughter. Very far away, as though submerged, and almost weary, the rhythmic resounding of the drums. Lídia thought of the stories of ghosts and spirits that old Fina used to tell her. One in particular used to startle her: the one about the witches whose tongues came free from their bodies, went creeping though the night, went into homes and attacked sleeping children, strangling them. Old Fina told how many years earlier one of her friends, still young, had woken up in the night, seen one of these tongues at the foot of her bed and killed it with blows from a machete. The next morning she discovered that her mother was mute.

Lídia awoke with a start. Her grandfather was beside her and he smiled at her. Father Christmas accompanied them to the station and when they arrived he put a little bag of caramels in her hand. He and her grandfather embraced at length. At last Carmo Ferreira drew apart, held the old man's head in his rough hands and said to him, 'Courage, this country will be ours yet.'

Chapter 4

Lídia liked telling stories about her childhood. There was one that struck me particularly, because it was not possible. Later I was amazed to discover various references to the case in the newspapers of the day. It all began on the Island, one Saturday afternoon, at Ermelinda's bar. Lídia and her grandfather were eating slow lupine seeds when Eduardo Ferreira Viana appeared panting with excitement. He was a powerful, restless creature, who seemed permanently on the edge of a nervous breakdown. He stopped beside Carmo Ferreira and dropped onto the floor a woman's hand. The old man was startled:

'*Sundu ya mamaena!!*'

A circle of astonishment formed around the table. Fat Ermelinda, an angel-faced mulatta, allowed herself to faint with a gentle cry into the convenient arms of the poet Vieira da Cruz. The dog ran off, did a lap of the house and immediately returned carrying a whole arm in its teeth. He barked, ran to the door, and barked again. The men looked at one another, and then followed him. Some hundred metres away, beside a little forest of acacia trees, the sand had been turned up and you could see – partly eaten away and half-buried – a human cadaver.

They found the bodies of seven women in that place, some of them already badly come apart, transformed into slime and mud and boiling with necrophagic life – tiny, pale and nervous. All were 'horribly mutilated', as the reporter from the *Província de Angola* would write the next day. To be more precise, the bodies were cut through right across the belly.

The mystery fed the conversations of Luandans over the weeks that followed. Luanda was a city of calm and mild crimes, and even these were infrequent, almost always anonymous. A week later the editor of *A Glória de Angola*, Vitorino Espírito Santo, was celebrating the discovery, writing that it was 'the proof that, counter to some people's incorrect arguments, Angola is finally entering the great club of civilised nations.' It's a good example of the acidic Luandan sense of humour: *A Glória de Angola* was then what remained of a once powerful nativist press, which the growing colonial offensive was practically suffocating.

Almost everyone agreed that what they were dealing with was a sexual crime. However, the suspects varied and the theories for explaining the case varied even more. Some colonials, particularly those lately arrived, recalled the 'cannibalistic practices, the savage orgies of the bushland blacks', many of whom had reached the capital and were seen wandering aimlessly through the dust of the streets, 'offending the eyes of our virgins with their shameless outfits'. I took these curious statements from a small article in the *Província de Angola*. Its author, one A.D. Ventura – possibly a pseudonym – suggested the creation of European neighbourhoods that were kept rigorously separate from the African neighbourhoods and watched over by a special police corps: 'Only in this way,' the writer of the article concluded, 'will it be possible to guarantee the security of our wives and daughters. Yesterday they were only black women, but tomorrow, who knows, perhaps the tragedy will come knocking on our own doors.'

Vitorino Espírito Santo, in a later article, wrote that 'a crime that is so refined, so imaginative, so filled with mystery and seduction, cannot honestly be imputed to the common herd. The people, the barbarous black man, kills simple beasts simply: he strikes a blow, he buries the blade and he flees. Some have resorted to magic. But none of them had the inspiration to carry out something of this kind and on this scale. A crime of this nature requires the learning of an educated man and the sensibility of an English Lord. I know the name of the guilty man and can reveal it to you now: Jack the Ripper.' The article must have caused considerable scandal, because the issue in which it appears would be the last published in the series.

The other newspapers I consulted didn't solve the mystery. But Lídia claimed to remember the sudden outcome very clearly. According to her, a few months after the discovery of the bodies, the killer handed himself over to the police to escape the people's fury. He was a fisherman from the Algarve, an insignificant sort of man, with sharp protruding bones, and a harelip. 'A real genetic disaster,' in Lídia's words. He had been deported to Angola for the crime of murder and having bought himself a little boat had spent the latter years of his life settled among the Luanda island fishermen. Without much luck at sea, one day he nevertheless began to appear with his barge laden with a new kind of fish. The people found it odd, especially the fact that the man from the Algarve only ever brought the scaly things' tails to land (quite big tails judging by accounts), on the grounds that they were the tastiest part of that new species. Shortly after the bodies were discovered, the man confessed: they were mermaids! The wretch had been killing them and then cutting their human appearance away, burying these pieces in big common ditches. The tails, rejected by the people of Luanda, would be salted and sold to bushland traders from the interior, who would then sell them on as though they were salt-cod.

The man was released after a few weeks. Lídia heard that he'd fled from Luanda hidden in the hold of a trawler and that he had later set himself up in Moçâmedes, where he'd opened a funeral parlour.

Chapter 5

It was in the July of 1994, in Porto Alexandre (Tombwa), in the extreme south of Angola. By chance I'd gone into an old ironmongers' shop. At first I thought it was empty. Then I saw him, sitting in the gloom. All I could make out were his thin hands. The tired gestures with which he shooed away the flies.

The shop didn't seem to have anything to sell. Just a few objects eaten away by rust. Nails, nuts, little things of obscure function. The man spoke slowly:

'You should have seen this place in other times,' he said to me. 'These houses, the ones out there, they were like palaces. And then there were the casuarinas too, tall trees that the government had planted to stop the advancing of the dunes.'

I had seen the houses. They looked like boats submerged in the sand. As for the trees, I hadn't seen a single one. The man raised his hands in a gesture of discouragement:

'What do you expect? They cut them down for firewood.'

Night was falling fast over the desert. Looking towards the door, out there, you could see the shadows growing. A dog went past growling, head down (could it be fear?). 'I've had plenty of money in the past,' the man continued. 'I was a fisherman.'

He laughed: 'I used to fish for mermaids.'

He fell silent. Silent and hidden in the shadows, it was as though he wasn't there. I sat down alone on the doorstep. I thought of Lídia. I had gone there, to this place at the end of the earth, in search of her. Lord, where could she be?

The red ants ran, forming strange pictures in the sand.

Chapter 6

'He was an odd guy,' Lídia said to me about Canon Froto, her godfather. His voice changed with the seasons, shining like a just-polished metal in the raw, dusty months. Hoarse in the rusty dawns, before the great rains: they said that he'd had his throat operated on and his vocal cords reconstructed in metal. Firm and definite on matters of custom, he could not abide ladies participating in religious rites with their faces uncovered, just as he would not allow gentlemen in shirt-sleeves into the church. On one occasion he publicly reprimanded the Governor General himself because he had tried to tell a slightly risqué story at the inauguration of the festival of August 15th. And yet his best friends were Carmo Ferreira and Canon Manuel das Neves, the first a committed republican, anti-clerical and with libertarian tendencies, and the other a fierce nationalist who plotted secretly against Portuguese rule and seemed much more interested in hearing the words of the People than in conveying to them the sacred word of the Lord.

There was another famous man from São Tomé in Luanda who also frequented the house of Carmo Ferreira: Dr Aires de Menezes, one of the first black doctors to develop a practice on Angolan soil. Tall and of athletic bearing, dressed like the hero of an American movie, a sober monocle in his right eye, with French perfume and a silver walking stick. The ignorant white men watched him with distrust. They looked at his haughty monocle, disconcerted at his incredible appearance and when he passed them they muddled their words, greeting him, 'And how's Y'Excellency's health?' But no sooner seen the back of him than they would spit out to one side: 'And now we've got this blasted black man!' The story goes, that one of them, wanting to humiliate the doctor, turned up at his surgery asking to have one of his feet operated on – he had chigoe fleas. Aires de Menezes wasn't troubled: he stretched the man out on the operating table, prepared his tweezers, his needles and scalpels, gave a local anaesthetic and carried on in every way as though this were a real operation he was performing. The *candungo* laughed to himself, thinking about the good story he would have to entertain his friends. He stopped laughing when Aires de Menezes presented him with the bill: 'You think it's expensive?' asked the doctor, surprised. 'You should know that when you're talking about treating parasites, it's cheap at any price.'

In spite of his proverbial rudeness, Canon Froto cultivated an old man's gentle tenderness for Lídia. He took her out in a sling, offered her sweets and little rag dolls and as soon as the girl had shown herself capable of holding a pencil he taught her to read and to write and spoke to her of the world. At D. João II School, where she had finished year four, Lídia stunned everyone with her precocious learning: she didn't merely read and write, she had already mastered the basics of arithmetic and geometry, recited whole poems by St Francis of Assisi, knew the secrets of the Bible and could conjugate the most obtuse Latin verbs.

D. João II School occupied the whole first floor of the Palace of Dona Ana Joaquina, a building with three centuries of memories, whose wide walls contained dramas of blood and love, of slaves and masters. Named a piece of national heritage, it was occupied in 1977 and debased and destroyed down to its stone skeleton. Nowadays Angolans back from Zaire light bonfires in its huge halls, raise chickens in its old confessionals crafted of valuable woods, and pigs where Luanda's Creole aristocracy used to waltz. With the innocence of those who know nothing they stretch out fabrics with the likeness of the President on the elegant iron-wrought verandas, and many-coloured underpants on the proud flagpole.

But all this came later. At the time, the Palace of Dona Ana Joaquina was still calm and heavy, and maintained an atmosphere of ancient nobility that fascinated young Lídia:

The ancient light intact,
preserved in each crevice, each cranny,
On each corner,
Clinging to the high hall ceilings
The dead dumbly murmur
Stealthily...*

---

* Lídia Ferreira, in *Ancient Stones*, Casa dos Estudiantes do Império edition, Lisbon, 1961

Chapter 7

You studied, Lídia, at the D. João II School, in the old Palace of Dona Ana Joaquina. What was your day-to-day life like in those days?

Lídia: It was almost always the same. I would get up at half past five in the morning. Angelina would give me a cold bath, comb my hair and dress me. At six o'clock it was breakfast, as my grandfather was heading out to take care of his business. At six forty-five Angelina, Maria do Carmo or one of the servants would take me to school. I remember the teacher clearly, a serious man, always dressed in black. He would take attendance, ask to see homework and punished those who didn't deliver with half a dozen strokes of a ruler on each hand. Repeat offenders would get theirs on the backs of their hands. They said that if you rubbed chicken droppings on your hands the ruler would slip and it would hurt less. But I tried it and it didn't work. There was a break at ten o'clock, and we would go out to the playground, where the domestic servants were already waiting for us with the snacks our mothers had prepared for us. The poorer of my schoolmates brought in a roll wrapped in brown paper.

And did you also have someone bringing you your snack?

Lídia: I was one of the few black children who had someone waiting for me, but it wasn't until much later that I noticed this. I remember another boy, also black, for whom a very white lady, dressed in a kind of cream-coloured tunic like a priest's, a colonial helmet on her head, used to come to bring his snack. She'd arrive pedalling an old blue bicycle, the lunchbox in a basket fixed to the handlebars. And the dogs ran along behind her in silence.

What?!

Lídia: That's exactly how it was. I remember seeing her pedalling. And the dogs behind her, running in silence.

(Interview with Lídia do Carmo Ferreira, Luanda, 23 May 1990)

Chapter 8

You wrote in one of your poems that when you were a child you used to hide to smoke. Is that true?

Lídia: I've always written about things that have happened. I remember smoking my first cigarettes, in the shade of the cashew trees, behind the high school – Caricocos. A pack of 300 cost nineteen escudos. There were even ads on the radio. (She sings): 'If you don't smoke Caricocos / You've no idea how good they taste... / Caricoco hey-la / Caricoco hey-la-la'. Then there were the French 'Number Ones' with blue and white stripes, which looked like they were wearing pyjamas. And Reys, noble tobacco, but which tasted revolting. Then Cuanhamas appeared, black and dangerous, no sooner had you lit one than it would come apart into little sparks. One day I arrived home with little holes all over my dress. Vavó Fina smelled my mouth, smacked her lips, made a rotten expression, went to fetch my grandfather. The old man laughed a lot and imitating the voice of the wireless started singing 'If you don't smoke Caricocos you've no idea how good they taste.' He opened his cigarette case and offered me a cigarette. I think I was furious. That day I stopped smoking.

(Interview with Lídia do Carmo Ferreira, Luanda, 25 May 1990)

Chapter 9

Lídia would write poems in the silence of her bedroom. As soon as it got dark she would go out into the back yard to gather bouquets of roses. The cicadas screamed. Then she would close herself in her room and pull the petals off the roses and chew them anxiously, feeling confusingly like a female praying mantis devouring a male. Out there the cicadas were burning, mad with amazement and lust. Lídia devoured the roses and scratched through leaf after leaf of paper with long incoherent poems.

She was afraid of snakes, and of the dark. She was above all afraid of her own body. She counted the days waiting for her period with horror. And while it was happening she would avoid going out, agonised by the idea that her scent preceded her. She felt herself persecuted by the restless gaze of the men, the mocking gaze of the girls, the sympathetic gaze of the old greengrocer women. She closed herself in, alone in her bathroom, and wept in silence, as she washed the cloths stained with blood.

Her best friend, Antónia Buriti, was in love with a classmate. She spent her days sighing, breathy, her little hand on her heart and her eyes moist. Lídia found her ridiculous and hated seeing her like that: 'You look stupid,' she would tell her. But in reality she was jealous of her. The cause of such sentimental exaltation was a dark mulatto who was known to be arrogant and argumentative. But he did have an incredible gift for caricature and published a few sarcastic poems in the school paper, *The Student*. The teachers said – in a whisper – that he showed great promise. His name was Viriato. Viriato Francisco Clemente da Cruz.

There were few girls in the high school and they had little to do with the boys. These formed their own groups. They organised big football tournaments, went swimming at Samba Pequena beach, they roamed through the city in a band, explored the slums, looked for cuckoos in the gullies, waged war against rival gangs, raided the old courtyards to steal fruit, or hunted birds. Basically, as old Fina used to say, they ladded about. Viriato was the leader of one of these groups.

Lídia had noticed him, as everyone had, but what captivated her was something quite new; something she could not explain. Antónia Buriti did know. She spoke slowly, languidly of his 'mysterious oriental eyes', glorified the boy's determined personality. With great excitement she would recount the stories circulating about him. None of this mattered to Lídia; it was something else. One day she wrote in her diary, VI-RI-ATO. A VITORI. VIA, RIOT. She didn't know what that meant. Sometimes she dreamed about him. They were walking down a long road together and she gave him her hand. And suddenly she realised that the boy beside her was not Viriato. It wasn't even a man. She had this dream again, many years later, by which time Viriato was dying in China and she was beginning to get to the heart of mysteries.

Chapter 10

The boys were cruel. Once they put birdlime on a small wall where birds usually landed. It was a habit in those days to catch birds with birdlime. Poor children constructed wicker or wire cages, caught the little birds and then went to sell them from door to door. The boys from the high school didn't want to catch the little birds to sell them, however. When there were already seven or eight struggling on the wall they started discussing what they should do. Some wanted to stone them, Viriato wanted to eat them. At this point a thin lad appeared:

'Killing little birds is a crime,' he said. 'Better let them go right away.'

His name was Rui Tavares Marques and he had recently arrived from Huambo. He was an outgoing little kid who entertained everyone with his impressions of the teachers' voices. I will be talking about him again later on, as he was the man who judged the mercenaries in 1976, and subsequently took part in the interrogations of the fractionists. Those who survived said that he was the worst of all: 'He was Macchiavellian.' Other adjectives: hateful, hypocritical, repellent, paranoid. He obtained his confessions by torture. They say that once in an attack of rage he put his hand into the mouth of a prisoner and tore out her tongue. And yet he still has many friends: 'He's absolutely delightful,' a Portuguese woman writer assured me, 'a cultured, fun, intelligent man. An excellent cook and gifted poet.' Other adjectives: brilliant, friendly, gentle, welcoming. I told her that he had once torn out the tongue of a woman who was tied up. The Portuguese woman raised her hands to her lips:

'How horrible! That's not true...'

Not true? Very well. Let us return to the birds. Rui Tavares Marques – whom we would later have to call Tovaritch Marx – confronted the boys:

'Killing little birds is a crime,' he repeated. 'If you don't free them at once I'm calling the police.'

A boy with an effeminate manner, Rosa-da-Ana – also known as Porcelain Rose – appeared with a pair of pruning shears:

'You want to free the birds? Then we'll free the birds.'

And while the others were holding Rui Tavares, he cut the birds' legs off.

Chapter 11

'Childhood is the season of malice.' It's your line. What does it mean?

Lídia: Just that, that childhood is the season of malice. Of course, it is also the age of innocence. I think a certain innocence is necessary for malice to manifest itself in its most exuberant forms. Did I tell you the story about the birds? It was me who gave Porcelain Rose the shears.

News stories about children who kill or torture other children don't surprise me. What does amaze me is that the phenomenon isn't more widespread. The great torturers – and I've known some – well, we've known some, haven't we? – the great torturers are almost always men who haven't had a childhood and so practise it later on.

Perhaps malice in men, deep down, is an expression of their innocence. That's why I always say that only the innocent are guilty.

(Interview with Lídia do Carmo Ferreira, Luanda, 23 May 1990)

Chapter 12

The Second World War had come to an end, and fragments of news were reaching Luanda of a world being restored. The defeat of Nazism struck at the very essence of the racist theories that had been embedded in Angola since the end of the previous century. Social Darwinism was treated as a joke in the Academy, and the arrogant Germanophiles – who just a few months earlier had advocated for the separation of races and for keeping the blacks and mulattos from all public posts – had fallen silent. Students organised marches to throw stones at the windows of the German consulate, while at the same time irritating the English consul with repeated demonstrations of support and gratitude. Salazar, meanwhile, continued to tighten the net of Empire, and the Angolans found themselves each day less in control of their own destiny. The older ones spoke of a time when it was the children of the land who dominated Angola's economic, cultural and even political life, but the young laughed at them. Some of these old people dreamed of a restoration of the old parties from the days of the monarchy: they spoke a lot of the Pro-Angola Party.

Some small number of tireless idealists, like old Carmo Ferreira, aged away at café tables, trying to bind the confused, rotting threads of rebellion to one another.

In this atmosphere poetry burst from the young as the most obvious means of cultural affirmation: 'They took everything from us, our dignity, our land, our men. And finally even our selves,' Lídia said to me; 'they took our whole past away from us and we looked around us and couldn't understand the world. Then we began to write poetry. Poetry was an unavoidable destiny for an Angolan student in those days.'

It was a poetry that was poor but generous, alert to the distortions of society and above all obsessed with the sacred space of childhood, this final and deepest stronghold of memory – general, not particular – which explained the world. The infancy of distant customs still preserved: *makèzu*, cola and ginger, the mixed-race *quimbundo* of the greengrocer women, the legends their grandmothers told, always inhabited by talking beasts and strange prodigious beings.

The young poets were aware of the messianic role they had to play. 'We were writing for History,' Lídia said to me. She told me that once she met Viriato da Cruz walking in the Largo da Mutamba. He was alone, but seemed to be concentrating on something. Lídia asked him what he was doing and Viriato replied that he was waiting for the echo. She thought this strange:

'Oh, really! The echo of what?!'

Viriato explained that that day he'd published a short poem in some newspaper from the city:

'You didn't read it? No matter, your grandchildren will certainly read it.'

That was definitely in the late forties. Viriato was recovering from TB. The illness and the lack of financial resources had forced him to abandon his studies. He spent his days reading. He received from Brazil books of the revolution that had been banned and he read like a man possessed. He read some literature too: Jorge Amado, Erico Veríssimo, Manuel Bandeira, Graciliano Ramos, the Russian classics, the first Portuguese neo-realists. He had a curious, excitable spirit. He had difficulty taking criticism, but was always the first to criticise. He spoke of the need for Angolans to rediscover Angola, he defended the study of *quimbundo* – our legitimate language – and dreamed of a general revolt of the countryfolk and the oppressed masses from the slums. At the same time he criticised with ferocious sarcasm the 'little bourgeois values' of the old Luandan aristocracy, got irritated with the intellectual limitations of his circle of friends and was known by many people as a pretentious and arrogant kind of guy. The truth was that he felt embarrassed when people spoke *quimbundo* in his presence, and whenever he visited his family in Porto Amboim where he'd been born he avoided the countryfolk because he didn't know what to say to them. He secretly envied those who left to study in Portugal.

On the day Lídia went away he appeared on the quay at the last minute, as the passengers were preparing to climb the gangway. He had brought a bunch of roses and was racked with fever. He didn't say goodbye to her. He said to her, 'Sis, don't forget us!'

It was raining. Lídia put her arms around his neck, pulled him towards her and felt his trembling body. It burned. And anxiety, the scent of roses.

THE SEARCH

'I no longer know who I was, nor who I am. I no longer know how much of me is, not life, but what gives life in some book I've read.'

Lídia Ferreira, in a letter to Mário de Andrade,
written in Lisbon, 30 April 1981

Chapter 1

António Guilherme Amo, Antoine-Gufflaume Amo, Antoine Willem Amo, Anton Wilhelm Amo, or Antoni Willem Amo, depending on your source, was born on the Gold Coast – now the Guineas – in 1707 and soon afterwards was offered as a slave to the Duke of Brunswick-Wolfenbuttel, Antoine Ulrich, who in turn passed him on to his son, Auguste-Guillaume. He was lucky: Auguste-Guillaume was a somewhat eccentric philanthropist, who defended an end to slavery and supported the theory that men were essentially the same everywhere, in their defects and their qualities, and that they were determined by their environment, rather than their environment being determined by them. As well as this, he also believed in levitation: 'The simple fact of gravity decreasing in inverse proportion to the square of the distance, should stop us from considering weight one of the properties of matter,' he would say. He had spent years studying the case of Cambrai, an entire convent of maidens who in 1491, possessed by a strange fury, set off running naked through the fields and climbing trees and roofs then throwing themselves into space, where they remained, floating.

Auguste-Guillaume was so struck by Amo's intelligence that he put him to study, and in 1729 the young African presented a doctorate at the Halle University, in Saxony. He continued to pursue his studies in Wittenberg, and by the time a few more years had passed he was already a professor there. Well versed in astronomy and philosophy, and having mastered Latin as well as Greek, Hebrew, French, Dutch and German, Amo accumulated various academic degrees, finally coming to be named State counsellor at the court in Berlin. Nevertheless, after the death of Auguste-Guillaume he decided to return to the land of his birth, Axim, where he soon acquired a considerable reputation as a saint and divine. The French traveller-adventurer Davi-Henri Gallandat discovered him there in 1753, living as a hermit, and gives a detailed and moving account of the meeting in his memoirs. It seems that Amo died in Chamah, at the fort of the Dutch Company of São Sebastião, around 1765.

It was in a monograph by Cameron that Lídia first came across a reference, albeit a brief one, to the life and work of António Guilherme Amo. She was so excited that even though she was in the middle of a period of exams she put aside her books on zoology, mesology and minuscule calculus to investigate the strange destiny of the Guinean philosopher. That year she only managed to pass in one subject, but it didn't bother her, for by now she had discovered that her vocation was not in agriculture.

The following year she signed up for History. From her passage through Agronomy she retained an apparent hatred for numbers and a cruel mania for assigning to everyone, in a particular kind of rule-less Latin, what she jokingly called 'the scientific designation of each, adding to Linnaeus' method certain psycho-physionomical notions'. In the letters that she wrote to Antónia Buriti, Viriato Cruz is *Lupus rex*. Later she took to calling him *Orago infelix*. Young Mario Pinto de Andrade, who travelled to Lisbon in the same boat as her, matriculating at the faculty of literature and languages, is *Mirabilis captiva*. Agostinho Neto, *Mantis religiosa*. One of her nieces, Paulete, a mulatta girl with large eyes, luminous skin the colour of palm oil, Lídia called *Ardenthia genitalis*.

In Agronomy Lídia also acquired the friendship of Amílcar Cabral. The future liberator of Guinea-Bissau, then a second-year agriculture student, he had attracted attention for the calm determination with which he faced the world, his implacable intelligence, his beautiful bronze profile, his voice that would charm the birds, and a kind of gallantry you no longer find. He also had another quality that made him popular at student parties: there was no one who danced the rumba like he did. Lídia remembered going with him and Mário Pinto de Andrade to the premiere of *Red River* – a western with John Wayne, which Mário de Andrade had insisted on seeing just because of the title. 'Either that,' he said, 'or *The Lady from Shanghai*.'

From that day the three of them began to meet up frequently towards the end of the afternoon, after classes, at the Tapada de Ajuda or in a café near the Botanical Gardens. They would have passionate discussions about the films then showing or the banned books which came to them from France or Brazil, and, of course, they would discuss Africa.

The fate of Amo excited Mário de Andrade in particular, whose life was obsessed with restoring to the black man his offended dignity. 'The Europeans,' the young man would say, 'wiped out from History all trace of the cultural presence of blacks in western civilisation; worse still, they now mean to destroy all our traditions, our whole memory.' And he added that it was necessary to take active measures: to make use of one of the watchwords created by Viriato da Cruz, 'We Will Discover Angola', and develop the foundations for the considerable project of rediscovering Africa. His eyes really shone as he said these things. He spoke of what the blacks were achieving in France. He showed translations he had done himself of poems by Césaire or Senghor: 'A thousand people and a thousand tongues / Have found voice in your red faith / Now the fire consuming you sets the desert and the bush ablaze / Now Africa rises up, the black woman and her sister, the brown. / Africa, become white steel, Africa, become black host / So the hope of man can live.'

Chapter 2

In 1986 in Malaysia, on the boat linking the continent to the island of Penang, I saw these black birds, that looked like crows, but broader, heavy and pensive. They fell from the sky and clutched onto the gratings on the deck, from where they addressed passengers with unusual words and the extravagant voice of a circus announcer. They spoke of everything and of nothing. They spoke about the state of the weather, the health of the king, the cost of living and the Buddha's sense of humour. The passengers asked them unfathomable questions, the kind you wouldn't expect anyone to be able to answer, but they always replied, and always with incontrovertible good sense. In Malaysia these birds reminded me of Little Joãoquin. Everyone knew him by this name, but he was an enormous man, with the solid head of a bull – Lídia called him *Capita taurus*. He had arms thick as the trunk of a baobab tree.

I met him when I ran away from home and went to Luanda, in November 1975. Then I spent four years imprisoned with him. Little Joãoquin used to fix watches. He lived with his godmother, Dona Diamantina, a placid woman of indiscernable age, with skin so white she seemed to be made of the same stuff as moonlight. She was an original woman. She almost always wore a cream-coloured tunic and faced the fury of the sun with one of those colonial hemlets, handmade in cork. She and Little Joãoquin didn't speak much, and only in murmurs, but it was clear that there was a feeling more powerful than love that linked them.

They arrested Little Joãoquin on an accusation of belonging to the Angolan Communist Organisation, the OCA. It was my fault, as I had hidden pamphlets from the organisation in his house. But this didn't seem a reason to arrest a man, and, mistrustful by nature and in principle, some of our comrades saw the event as a tortuous manoeuvre on the part of state security to infiltrate the movement; but they were soon captivated – as was I – by the charm of his archaic discourse and above all by his bull-like stoic good sense.

When the Information and Security Directorate finally released him, we had already named him by default, and so secretly that even he himself knew nothing about it, secretary-general of the future Workers Communist Party (of all the people we knew he was the one who most closely resembled a worker).

I'm recalling Little Joãoquin because he more than anyone understood the importance of António Guilherme Amo in Lídia's life, and how she had been transformed by discovering him. In prison we organised a series of courses on subjects that ranged from modern languages to medicine. In Cell J, where I was being held, there were a number of university students, two doctors, an engineer and an English teacher. There was also a young tractor-driver suspected of belonging to the FNLA – he gave us *quicongo* classes – and a famous torturer from the Portuguese army, Colonel Aristides Lobo d'África, who agreed to guide us through a course on classical music.

Lídia, who was being held in the women's wing, started collaborating in these courses, getting manuscripts to us with lessons on Angolan history, slavery, Portuguese discoveries, the French Revolution and other general subjects. Inevitably she ended up telling us about Amo too. Lídia's manuscripts were usually read by Little Joãoquin, who fulfilled his task with the greatest gravity. The story of the Guinean philosopher excited him, and when Lídia made mention of him again for the third lesson in a row I remember that he paused in his reading and commented, 'Miss Lídia speaks to us as though she were him, Amo himself.'

A lovely anachronism, that 'Miss': in the midst of that revolutionary fervour Little Joãoquin always refused to refer to anyone as 'Comrade' and continued using 'Mister' and 'Miss', and sometimes even 'Sir', or when dealing with the high leadership of the party or the regime, 'Your Excellency Such-and-Such'.

When pressed very hard he would resort to a new mode of address: 'Your Esteemed Comradeness'.

Chapter 3

'The Life and Work of António Guilherme Amo, Black African Philosopher' was the subject chosen by Lídia for her degree thesis. The professors tried to dissuade her: there wasn't, they said, enough information on Amo to write an article, still less a thesis. So Lídia confounded them, showing them the notes she had been collecting over four years.

Another professor, a former minister under Salazar, objected on the grounds that a thesis on a black philosopher – and a completely unknown one – seemed to him an inglorious task, and besides, it could lead to uncomfortable interpretation:

'I can see that you are a student from the colonies,' he said to her. 'Why don't you develop – for example – a subject linked to discoveries, to our amazing maritime adventures.'

'*Your* adventures,' corrected Lídia. The professor looked at her with an expression of alarm. The young woman surprised herself at her own audacity, and then she remembered her grandfather. She saw him sitting in the yard, talking to other old men about his usual dream: the independence of Angola. Carmo Ferreira wrote to her every week. To begin with they were very formal letters, only news of family and friends; bit by bit, however, they came closer, became more intimate, full of nostalgia and of a kind of urgency she could not define. 'Now,' Lídia told me, 'I know that he was dying.' The final letters seemed like fragments of a diary. In them the old man spoke mainly of his ideals: 'In each letter to me he would repeat that I was Angolan, and that I must not disillusion those who had put their trust in me.'

Chapter 4

December was when Lídia missed Luanda the most. In December it is cold on the streets of Lisbon. A spider-web rain clings to your clothes and your hair. People become more bitter. In Luanda, on the contrary, the vigour of nature infects everything. The sun burns. The birds sing with delight. December is a month of laughter and heat – the good heat that comes from the ground. Men sit in the shade and drink beer. They talk at length. Women in-laws forgive each other ancient offences. There is a splendour of red acacias on the streets. The stars, like diamonds, ornament the nights with a new sparkle.

On Sundays Lídia would go to the beach with her aunts or a group of girlfriends, and when they returned old Jacinto would give them a hose bath in the yard.

Jacinto do Carmo Ferreira died in December 1953, now already a centenarian. Lídia received the news in the Lisbon cold. If she had been in Luanda it would certainly have hurt her less. But it was in Lisbon and the sky was dirty. The air was secreting a thick slow rain.

Lídia arranged her things, sold everything she couldn't take with her, got all the money together and bought a ticket to Berlin. She left without saying goodbye to anyone.

'It was a snap decision,' she explained to me; 'I wasn't myself. With my grandfather's death I felt there was no ground beneath my feet. I felt that life didn't make sense. I was very confused, and to make matters more complicated, Mário was angry with me.'

It all began with a big discussion about *négritude*. Mário Pinto de Andrade was planning to include some poems of Lídia's in a collection of black poetry in Portuguese. By this point he was already in correspondence with Césaire, Senghor, Diop and Depestre. He had written dozens of articles and lectures on subjects like 'The Expression of Kimbundu', 'Black Literature and its Problems', 'The Black-African Linguistic Problem' or 'Folklore in Bantu Culture' and had helped to establish – with Francisco José Tenreiro, Agostinho Neto and Aldo do Espírito Santo, among others – a Centre for African Studies.

The 'Book of Black Poetry in Portuguese' would, said Mário de Andrade, be 'the first collective manifestation of *négritude* in the Portuguese language. The ultimate proof that Portuguese-language black poets had begun to forge a trail of their own and were also exercising the timbres of their voices to sing in the great human symphony.' Lídia, however, didn't feel that her poetry was black.

'It's a mistake,' she tried to explain to Mário de Andrade. 'What I write doesn't have anything particularly to do with the black world. It's to do with my world, which is as white as it is black. Mainly it is my world! If you want to include works by me then change the name of the anthology to "Book of Black Poets", but even then it would be a nonsense, like putting together a "Book of Tall Poets", or "Collection of Poems by Obese Women…"'

Mário de Andrade lost patience and with his voice raised accused her of a lack of solidarity with her comrades and fellow-countrymen: 'And at this point in our struggle,' he added, 'a lack of solidarity could be mistaken for betrayal.'

Lídia was a woman with a careful and meticulous heart. She weighed her words before answering:

'Deep down,' she said, 'the truth is that I don't identify with *négritude*. I understand *négritude*, I feel solidarity with black people all over the world and I like Senghor's poems and Diop's stories very much, but I feel that ours is a different universe. You, like me or like Viriato da Cruz, we all belong to another Africa; the same Africa you can find in the Antilles, in Brazil, in Cape Verde or São Tomé, a mixture of deepest Africa and old colonial Europe. To claim otherwise is a fraud.'

Mário de Andrade looked at her, simultaneously indignant and victorious: 'That's Gilberto Freyre!' he said firmly, 'it's that damned luso-tropicalist mysticism!' He came alight. He had her now, trapped in the web of his irrefutable argument, and for half an hour he crucified her with harsh words. When he left he seemed genuinely offended and Lídia thought she had lost him forever.

In the days that followed she couldn't stop thinking about all that, but the more she thought, the more she was convinced that she was right: 'Senghor himself suffers from nostalgia for the Creole universe where his childhood happened.' And she thought of 'Joal':

'I remember the regal *signare* women under the green shade of verandas, / Those mulatto *signare* women with eyes as surreal as moonlight on the shore... I remember the pagan voices singing the *Tantum Ergo...*'

And if Senghor was like this, what could be said of the poets Mário de Andrade wanted to include in the anthology? Alda do Espírito Santo, a black woman from São Tomé, the singer of her island's Creole landscapes. Francisco José Tenreiro, also from São Tomé, mixed-race and Creole, who had lived almost all his life in Portugal. Noémia de Sousa, a young Mozambican who carried on the surface of her skin the disquiet of many mixed bloods: her father a native of Mozambique, with the inevitable Indian, Arab, Bantu and Portuguese ancestry, her mother a mulatta, the daughter of a black woman and a German man.

Noémia also studied in Lisbon. Her poems were read at recitals and many African students knew two or three of them by heart. One of them spoke of her distant childhood. It spoke of Indian fishermen, the cries of the fishing-boat blacks, the black mamas softened by the heat. It spoke of the fishing companions, 'Black and mulatto, white and Indian boys, / servant children, of the baker, / of the fishing-boat black man, of the carpenter, / who have come from the wretchedness of Guachene / or the fishermen's wooden houses.' All of them 'Companions in the disquieted feeling of the mystery of the Island / of Lost Ships / where no cry is without an echo.' Lídia liked the poem because it reminded her a little of her own childhood.

Viriato da Cruz and Agostinho Neto were also to appear in Mário de Andrade's collection. Neto, though born in a rural area, was the son of a protestant pastor and his poetry frequently showed traces of the Bible and a familiarity with religious chants. Once he showed Lídia a poem which began like this: 'My Mother / (all black mothers / whose children have left) / you taught me to wait / like you have waited at difficult times / But life killed this mystical waiting in me / I no longer wait / I Am the One Who is waited for.'

Lídia was so disconcerted by this last line she didn't know what to say. It took her some time to realise that a prophet, in order to be authentic, merely needs to feel he is authentic.

The most curious case, however, was that of António Jacinto, the

Luandan son of Portuguese parents, very active in the cultural arena and with whom Mário de Andrade had been in correspondence. At first the young philology student didn't want to be included in the anthology: '*Négritude* doesn't exclude people who are mixed-race, but it does exclude whites,' he explained to Lídia. Apart from this he distrusted white Angolans, from his deepest roots. Lídia did too. Both of them knew that whites liked to take part in cultural initiatives, but only up to a certain point, and they were rarely willing to forego their privileges of race and class. For example, at the revels of the African students the young whites would show up for the first few hours. Then they would spend the rest of the night at the sparkling parties of their metropolitan classmates, where neither blacks nor *mestizos* were anywhere to be seen.

Jacinto's poems were nonetheless some of the most interesting, not only from an aesthetic point of view but also in political terms. 'Monangambé' is an extremely strong, electrifying poem: 'In that big plantation there is no rain / it is the sweat from my face that waters the fields / In that big plantation there is mature coffee / and that cherry-red / is drops from my blood made sap'; this is how the poem opens, and then continues with a cry of protest against colonial exploitation: 'Who gives money for the master to buy / machines, cars, ladies / and heads of black men for the motors? / Who makes the white man prosper, / makes his belly grow – makes him have money? / – Who?' Mário de Andrade would have liked to have written it. When he decided to include Jacinto in the collection – in place of Orlando da Costa, an Indian poet born in Mozambique but who had lived in Portugal since childhood – he said to Lídia that that way they wouldn't be able to accuse him of racism: 'And what's more,' he added, 'outside Angola nobody knows that Jacinto's white.'

Finally Mário also wanted to include in his 'First Book of Portuguese-Language Black Poetry' the Cuban poet Nicolás Guillén, according to him 'the greatest voice of *négritude* in the Americas.' In Lídia's opinion the inclusion of the Cuban essentially defined the collection, which wasn't about *négritude*: 'What was brilliant about Guillén was that he managed to bring the Cuban Creole soul to cultured poetry; he didn't recover the Yoruba traditions. What he did was reproduce the models of miscegenation that had happened on the island for centuries. He merged the African tradition with the European tradition.' The choice of the poem 'Sound number 6', from *The Whole Sound*, is almost a flag of Creoleness: '(…) We've been together since long ago / white and black, all mixed; / one commanding, another sent, / all mixed; / San Berenito and another sent / all mixed / (…) / Come out mulatto, / loosen your shoe, / tell the white man he's not leaving… / No one cuts himself off from here; / look and don't stop, / hear and don't stop, / drink and don't stop, / eat and don't stop, / live and don't stop, / for everyone's sound is not going to stop!'

Lídia thought about all this. At a different time she would have found the paradox amusing. She would have tracked down Mário who would have received her with that glow in his eyes, would have said something, some gallant phrase, and the laughter of the two of them would have wiped away the bitterness of their discussion. But it was December and old Jacinto was dead. Amílcar Cabral had got married and returned to Guinea. Viriato da Cruz hadn't replied to her most recent letters.

Lídia was confused. Tired. She wanted to continue investigating Amo's past and knew that Berlin still bore many traces of his time there. Besides, she had some friends in the old German city. So she sold all her books, bought a plane ticket and went.

EXILE

'L'exilé partout est seul.' [The exile is alone everywhere.]

Viriato da Cruz in a letter to Monique Chainowiez,
written in Peking, 23 July 1971

Chapter 1

When Diogo Cão and his sailors disembarked at the mouth of the Zaire River and asked the inhabitants what that region was called they were told they were in Soio. But it seemed to Diogo Cão that the natives were replying to him in good Portuguese that they were in 'Sonho, Senhor' – that is, in 'Dream, Sir' – and he was amazed, not so much at having found people at the ends of the earth schooled in the Portuguese tongue, but mainly at the excellence and aptness of the name.

The sky moved and cried with long birds, the marshes pulsed with strange forms of life and the river spread itself out, dark and heavy, into the sea, and there it was so wide that one couldn't distinguish the far bank from the horizon.

In 1953 the landscape was still almost identical, but the place was no longer named after a Dream, but São António do Zaire. In that year, the same year Lídia moved to Berlin, a boy was born there who was given the name Tiago, or more properly Tiago de Santiago da Ressureição André. He was the first boy, after seven sisters. The father was a nurse's assistant, native to the area, and the mother a lady from M'Banza Congo, who dedicated herself to the trade in fabrics and boasted of belonging to the Bacongo royal line.

Santiago had a prodigious memory. He recounted events from his childhood, specifying the tiniest details, in such a way that I became convinced that he was making them up as he went along. Later I became certain that he did not. We used to play a game: I would read him a page from a book, without pausing or repeating anything, and a week later he would come back to me and repeat word for word what I'd read to him. He rarely made a mistake.

Tiago's mother wanted him to be a priest. As soon as the boy was of age she thought of sending him into the seminary. But that was not how things turned out. One day, in February 1961, Tiago's father arrived home very anxious. 'It would seem,' he confided, 'that something appalling has happened in Luanda, a chaos of blacks against whites, whites against us. A terrible misfortune.' The next day it was known that the capital's prisons had been attacked by groups of men armed with knives and katanas and that the Portuguese, mad with hatred and even more with terror, had fallen upon the slums and were killing people.

That same evening, the old man buried his fine Sunday suit in the back yard, alarmed at the rumours that were coming in from the South: they said that the Portuguese were arresting any natives who wore black. A civilised black man who dressed himself in black was a black man who got himself beaten up on the street – they came at him with headbutts, kicks, they tore up his documents and perhaps even killed him, many people were being killed like that, it was said. A few details, according to Santiago: 'I remember that on that day it was raining a lot, in Soio, and I ran away from school. At night a man came to see Kota. He was a relative from the North. He spoke *quicongo*. He talked, and he talked more: he said that the time of redemption was coming, that we should flee into the bush and he spoke of the UPA. He said that Holden Roberto was going to arrive by plane to expel all the *candungos* and also all the mulattos and also all the blacks who were friends of one or other.'

Santiago remembers that they ran away one moonlit night: 'We got into the bush and just walked like fuck.' They walked for several days. Along the way they joined up with other families and there were more and more people each day, all talking about the rumours of war. Many sung in *quicongo*: 'Oh Lord, look at your children, / Look, Lord, at the children of Israel / and Angola, Lord; look at your children / Slavery will end.'

There were some men who were carrying little round stones and they said these stones were bewitched and when you threw them at the Portuguese they'd explode as though they were bombs. There were also some who carried old homemade rifles and others katanas or long sticks. They were singing: 'He who eats at Flemish tables / Struck with fear his heart should be. / But not we! / For with Ninganessa near us / We need fear no tyranny!' Another chant spoke of the changes that were taking place: 'The land, yes, the land will change. / These apostles will rise up / On the Saviour's appointed day. / Let each man abandon the loincloth of despair / and wear the white cloths of joy! / Hope – the white man will leave! / We will never pay taxes again!'

The further they went into the bush the more people started abandoning their clothes and dressing themselves in leaves and tree-bark. The name Antoine Ninganessa was heard more and more and after a certain point all the songs were about him. They said that he had been sent by Holden Roberto to announce the good news. He was a prophet.

Little Tiago felt fear in his heart. He felt fear as though he had an enormous stone crushing his chest.

He looked around him and saw people he had known in the city, people who were usually sober, shy people, shouting and jumping, possessed by strange convulsions. Some women were assembling little mountains of herbs on the ground, piles of animal skins, of human hair and other things he couldn't name. Things he had never seen before. The women made these little piles and then set them on fire. He saw wonders: men who went onto the bonfires, remained there for long moments and came out again unharmed and dancing.

The women brought baskets full of a white earth and gave it to the people to eat, saying it was the earth where the nationalist Simon Kimbangu had been buried and that whoever ate it would be immune to the bullets of the Portuguese. They spoke of the war. They said that right across the North the people were killing the whites, they said thousands of Portuguese had already died. And they said too, that Ninganessa ordered women to kill their mulatto children and when they didn't they were killed too; someone would have had to kill them anyway, as after strangling their babies they went mad with the pain and started screaming incoherently and making such noise that it started bothering people.

One evening Tiago met Antoine Ninganessa. He was a very tall man, so thin that he looked as though he was about to split in two. He had long dishevelled hair and extremely red eyes which shone at night as though they were burning coals. He spoke constantly. As he ran to and fro he didn't stop talking, giving orders or praying aloud lifting his long spider arms to heaven. He was always saying that people should stop imitating the whites. Nobody should wear trousers or shirts, nobody should eat from aluminium plates, nobody must use toilet paper. Sometimes he became excited and shouted that it was necessary to do everything just the opposite of the Portuguese. And then he set an example himself, beginning to walk backwards like a crab, or sat in a chair with his legs folded the wrong way and turned his head towards his back and spoke not through his mouth but through his anus.

Seeing this, Tiago's father dared to ask whether he shouldn't turn himself completely in reverse, inside-out, thus making himself beyond any doubt the opposite of the Portuguese. He spoke gravely and seriously. However Ninganessa looked at him wildly and shouted at him, you're still white, a fucking white man, because no one but a white man could have thought something like that. He immediately ordered two men to grab him and when he saw him held securely he took a katana and cut off his head with a single stroke. 'The mouth of a foolish man is his only ruin,' he shouted, 'his lips are a trap for his only life.'

Tiago de Santiago da Ressureição André told me all this. It was in the São Paulo Prison. Santiago was a warder and liked to alarm us by telling us tales of violence and witchcraft. He had his own distinctive way of telling them. He laughed a lot. He always laughed at the most tragic parts. He told us how he had seen his father's head spinning in the air and he began to laugh.

God! He laughed with his whole body.

Chapter 2

In Berlin Lídia met a Brazilian painter called Alberto Rosengarten. He was a large, heavy man, twelve years older than her. But he had very blue eyes, filled with a chuckling light, and to Lídia he looked like a boy.

Alberto was militating in the Brazilian Communist Party. He was an agreeable communist, given to petit-bourgeois tolerances, a good drinker and an even better eater, who liked parties, expensive cigars, boxing, horses, and all kinds of games of chance. His friends would say he was immune to the tricks of love, but he fell in love with Lídia at first sight.

It was at the Akademie der Künste. Lídia had gone in by chance and was getting bored surrounded by Renaissance pictures, with fat nymphs and sad landscapes, when she heard someone behind her saying in Portuguese, 'This isn't the place for you.' She turned around and met sudden blue eyes. The eyes were laughing. It was a big red-headed man and he was laughing: 'I'm sure you're Brazilian,' he said.

Those were nervous days in Berlin. The cafés were full of young people. They drank hot chocolate with a lot of cream, they ate fruit cake and had enthusiastic discussions about the fate of the world. Lídia still barely spoke German, and unable to understand everything that was going on around her she felt lost. A former Agronomy classmate had let her have a room in a nineteenth-century building, which retained a façade completely riddled with bullets as a reminder of the war. And while she waited for the German government to award her refugee status and a study grant she spent her days wandering about, or closed away in a library, trying to find signs of Guilherme Amo.

Alberto Rosengarten took charge of her. He arranged a job for her in a publishing house and introduced her to his vast circle of friends – painters, sculptors, writers, professional agitators, lorry-drivers, students, Polish aristocrats… basically the many and varied people without any fixed job who had made Berlin their temporary port of shelter.

Nanaya Mestre was one of the first people Alberto introduced to Lídia. Nanaya sang jazz in a little nightclub, El Perro Loco. She had a hot, hoarse voice and natural Brazilian exuberance. She had come from Bahia five years earlier – pursuing an adolescent love – and quickly became very popular. She was also known for her talents as a medium and regularly practised cartomancy. She lived in Ceciliem Garten, on the second floor of a brick-coloured building, and it was there one autumn evening that she suggested reading Lídia's tarot.

First she laid out the Tarot of Marseilles. In the recent past – still capable of influencing the present – was the Tower, the most ominous card, a sign of inevitable destruction. Next – for the present – came up the Lunatic and the Hanged Man, indicating isolation, disorientation and instability, linked to betrayal and abandonment. Nanaya interpreted the cards with nervous gestures, entwining her fingers and separating them again:

'The Hanged Man,' she said, 'is also a card that foretells sacrifice and self-denial.'

Lídia smiled at her. She looked through the window and saw a solemn garden, with big golden-leaved trees. 'In the middle, around you, is the Star,' Nanaya continued, 'which is a card of creative inspiration and energy. It's also the appearance of new ideas and of profound optimism. The obstacles, the Devil, will be irrationality, powerful sexual desire and irrepressible instincts. In the House of aspirations, Justice represents the desire to triumph over obstacles, impartiality and perfect balance.'

Then Nanaya laid out the Egyptian Tarot: 'The first oracles confirm that this is a period of great disquiet for you, and economic troubles,' she said, holding Lídia's gaze with hers.

The Angolan smiled at her again: 'That much I know already.'

'There is another thing too,' Nanaya added, 'the oracles say that you are involved in a romantic relationship that is important but which will not last your whole life.'

'Amazing!' Lídia joked, 'and there was me thinking that even two lives wouldn't be enough for so great a love.'

Chapter 3

Just a few months after arriving in Berlin, Lídia resumed her correspondence with Viriato da Cruz. The young revolutionary wrote her lengthy letters, giving news of friends and polemicising passionately, discussing politics and literature. I have read these letters, and they seem to me to be important for understanding the evolution of the modern nationalist movement. Some are fine works of literature. The style, while colloquial, is pure and somewhat distant, as though Viriato were addressing himself not only to Lídia but to a whole audience of listeners – the future.

Lídia also showed me a watercolour he had signed; it's a picture of Tundavala, the grasses tall and green along the edges of the abyss. By my calculations it was painted in 1951, the year Viriato served in the office of the Diogo Cão high school in Lubango.

In 1954 it was Mário de Andrade's turn to abandon Portugal, settling in Paris. Lídia heard about this because of an Algerian friend of Alberto's who appeared in Berlin, having come from Paris where he had been at the Maison du Maroc with an Angolan called Buanga Fele. The Algerian had been very struck by Buanga Fele: 'When he speaks it's like he's on fire,' he said. And he added that the young man was working at the headquarters of the magazine *Présence Africaine*.

Lídia asked for a week's holiday from the publishers and went to Paris with Nanaya. They didn't find Mário de Andrade at the headquarters of *Présence Africaine*, at 17 rue de Chaligny, and the young woman left him a note – 'Have I found you?' – and the address of the little pension where they were staying.

Mário appeared that same night. He was very thin, so thin that he hardly seemed to have a body inside that heavy dark gabardine. But his eyes lit up his little round-rimmed glasses. They shone more than ever. He embraced Lídia like a shipwrecked man embraces a plank of wood. It was only when he let go of her that he noticed the presence of Nanaya:

'I'm sure I know you,' he said. 'I think I've seen you in my dreams.'

They talked till the early hours. Lídia told me, 'It was the longest conversation I had with Mário, and listening to him talk I knew that he had found his destiny.' Nanaya, whom I didn't meet until March 1991, in Baía, did not forget that night either:

'Mário spoke a lot about his work on *Présence Africaine*. I think he worked as secretary to Alioune Diop, and through this role he seemed to know everybody: Senghor, Césaire, Nicolás Guillén, Aragon, even Sartre himself.'

The conversation was proceeding in a lively fashion – so Nanaya recalled – when Mário suddenly lowered his voice, put his hand in one of the pockets of his gabardine and pulled out an envelope which he handed to Lídia: 'They want to form an army to liberate Angola and they've written to me to ask for weapons,' he said. Lídia looked at him stunned, opened the letter and read it: 'I don't know what to think,' she murmured. Mário was ecstatic:

'Algeria has already taken up arms to rid themselves of the French. So what about us, what are we waiting for?'

Chapter 4

In order to try and reconstruct this whole period in Lídia's life – the years of exile, between 1953 and 1974 – I have mainly been using the interviews she gave me. Nanaya Mestre and other people who were close to Lídia also gave me valuable pointers. Nonetheless I only know very little.

I know that the week she spent in Paris was important to Lídia. I know this because she said as much in a letter to Mário Pinto de Andrade, written in Berlin and dated 20 January 1972: 'I think back to the few days we spent together, in Paris, when anything was possible. We were going to liberate Angola, remember?'

I also know that about a year later Lídia left Europe and went to live in Olinda, in the Brazilian north-east, with Alberto Rosengarten. That much I know but I don't know the details, the circumstances, what it was that weighed on Lídia's decision.

Let's assume: Alberto loved her. Alberto wanted to return to Olinda, the city of his birth. Every day he would dream about the Olinda skies, the light of dawn, the Portuguese-style houses, those happy coloured façades. Alberto loved Lídia and he wanted her to see his country. He began to paint watercolours that were sad, almost transparent and yet haunted by an immense bitterness.

I suspect that Lídia didn't love him. Another assumption: Lídia accepted Alberto's love gladly but without enthusiasm. 'Alberto is a friend who makes me happy,' she explained to Nanaya once. The Brazilian's anxiety began to infect her, however. The simple vexations of everyday began to seem intolerable to her – the little bureaucratic obstacles relating to her stay in Germany; the way people looked at her in the street, the lack of sea, the harsh Germanic language. She wrote long letters to Viriato da Cruz and then tore them up; she said to him (I'm still assuming): 'German men are very tall and blond: I hate them. Their wives are precise and methodical: I hate them. The gardens of Berlin are totally aseptic. I can't bear the silence of the trees.' In reality these were the same tall trees which had once fascinated her, but when she looked at them now she no longer found in them signs of her childhood. 'Exile is where we don't recognise ourselves in anything,' she wrote in a poem from the time; 'Exile is the hostile silence of things.'

It is possible for us to imagine this bitterness evolving: one December morning, when they awoke, Alberto said wistfully: 'In Olinda the first light of dawn still carries the fragrance of the sea.' They were lying down and Alberto looked bigger. Lídia climbed on top of him, kissed him on the mouth and looking straight at him without a smile asked simply:

'When do we leave?'

Chapter 5

Olinda is a genial city, the twin of old Benguela with its same tranquil people, identical in the slow breathing of the streets and the houses beneath the sun. Lídia recognised herself in it, and perhaps would still be living there had she not been suddenly awoken on the night of February 4th, 1961 by the telephone ringing:

'You have to join us, now you can't refuse any more,' Mário's voice on the other end sounded anxious and bewildered, 'they've started the war!'

'They who?' asked Lídia. There was a brief but dense silence and she regretted having asked the question. Mário spoke again. Lídia imagined his face tense. She imagined him moving the phone to his left hand and wiping his sweat with the right; it must be very hot in Conakry:

'They who? What the hell! Switch on the BBC and listen to the news. We've started the war. Luanda's burning!'

Mário seemed anxious. The truth was that he didn't know himself who it was that had started the war. In May 1960 he had flown from Paris to Conakry where Amílcar de Cabral, Viriato da Cruz and Hugo de Menezes – the son of Aires de Menezes, the doctor from São Tomé whose amazing appearance had had such an impact on Lídia's childhood – were already waiting for him. Mário had met the president of Guinea-Conakry, Sekou Touré, in Paris. Around the same time he had befriended many other Guineans who had come to occupy important roles in the regime, and after the independence of Guinea-Conakry he would use these contacts to secure support for the Angolan cause. Meanwhile Viriato da Cruz had also gone into exile. The People's Movement for the Liberation of Angola, the MPLA, created in Luanda, inspired by Viriato, was beginning slowly to make its presence felt and Mário was elected its secretary-general. In Angola the Portuguese political police arrested dozens of nationalists, in an operation which marked the toughening of the Salazar regime's stance towards the colonies and which would become known to history as the 'Case of the Fifty'.

The structures that were opposed to Portuguese colonialism were multiplying all over the place, overlapping with each other and muddling up together at a vertiginous speed: the National Liberation Movement of the Portuguese Colonies, the MLNCP, was transformed into the Anti-Colonial Movement, the MAC, and then into the African Revolutionary Front for the National Independence of Portuguese Colonies, FRAINCP, and finally the Conference of Nationalist Organisations of Portuguese Colonies, CONCP. During the course of the 'Case of the Fifty' a number of nationalist organisations were mentioned, from the (by then already extinct) Angolan Communist Party, the PCA, to some 'Firm for the Liberation of Angola' or other, via the Union of Angolan Populations, UPA, led by Holden Roberto, a *quicongo* aristocrat living as a refugee in Léopoldville. In the National Assembly in Lisbon, António de Oliveira Salazar commented ironically, 'There aren't many of them, but they keep changing their name so it seems like there's lots of them.'

With the support of China, Algeria and Conakry, the MPLA began from 1960 to develop certain diplomatic and propaganda activities. In December of that year, at the House of Commons in London, Mário de Andrade read a communiqué to a group of journalists, in which the MPLA asked Salazar to abide by a recent UN decision requiring that Portugal concedes independence to its colonies. If they did not, so said the communiqué, the MPLA would launch itself into direct action for the liberation of Angola. However when the BBC began to release the first pieces of news about the attacks on prisons in Luanda, on February 4th, 1961, Mário de Andrade, Viriato da Cruz and the remaining handful of Angolan exiles who made up the MPLA were worried: who was it that had plotted that madness?

'It was the people!' said Viriato. 'Or rather, it was us!'

The brains behind the attack on the Luanda prisons had in fact been Canon Manuel das Neves, a *mestizo* Luandan of whom Lídia retained contradictory memories: 'I found him a fascinating character,' Lídia said to me one of the last times we were together, 'even when he was talking about something simple it was as though he was really talking about other things. My grandfather was a great friend of his, but every once in a while they would have terrible arguments and then they'd go for months without speaking. Some said he was a Bolshevik. I remember the first time I heard anyone use that word it was in relation to him.'

It's said that a few days after the attack on the prisons, the PIDE found bloody katanas hidden in the Sé Church at which Manuel das Neves officiated. Many of the young people who took part in the operation were students at the São Domingos seminary. They had dressed themselves severely in black and apart from the katanas and the sticks they also carried rosary beads and wooden crucifixes. Some of the survivors admitted that the sticks were bewitched and the katanas had been blessed by the Canon. The Portuguese papers never reported these details; on the contrary, most of them believed the rumours that credited the organisation of the attack to certain foreign powers and organisations, 'enemies of western Christian civilisation'. One political official drew attention to the fact that 'many of the terrorists arrested only speak French' and some media went so far as to note the discovery of machine guns that were Czech-made. And not one newspaper referred to the 'Queen' – Engrácia Francisca Cabenha, a fifteen-year-old virgin who (for some magical function) accompanied the attackers – nor to the obscure ceremonies and rituals to which they subjected themselves.

When the MPLA claimed authorship of the operation, explaining that it had sought to liberate many of their comrades arrested following the 'Case of the Fifty', the Portuguese ideologues and high command breathed a sigh of relief: the world was making sense again.

Canon Manuel das Neves was transferred in secret to a little town in the north of Portugal, Soutelo, where they removed him from existence, isolating him between the austere walls of a Jesuit friary. The very little that was left of him died ten years later.

Chapter 6

In 1961 you went to work for Guinea-Conakry at the National Research Institute, where Mário Pinto de Andrade already was. Did you take on any role in the leadership of the MPLA?

Lídia: No. I took part in a lot of meetings, but I never agreed to represent the MPLA at meetings with foreigners. Mário got annoyed with me, he repeated that I had to choose my class allegiance and commit myself completely to the struggle of the people. I laughed. My grandfather, while he was an anarchist-unionist and a romantic by nature, had taught me to be a sceptic. Above all he taught me to mistrust those enlightened people, those people who knew the fate of the world. He'd say to me, 'You get wings on angels, just as you get them on demons, just as you get them on parrots. To be safe it's best to treat everyone as though they were parrots.'

In those days were there more angels or demons?

Lídia: In those days we were still just half a dozen intellectuals without malice, people of a revolutionary morality resistant to everything. That's what the MPLA was. I remember once when Viriato went to China to try and find support and returned with his pockets stuffed with twenty-dollar bills. The money was divided strictly among the different committees and there was never the least trouble about this. The trouble began later when the movement grew. Then some of those who'd been angels became demons. Others turned parrot.

On March 15th, 1961, the UPA began its armed struggle against the colonial regime. How did the MPLA react to this?

Lídia: Well, first of all I'm not so sure it was the UPA. It was certainly a rural revolt, instigated by the UPA, but which got out of the control of its leaders. The Portuguese response was terrible. A few days ago I read an article from a newspaper of that time. It was describing how some white farmers, 'understandably desperate at the loss of all their goods and the death of their loved ones' – I'm quoting the paper here – dedicated themselves for weeks to games of death. The most popular was the Queuing Game: they'd line up a number of prisoners in single-file, put the barrel of a gun to the chest of the first and fire a single shot, and the winner was whoever managed to get through the greatest number of them. But what was the question again?

I wanted to know the reaction of the MPLA to March 15th.

Lídia: Bewilderment, of course. The UPA was a movement of the right, Holden a puppet of international imperialism (that's what they said), but it was the UPA that had the support of the country-folk, and that was intolerable. And what was worse, no one could say it.

(Interview with Lídia do Carmo Ferreira, Luanda, 23 May 1990)

Chapter 7

Blind airplanes bombarded the forests of the North for almost six weeks. In his desperate flight to Zaire, Tiago de Santiago da Ressureição André saw the villages devastated by the fury of the Portuguese, the rivers and forests devoured by napalm fire. Close to Nova Caipemba, he told me, they found a wood made entirely of unvarying ash, and within it a few huts also of ash, and inside the huts, mats and water jars; and a variety of utensils, all of ash. Fixed to the smallest branches of the trees were hundreds of little birds, also of dead ash, with their happy songs of rain crystallised at the tips of their beaks. The bombs of the Portuguese had frozen the passage of time over the wood, enclosing that anxious instant in a bell-jar of ashes. When a moment – a moment that everyone felt was never ending – had passed, someone raised his arm and with the tips of his fingers touched the fragile ash structure. Then the whole wood began to collapse, with a slow whisper of light rain, and with it the birds and the huts and the domestic utensils, and soon there was nothing around them but a broad plain of unchanging ash.

Chapter 8

How did the world react to March 15th?

Lídia: The revolt of March 15th and the subsequent response of the Portuguese launched Angola into the centre of the world's attention. The UPA, in spite of receiving American support, managed to arouse sympathies in certain sectors of the revolutionary left, forcing the MPLA to radicalise their position. In interviews and statements to the American press, Holden Roberto denounced them as a group of communists enfiefed to Moscow. At the same time, realising that the UPA would never be able to assert themselves nationally and internationally as long as they were tied to the old ideals of restoring the Kingdom of Congo, having been present at its creation, Roberto tried to establish alliances with other groups and individuals of different ethnic origin; and this was how the National Front for the Liberation of Angola, the FNLA, was born. In hallway discussions the directors of the FNLA characterised us as the children of the colonisers, mulattos and whites, who wanted to usurp power from their parents. It was the best definition I've heard of the MPLA to this day.

Maybe it is a good definition. But it's worth remembering that in the United States or in Latin America it was also the children of the colonisers who brought about independence.

Lídia: That's true, but they were careful to eliminate the Indians first. Whatever the case, the FNLA sought to emphasise our petit-bourgeois origins, insinuating that not one of us had links to the rural masses and that we weren't capable for this reason of structuring a movement of armed action against Portuguese domination. Frantz Fanon, who at the time was held in very high regard by the European left, owing to his support for Algerian independentists, was one of the first personalities to defend this position.

How was it that the MPLA reacted to these kinds of accusation?

Lídia: In 1962 the Portuguese Communist Party managed – with Soviet support – to liberate Agostinho Neto and he was elected President of the MPLA at National Conference, now in Kinshasa where the leadership of the movement had been transferred. It was clearly a manoeuvre to silence the UPA's insinuations. Neto was black, he was the son of a protestant pastor and had great popular support from Catete, the area he was from. Beside this, his imprisonment in 1960 had made him a hero of international renown. In Paris there was even a petition demanding that the Portuguese government free him. Sartre signed it, for example.

At that point there was still nobody disputing Agostinho Neto's leadership?

Lídia: Nobody! Except, of course, for Viriato da Cruz. Viriato never accepted the decision of National Conference. He was mad with rage: 'This man's an autocrat!' he shouted in the middle of a meeting, pointing his finger at Neto. He was completely alone. Mário de Andrade and all our companions from Conakry remained silent. Some stood up to denounce him as an opportunist or a radical. And I, I hardly knew what was going on, I got on a plane and flew to Kinshasa in an attempt to reconcile the two positions. I didn't succeed at all. Viriato thought we were against him because he was a *mestizo*, and Neto, with that bovine obstinacy of his, refused to have his name at the top of a list on which Viriato's name appeared.

(Interview with Lídia do Carmo Ferreira, Luanda, 23 May 1990)

Chapter 9

Understanding that the break had already become irreparable, Lídia returned to Conakry. She spent another year in Guinea, watching with bafflement and alarm as the totalitarian delirium of Sekou Touré proceeded. One day they came to tell her that Viriato da Cruz had joined the FNLA. Soon afterwards she learned that Agostinho Neto was getting ready to form an alliance with two small movements inspired by the Portuguese, and almost immediately afterwards received a phone call from Mário de Andrade, telling her in confidence that he was going to offer his resignation as secretary for external relations: 'For me that was the final straw. I went to Alberto and told him I missed Olinda.'

Alberto Rosengarten was arrested in Olinda in April 1964, following the military coup that installed the dictatorship in Brazil. Lídia spent two months in the jails of Rio and São Paulo and then was expelled, managing to obtain asylum in Germany.

The communiqué announcing the death of Alberto Rosengarten said that the painter had committed suicide, throwing himself from a sixth-floor window (Lídia: 'It's possible, it's well known that prisoners like to fly'). It also said that he was an agent of the Soviet KGB, and that he had developed subversive activities against the integrity of a brother-country.

A few months later, a group calling themselves the Rosengarten Committee detonated a bomb close to the American embassy in Brasilia. On the broken wall it was possible to make out a sentence, in large red letters: 'Rosengarten did not die! He lives in the hearts of the p–' That was where the sentence was cut off by the explosion.

THE ETERNAL DAY

'OUR VICTORY IS INCURABLE!'

> Headline occupying the whole front page of the *Certain Victory*
> newspaper, the official organ of the MPLA, on 31 March 1975

Chapter 1

In Mayday Square Zorro was trying to make his way through the crowd to get close to Paulete. He could see her. She had her arms raised and she was dancing. Zorro imagined the young woman's face. He remembered the first time they had danced together. Fear. (Could it have been fear?) Anxiety, disquiet. They were dancing together and he'd lowered his eyes and saw her with her eyelids closed, smiling. Now she was too far away and had her back to him, but from the movement of her arms, her torso and her vast black hair – thicker than night itself – Zorro was sure that she was smiling. She had her eyes closed, and she was smiling.

Around him the crowd was shouting. Singing. Zorro heard loose phrases, 'Long live people-power!' 'MPLA! MPLA!' 'Victory is assured!' A tall, strong man, who smelled of garlic and alcohol, hugged him.

'A hug, comrade! Long live our MPLA!'

Zorro drew people's attention. A fair *mestizo*. Tall, slender-bodied, with an energetic face (which people used to call chiselled) burned by the sun. He wore his hair long, tied at the back of his neck with a kind of slide in blackwood, in such a way as to resemble a horse's tail. That gave him the look of a rebel. He was only twenty, but usually said twenty-six.

In the previous twelve months he had experienced more than in the previous twelve years: he had left for exile, become involved in the political struggle, lost the woman of his life and gone to war. He understood very quickly that this war was a strange kind of suicide. Dazed, he discovered that almost nothing he had believed in hitherto made sense.

In 1974 he had decided to leave Angola. He was in the second year of Economics at the University of Luanda, when he learned that his name was on the list of recruits for the colonial army. He said goodbye to his mother and left in secret for Lisbon. He wanted to make it to Paris, where hundreds of Angolan and Portuguese deserters were living. He had already managed to make contact with a network that helped to bring emigrants clandestinely onto French soil, when the Carnation Revolution broke out. 'I wanted to get back at once,' he told me, 'but then Paulete happened to me. Women like that always happen to you suddenly.'

It was at a party at the home of some Angolan students to commemorate the liberation of a group of MPLA prisoners. The young militants were of course the centre of attention, but they were not the ones who caught Zorro's notice:

'There were lots of people, a lot of hysteria. But she was calm. She was standing in a corner, pretending to listen to someone.'

She was wearing a black dress and a broad leather belt with brass figures on it. Her hair was hidden by a red and yellow handkerchief. The dress, very short and tight, drew the shape of her firm breasts, her broad hips. Zorro just waited for the other man to move away and approached her. 'My name is Carlos Umbertali de Miranda,' he said, 'but everyone knows me as Zorro.' The girl laughed:

'The crusader for justice?!'

Zorro was tired of the old joke. That name was a childhood scar. But the young woman laughed, and her laugh echoed fresh and brilliant like a shattering of glass. The lad laughed too. He asked her to dance and only then did she introduce herself:

'Paulete,' she said, 'Paulete do Carmo Ferreira Bastos.'

Zorro looked at her, astonished:

'Carmo Ferreira? Daughter of Lídia Ferreira?'

Lídia do Carmo Ferreira. Once in a cultural soirée Zorro had recited one of her poems. The poem described a house by the sea: 'In the ancient house where I was born and was / happy for ever / it all persists, the same and eternal, / still the same too is the light / of dusk / in the rooms. The immense moment, / And on the broad open verandas / over the sea / still the same too is the fragrance / of the wind.' In the final lines the metaphor became obvious: 'Somewhere the House is waiting / for me, for us. / Somewhere the House lives. / I hope. We hope / with the secret learning of the trees / and of the sorcerers. / A House like that, nothing / can consume. Nothing!' This was in 1973. A few classmates got up and clapped at length.

| 80 |

Most, however, were unable to understand the poem. To tell the truth, they didn't even know Lídia Ferreira.

The university students in Luanda were almost all white, the children of the Portuguese, and lived in an odd world that was politically aseptic, where the serious disquiets of the present didn't reach. In that universe of parties, clubs, beaches, American music, Coca-cola, drinks and joints, mopeds and beauty contests, Africa was just a distant rumour. A landscape of baobabs and ruddy acacias, tall grasses, and black women bare-breasted.

At the end of the soirée one of the professors summoned him discretely to his office: 'What you did was insensitive,' he told him. Zorro remained silent. No one knew this man. He had arrived just a few weeks earlier from Portugal and seemed to avoid the students and even his colleagues. Rumour had it that he was a PIDE informer. The professor stood up: 'What you did was insensitive,' he said again, 'it was gratuitous provocation, and it was childish, but I want to congratulate you on your courage.' He held out his hand. Zorro hesitated a moment and then did the same. That gesture was the beginning of his political training. The Portuguese man belonged to a tiny Maoist party whose leadership was in exile in Paris, and he had access to banned books and leaflets. Zorro began to spend time at his house. He would close the blinds, turn the radio up to its maximum, and spend hours and hours discussing revolutionary strategies, the colonial problem, the successes and mistakes of the nationalist struggle.

The professor was very critical of the role of the Portuguese Communist Party and even the MPLA itself: 'They are both in the hands of a revisionist clique,' he would say, 'they've sold out to Soviet interests. The MPLA wants Angola's independence so that Soviet imperialism can extend its clutches to western Africa. Viriato da Cruz denounced this and had to take refuge in China. Whoever rules western Africa will rule the world.' Zorro was amazed, he had never seen things through that prism before. When he decided to leave for exile the professor showed him a list with names and addresses of comrades in Portugal and in Paris: 'I want you to memorise this page, then burn it.' Zorro agreed. A week later, already in Lisbon, he discovered that he had forgotten everything.

Paulete laughed at Zorro's question:

'Lídia's daughter? Lídia's my aunt, and as far as I know she doesn't have children. She's teaching in Berlin, at the university.'

They went to dance. Someone had put on Angola 72 and Bonga was singing 'Kilumba diá Ngola'. Zorro felt Paulete's heat in his arms. He felt her scent and her rhythm, the urgency of her rhythm. He heard, as from within, the hoarse voice that sang: 'Kilumba ayá mié, Kilumba ayá mié, Kilumba ayá mié mu Angolá, kilumba ayá mié.' He lowered his eyes and saw her with her eyelids shut, an absent smile.

On Mayday Square he felt fear again. (Doubt? Disquiet?) 'She's escaped,' he thought as he approached her. 'She isn't a woman, she's a premonition.' He touched her shoulder. The girl turned and opened deep eyes to him:

'Zorro!' she shouted, hugging him, 'when did you arrive?'

'I'm just arriving,' said Zorro. Burying his face in her thick hair he whispered something in her ear. The girl laughed:

'You're a reactionary,' she said. 'A real son of a whore!'

'Much worse,' Zorro murmured. 'A real son of a war.'

Chapter 2

'In Catengue,' Zorro told me, 'there was a moment I thought about ending it all. Because there was nowhere to go. I didn't believe in anything any more, but I knew I didn't have the right to contaminate other people with my disbelief.'

Zorro's story: he was in Catengue. One morning he woke up and saw the purple earth, the mountains sinking into the mist. He heard a groan and discovered a girl dying next to him. She was sixteen years old: 'She gripped a KA-2 tightly and she smiled at me. She said to me, "We're going to thrash the *carcamanos*, commander. We're going to win!" I knew we weren't.'

Zorro was a political controller for the squadron. In October they named him as the man in charge of logistics for the Emergency Committee for the Defence of the City of Moçâmedes. However, when they informed him of this, Moçâmedes had already been occupied by South African troops. The group that defended the city to the end was made up of sixteen-year-old boys. Not one escaped. Zorro knew this too. And yet he got into an old Dakota and flew to Benguela.

'I took part in the fighting to occupy the city,' he told me, 'it was easy because the UNITA delegation was militarily very weak. There was almost no bloodshed.' Meanwhile the South African column had gone up to Coporolo. Here it divided: fifteen armoured vehicles set off for Benguela and five for Cubal. Zorro watched these manoeuvres from a distance: 'I saw it all with my binoculars. Later I learned that the five armoured vehicles had been received by the FAPLA with festivities. In order to calm their soldiers the FAPLA high command had sent a message assuring them of the quick dispatch of reinforcements. The soldiers in Cubal saw the South Africans arriving, thought they were the reinforcements they'd been promised, abandoned their trenches and started dancing in the middle of the streets.'

Simon du Plessis, a young South African lieutenant I met in São

Paulo Prison in Luanda, was in one of those armoured vehicles: 'We arrived in Cubal,' he told me, 'to find the road full of blacks who were all dancing. I wanted to stop the car. I caught the attention of the gunner, and said to him, "The savages are dancing. Why the hell are they dancing?!" He laughed. "I don't know," he replied, "there are some things we can't know. The bastards aren't like us." And he opened fire. That day we killed a lot of your people.'

The priority of the FAPLA military commanders was to protect Luanda. Nobody knew exactly what should be done regarding the South Africans, and the rare instructions that arrived contradicted one another. In Catengue, a Cuban, Captain Rodriguez, took command of operations. 'We made mistake after mistake,' Zorro told me, 'first because we could have abandoned the positions we knew were unsustainable at the right time, and retreated to the interior, to the area of the Mumuilas or the Mucubais. But at that time the order wasn't to retreat. Later we retreated when faced with the South Africans, leaving our weapons and luggage behind us. Catengue was a continuation of that disaster. We set up a defense based on three rows of artillery. One at three kilometres from the fork in the road, one at four and the last at five. Captain Rodriguez wanted me to be the one to fire the monster-gun and with the first shot – I was lucky! – I smashed the front armoured vehicle. But then the South Africans began to respond, and they quickly silenced the first line, then the second and finally the third.'

They then retreated to a site twenty kilometres from Coporolo, a valley through which the road snaked. Captain Rodriguez explained that it was necessary to dig up some trenches and wait there for the South Africans to arrive. Zorro protested, it seemed to him more sensible to set up the ambush in the mountains. Rodriguez silenced him with a shout:

'Coño, it's going to be like I say it is!'

They were still digging the trenches when the South African armoured vehicles rose up behind them – they had abandoned the road and cut up along a trail – and they opened fire: 'Our watchword was run-run-run-run-run...' Zorro told me. 'We got ourselves into the bush and didn't stop till we'd reached Benguela!'

Early in the morning of the Catengue battle Zorro woke up and saw a girl next to him, dying. 'She was half-dead already,' Zorro told me, 'she had a bullet in her chest and was losing a lot of blood. I asked her where she was from and she told me she'd been born in Moçâmedes. I'm from Namibe too. I was curious and asked her what she was called.'

The girl looked at him with a strange expression of pride.

'I-Shall See-the-End.'

Chapter 3

'Zorro? I already knew him by name.' Paulete:

'I already knew him. Everyone knew him. They said he was nuts, that he wasn't afraid of anything. I liked him because he knew how to dance and he was shy and delicate. He didn't try to get me into bed right away like the others did.'

Paulete at the time was coming to the end of her high school course. Her parents had sent her to the house of an aunt in Lisbon following a scandal that had shaken Benguela.

'A stupid story,' Paulete explained to me. 'A teacher who fell in love with me. He was married and much older than I was. One day he asked me to go with him to his house because he had something important to tell me. He didn't get a moment to tell me anything. His wife appeared with a gun in her hand, shot him and then tried to kill herself but was shaking so badly that she couldn't do it. The man, poor thing, was left with a hole in his neck. He wrote me a letter while he was in hospital, and that was the last I heard of him. Then my parents sent me to Portugal.'

The story that was told in Benguela was slightly different, but that is always the way: whoever tells a tale adds a little bit to it, in Luanda two or three little bits, in Benguela a tale becomes a novel. What is for sure is that Paulete went to Lisbon, and she was there when the April Revolution broke out. She was with the people walking the streets, shouting; she went to rallies; she took part in the endless student gatherings, demanding the end of the elitist system of awarding grades, the expulsion of reactionary professors and insisting on not a single soldier more being sent to Africa. She was at the secret MRPP meetings where they discussed whether or not long hair was reactionary, with its defenders pointing to the good example set by Marx, its detractors rebelling against the hippy movement as a symptom of the irremediable decadence of capitalist society.

By the time she met Zorro she had already read the basics of Mao and Enver Hoxha and supported the creation in Angola of a new party 'of the revolutionary left, able to represent the workers, the countryfolk and the oppressed masses from the slums.' Zorro was impressed at her energy: 'We went out every night, we'd go to put up posters or photocopy manifestos and didn't return home till the early hours. I'd rented a room in Graça and Paulete left her aunt and came to live with me. We would make love still dirty from the paint or the glue, but at seven in the morning she was already back on her feet, clean and fresh, as though she'd slept all night long.'

Chapter 4

When he had released himself from Paulete's arms, Zorro realised that the girl was accompanied by a young white man, strong
and with long hair and beard, scattered thinly, and round-rimmed
glasses that looked very small in the middle of his broad face. Paulete
introduced him to Zorro with an ambiguous smile. 'Francisco Borja
Neves, a friend from Benguela. You may have heard of him, he's got
this crazy idea that he's a poet.'

Zorro put out his hand which the other shook firmly: 'Indeed,'
he said to him, 'I remember having read something of yours in the
Jornal de Angola.'

In fact Paulete had talked about him a lot. He had been her first
boyfriend. 'He was a boy from a good family, from Lobito, the son of
an engineer on the Railroad.' Paulete spoke of him in a neutral tone
(that was the most appalling thing about her, that tone of voice). 'I
met him when I was sixteen. I was a virgin but I thought of myself as
a *femme fatale*. I'd go out at night, on my own, in my red miniskirt,
very short, and a velvet hat.'

People would make comments. At high school the boys would
fall silent as she passed. Her mother made big scenes at home:
'That's what I was trying to do, *épater les bourgeois*!' One night a
car horn sounded behind her. Francisco Neves, at the wheel of an
E-type jaguar convertible, was striking a pose. He laughed:

'What's a woman like you doing in a place like this at half past one
in the morning?'

An American film, from the fifties. 'We were so stupid!' Paulete
looked at him intensely:

'I've been walking,' she replied. 'Walking my anxiety.'

They started going out. 'We went out for a year, or a little longer.
Every week there was a party at someone's house. There was a lot of
drinking, smoking weed, discussing music and football. On Saturdays we'd go by car to Baía Azul, to Caotinha or to Sombreiro. Chico
went deep-sea diving and I sunbathed. At night we would swim naked

and it was incredible: in the moonlight the seawater seethed with fish. We remained very still and they would come and nibble at our bodies.'

The romance lasted until a Spanish singer appeared in Benguela, who did Elvis Presley impersonations at a fashionable club. Paulete fell in love with the Spaniard and started going everywhere with him. Borja Neves was disoriented: he cried, he made promises and threats, pursued her for days on end around the streets of Lobito and Benguela (Paulete: 'Love makes people ridiculous. Hatred is a more respectable feeling.'). Meanwhile there was the incident with the teacher and Paulete was exiled to Lisbon. In September 1974 she returned to Angola with Zorro, and no sooner had she arrived in Benguela than she discovered a quite different Borja Neves. The boy was now youth representative for the MPLA and went around enthusiastically preparing for the revolution. He spoke musically, imitating the speech of the people. He had let his beard grow and proletarianised his beautiful jaguar. The car resembled an old bus, always full of people and bits and pieces and covered in the dust of the slums. Stuck to one of the doors it had an enormous poster with the beautiful face of Commander Valódia, treacherously assassinated, and the slogan, 'Victory is assured, the struggle continues.' His car was stolen not long afterwards, but Borja Neves didn't seem to mind: 'It was merely an excrescence of my bourgeois past,' he said to his friends; however, immediately afterwards he learned that the car had passed into the hands of the local FNLA representative and he was furious: 'Clowns!' he exploded, 'don't they have any idea how much it cost my parents to make me bourgeois?!...'

Borja Neves's parents had returned to Portugal, but he refused to follow them and lived alone in the huge family residence in Restinga. Not exactly alone, in truth: he shared the house with a servant, André Calandula, the main object of his political indoctrination.

'It was an enormous house,' Paulete told me, 'with something like nine or ten rooms and about five bathrooms. Francisco thought that a communist couldn't have servants and so he promoted Calandula to be his collaborator – at least, that's what he called him – and set him up in one of the guest bedrooms. When he went to Luanda Calandula stayed in the house and in the MPLA. He died during UNITA's occupation of the city.'

Zorro remembered him: 'After the Catengue disaster we went on foot to Benguela where we stayed a little while. Almost the whole population supported UNITA and when they realised that we'd been routed they chased us out throwing stones, with boos and insults. Calandula's someone I can't forget, because in the middle of all that confusion, while our military bosses were burning the stores and fleeing at the head of their troops, he behaved with great courage. He insisted on staying, even on his own, and he stayed. I never heard of him again.'

At the end of 1974 Borja Neves went to Luanda, to study economics, and became involved with the Active Revolt group: 'I was the person who introduced him to Lídia and to Mário Pinto de Andrade,' Paulete recalls. 'At that time he had begun a collaboration with the *Diário de Luanda* and wanted to get an interview with my aunt.'

Lídia had been in Luanda for some three months, and spent her days at meetings, trying to set up bonds of understanding between the different groups warring within and around the MPLA: 'Borja Neves approached me to ask for an interview, and that was when he began to show an interest in Active Revolt. I think he came to three or four meetings. He seemed like a good lad, but he talked too much, he was always justifying himself. He had a great need to demonstrate that he knew everything and that he was just as Angolan as any of the rest of us.'

At one of the first meetings, also attended by Mário Pinto de Andrade, it was decided that as a matter of security everyone present had to choose a war name. A *mestiza* doctor said she would be called Ginga. A tall young man lately arrived from a long exile did not hesitate a moment: 'I am Kalungá,' he said. He spoke with a heavy Parisian accent and using words and constructions from French: for example, he would always say *affaire* instead of subject, and when people were distracted he would rap on the table with his knuckles and shout, 'You must make attention!'

A second young man, seated in front of Borja Neves, and whom everyone treated with great friendliness, smiled: 'As for me, I choose Kalengue, the name my grandfather gave me.'

Borja Neves had often thought about getting himself a war name, but had never come to any conclusion. As his turn approached he began to get nervous. He tried to recall what little *umbundo* he knew, but all he remembered was *tchipepa* (meaning 'sweet', or 'good'). In *quimbundo* he was a little more fluent: *quimbanda* (sorcerer), *candengue* (child), *camba* (friend), *monangambé* (slave, servant). But none of that would do: 'Jesus!' he thought, anxiously, 'they're going to say I'm Portuguese.' He tried to concentrate: *jinguba* (peanut), *jindungo* (pepper), *kiabo* (a common local vegetable), *kitaba* (an Angolan delicacy). Damn it! Now all he could think of were names of food. Someone asked: 'And Chico Borja Neves, have you decided yet?'

'Oh, don't know,' said Francisco, sweating heavily. 'Will *bitacaia* do?'

'It means "chigoe flea", Lídia told me. 'That's how he came to be known as Chigoe Chico.' At the same meeting there was also a young protestant pastor, originally from Dondi. His name was Nendela Epalanga; when they asked him what name he had chosen, he thought for a bit: 'José,' he said, 'I would like to be José.' There was an embarrassing silence. Lídia smiled: 'If he is to be Joseph, then I shall be Maria,' she said. 'Maria is quite appropriate!'

Chapter 5

Ángel Martínez, the mercenary, opened his eyes and saw the night bursting into flames. In front of him, the Quifangondo hill was silhouetted against the sudden splendour of the sky. He closed his eyes and saw the fire, the chaos, the panic: 'I'm in hell,' he thought.

He was very close.

Just a few metres away, in the middle of the road, a Panhard armoured vehicle burned. The marshland itself burned in various places; suddenly something would light up, and another, and another, like sudden shooting stars. They formed lines, shapes, rapid constellations, and for some moments he thought the world was changed around: 'Here I am,' he thought, 'lying on my back on top of the night, and it's the earth that's concave and burning.' He thought about his grandmother, happy Rosalia Hernandez, saying to him in her lovely Cuban Spanish that at the end of the world everything would change places: 'Light will spout from fountains. The stars will fall onto the earth and transform the waters of the sea into blood and the rivers into absinthe. Night will become day and day night. The air will fill with locusts as big as horses and their faces will be like ours, with long women's hair, and the crashing of their wings will be like a thousand chariots racing towards war. And there will be lightning, and voices, and thunderclaps. The deserts will be covered with snow and the sun will set the polar ice alight.'

The wounded leg was making his whole body hurt and he was thirsty, an anxious, unreasonable thirst: 'You're fucked, Ángelito,' he said to himself in Spanish. He always spoke to himself in Spanish. In fact, he only spoke Spanish to himself. Even as a child, at home, he only used English because he was afraid of being teased for his accent. The grown-ups called him 'the little gringo'.

'Who told you to get involved in this black man's war?!' he spoke slowly, feeling the words form in his mouth. Oranges. He'd like to eat oranges. Three weeks earlier, in Kinshasa, he had been offered some marvellous oranges, sweet as honey. In Miami there were oranges too and in November they were in season. 'I will never eat oranges again,' he thought.

He had been hit by mortar shrapnel and not one of the damned Zairean soldiers had stopped to help him. He saw them running away like rats, hanging in bunches from the trucks, or running wildly, as the missiles burst, throwing pieces of trees and slime and the deep muds of the marsh into the air. He had just fallen, injured in his right leg, when an incredibly violent explosion threw him off the road. Stunned, he saw the Panhards of the Portuguese commandos being destroyed one by one. He knew that the people operating the Katyushas up on top of the hill were Cuban soldiers: 'One of them could be my brother.'

He had thought this many times. Three days earlier, when they were camped out on the Morro da Cal, he had seen a group of five soldiers advancing up the road. With his binoculars he could make out perfectly clearly the olive-green uniform of the Cuban army. The soldiers were advancing unconcerned, laughing and talking. Ángel got them in the sights of his MG-42, waited till they were within range and shot. One of the soldiers fell, then got up quickly and started to run. Ángel shot again, and again the soldier fell. This time too he got up again, helped by one of the others, and continued to run. Ángel was going to fire again when it occurred to him that that man might have the same name as him:

'I felt sorry for him and I shot the other one; he fell and didn't get up. You won't believe it, but when we took his documents I saw that he was called Martínez. José Martínez.'

Ángel Martínez joined Holden Roberto's guerrillas at the start of October, after reading a brief ad in *Soldiers of Fortune*: 'Attention. If you are an adventurer or a military technician and you want to fight communist imperialism in Africa contact Lieutenant-Colonel Brown, S.F.' Ángel was twenty-seven years old, and had been unemployed since returning from Vietnam. Taught to hate communism, he was militating in a movement of exiled Cubans whose main occupation consisted in elaborating detailed plans for an armed uprising against the regime of Fidel Castro. He picked up the telephone and called the editorial desk of the magazine.

Lieutenant-Colonel Brown ran *Soldiers of Fortune*. Ángel met him in his office. He was a strong man, healthy-looking. He was wearing a white T-shirt with the words, 'Fly – death comes from above'. Behind him a poster read: 'Become a mercenary. Travel to distant lands, meet interesting people... And kill them!'

Brown told him that he had also been in Vietnam. They spoke for a while about the war and discovered they had common friends. Finally Brown looked directly at Ángel: 'I think you're the right man!' Then he explained that a representative of the FNLA, a movement that was fighting in Angola against the Russians and the Cubans, was looking for a special man capable of fulfilling a mission that was difficult but would be well rewarded:

'An FNLA leader was forced to hide a briefcase with diamonds in a small city in the north of Angola, Damba. Now the whole of that area is iron and fire, with the FNLA soldiers fighting against the communists from the MPLA and also – we have reliable information about this – against Cuban soldiers supported by technicians from Russia and Red Germany. Your mission will be to recover that bag.'

Ángel wanted to know how much the diamonds were worth.

'A lot of money,' said Brown. 'Enough for the FNLA to continue their struggle another two or three years. And you're entitled to ten per cent.'

Ángel thought a little:

'It sounds good to me,' he replied. 'Even shit will walk when the dollars talk. Anyway, if the dollars really are to fight Fidel I don't even want that much. Five per cent is enough for me.'

When he arrived in Kinshasa he was told that South Africa had entered Angola and that the military situation would have to be decided by November 11th, the date set for Angola's independence. But it wasn't totally certain: Luanda was seeing the arrival of hundreds of Cuban soldiers, well trained, armed and munitioned and this could alter the course of the war. It was important to recover the briefcase with the diamonds, but even more important was to help with the taking of the capital. They offered him 300 dollars a week to lead a battalion of soldiers from the ELNA, the army of the FNLA. Ángel said yes. Less than a month later he was in Quifangondo.

By this point he had already become a mythical figure among the ELNA troops, the Zaireans and the Portuguese commandos. It was he who had the idea of intercepting a small plane that supplied the Margarida farm, occupied by FAPLA soldiers. A Portuguese pilot, a short, lean man full of nervous tics, whom his colleagues called Good Alvega, agreed to fly with him on a Beechcraft twin-engine.

They took off from Ambriz airport and climbed to six thousand feet. They circled for almost two hours, without any trace of the MPLA plane, until they decided to make towards Luanda. Then they saw it: it was a Cherokee Six, single-engined, and it was flying ahead of them, at the same height, back to the capital. The Portuguese pilot brought the Beechcraft down a few feet, moving it slightly to the right of the target. Ángel had a perfect sight of the belly of the craft. He set up a Browning 30 machine gun at the window to his left and began firing short bursts, again and again. Over the radio Good Alvega witnessed the other pilot's despair: 'They're shooting at us!' he heard him cry, 'Fascists! Fucking puppets, we've been hit!'

The single-engine dived deeply in an attempt to escape Ángel's fire, beginning to snake between the hills, flying low, some five or six metres from the ground. Good Alvega plummeted after him, pursuing him close. Ángel replaced a box of 250 bullets and resumed fire, trying to hit the engine. Suddenly the Beechcraft shuddered, and it was only then that Good Alvega realised that one of the tanks was empty. He pulled the control stick and the plane rose hiccupping. Growling curses and expletives Good Alvega changed the tank selector, opened the whole mixture control and pumped the fuel manually. When they had recovered from the fright, the Cherokee Six had disappeared.

Ángel Martínez smiled to think about the adventure with the plane. That had made a hero of him in the eyes of the Zaireans and the wretched ELNA fighters, but that didn't count for much during the attack at Quifangondo. His own soldiers had refused to advance, and only changed their minds when he drew his pistol and shot the one who seemed to be at the head of the revolt. Then they picked up their weapons and went down the Morro da Cal, but no sooner had they entered the Panguila marshes and the missiles began to rain down, than they dropped everything and ran. Some of them must have seen the shrapnel hit him: 'They definitely saw me fall,' he thought, furious, 'they saw me fall and didn't even stop to help me.'

The night was silent again and the stars were already shining in their thousands. The spectacular volley of fire seemed to have ended and it was only then that Ángel understood what it was for: 'Those bastards are celebrating independence,' he thought. 'It's past midnight, it's November 11th and we didn't make it into Luanda. Fidel won again!'

Thinking this filled him with rage and with energy: 'They're not going to take me!' he shouted. He tried to stand and it was as though night had fallen on his head. But he tried again and this time managed to drag himself a few metres. He rested a little, got up, grasped the leg with both hands and took a few more steps; suddenly he tripped and fell. He touched the ground and felt something cold and soft. He pushed away the grass and saw the face of a white man, his eyes open, his head buried in the mud up to his ears. He didn't have to look twice to know that he was Cuban: 'Holy Mother of God!' he exclaimed in Spanish. 'I think you're in a worse way than me, *compañero*.' He sat down beside the dead man and remained like that a good while. The night seemed bigger to him, now. Quick images of Havana came to his memory: the green and the green, the blue and the blue, the leaves of the palm trees under the sky. The casino lights. His father walking with him through the flooded streets in the rain, grumblingly pointing out the cars of the gringos: 'Look,' he said to him, 'that one's a Plymouth Sport Fury, one day we'll have to get one of those. The red one's a Cadillac, a fine car, such a shame it guzzles petrol; the convertible is a Lincoln, with power steering, I wouldn't mind having that one either.'

And then the revolution: the cries of his mother and the servants. The flight to Miami on a trawler laden with people. Grandmother, Dona Rosalia Hernandez, squeezing his hand: 'Don't worry, Ángelito, your father will come to be with us.' He never did. Some said he had been arrested, others that he had fled to Guantánamo, others still that he remained in Havana with his lover and two children a little younger than him. That was the most likely.

Ángel began going through the dead man's pockets: 'All I need is for this one to be called Martínez too,' he muttered. His name was Pablo Vivo: '*Vivo* – Alive? It's not a name that suits you,' said Ángel to the dead man. He gave a laugh: 'To tell the truth, it suits me much better.' He was pleased, the game hadn't come to an end after all. He stripped; he stripped the body and put on the olive-green uniform. Then with his hands he opened a pit in the drenched earth and hid the body of the Cuban inside: 'You see, Pablo? Turns out you're not dead yet. I'm the one who died!'

Chapter 6

While the President was giving his speech on Mayday Square, and Zorro was making his way towards Paulete through the crowd, hugging her and then greeting Borja Neves. While Lídia was thinking about death, closed away in her room, and Ángel Martínez was burying a dead man to take his name. While all this was happening, I was getting ready to flee from Huambo.

It was an intense night filled with gunshots, I remember it very well.

It began when Angola was not yet independent, and continued through till dawn. I don't think anyone slept in Huambo that night. Grandmother spent the whole time sitting in the big wicker chair in the living room, arms crossed, her face sombre. She looked at us, but didn't say a word. Around her a chaos was accumulating, of suitcases, crates, cardboard boxes, books, clothes, crockery, plates and cutlery. My mother was trying to help with arranging it all, but as soon as the shooting started she began to cry: 'I did say that we should have left in September, but nobody wanted to listen to me. So much shooting, so much shooting. Now the communists are arriving!' My father pretended not to hear her. At such times he used to recall the words of a Scottish grandfather:

'If you're afraid of fire, don't enlist as a fireman!'

In the middle of the night we learned on the radio that the shooting had begun as fireworks, to commemorate independence; however at the height of the festivities a stray bullet killed an FNLA officer. The soldiers of the ELNA took the accident to be provocation and responded by firing on UNITA people. Within minutes a battle had begun between the two allied forces.

I was pleased when I heard this: 'The puppets are going to kill one another,' I thought. But immediately afterwards I realised that that new civil war might bring me certain complications. I wanted to flee to Luanda together with a friend, Tito Rico, four years older than me. The last plane to Portugal was leaving that morning and my family and Rico's had everything arranged to be on it. We had agreed to leave at dawn. Rico had forged a UNITA safe-conduct and knew how to drive. We would escape in his father's Land Rover.

The previous day I walked around the city. The streets were filthy and packs of dogs were turning over the wreckage; there were German shepherds, Alsatians, a boxer, pointers, Dalmatians and many other pedigree dogs. The beautiful houses had their windows closed, the doors and gates closed, the spacious gardens empty and that vague and desolate look of things that no longer make sense. I went to the zoo, a place I'd known since childhood. The soldiers had killed the gazelles, the peacocks and the ostriches to eat them; the elephants to steal their tusks; and the lions, wild dogs and tigers just for fun. But they had let the monkeys go free and the old alligator remained unharmed, his mouth open, waiting for some bird or other to come clean his teeth and appease his hunger.

The monkeys, hanging from the eucalyptus trees, began to shriek when I approached. Some leaped down from the lowest branches and came to me. They shouted, they jumped somersaults and shouted, moved a few metres away and went back to their shrieking. I took some apples and pieces of bread out of a bag. The ruckus grew and the monkeys that were still up the eucalyptus trees started to copy the others. I was afraid, I threw them the bread and the apples, and I left. At that moment it began to rain.

It rained all night. A furious thundering occasionally drowned out the crackle of the machine guns. Grandmother got up and went to cover the mirrors with a sheet. She always did this when there was thunder. From my room, by the sudden flares of the lightning I could make out images of the war. Men caught running as in a photograph, petrified mid-run by the lightning flash.

I got together two pairs of trousers, some shirts, socks and underpants into a little rucksack. I added to this a flask, a toothbrush, my camera and a book, *The Historical Process*. In the living room, Grandmother was still in silence. 'Go rest,' my mother said to me, 'when it's time to go to the airport I'll call you.' I went back to my room and I wrote a note: 'Grandmother, when you read this I will already be very far away. I am going to join the MPLA to fight for our country. I know you understand. Tell them that we will meet again when all the puppets have been driven out and Angola is free. Revolutionary greetings.' Do you laugh? In 1975 I was fifteen years old and this was not ridiculous.

Five o'clock in the morning. I put on a pair of trainers, my old bell-bottomed jeans, my red shirt, and jumped out the window. I crossed the yard; on the other side of the wall there was a patch of open ground that connected to the land of the Athletics Club. There no one would be able to see me. I dropped down and buried my hands in the damp earth.

Tito Rico was already waiting for me at the main gate to the Club. We exchanged an MPLA-style handshake, sticking out our middle fingers and index fingers in the victory sign. 'I was afraid you wouldn't come,' Rico said to me, 'it's past the time.'

We found a checkpoint just outside the city. They were three soldiers from the ELNA. One of them stuck his head through the window and Rico showed him the safe-conduct. The man grabbed the piece of paper and shouted something to the others. 'Shit,' muttered Rico, 'they're Zairean!' We got out of the car and the soldiers searched us. The one who had the safe-conduct turned to us very excited:

'*Qui êtes-vous?*' he shouted. '*Où allez-vous?*'

Rico jumped on the soldier and with a quick gesture tore the safe-conduct from him:

'Go fuck yourself!'

'That's it!' I thought. 'We're dead.' The other soldiers raised their guns and looked at the third as though awaiting orders. That one had lost all his arrogance now, though, and seemed just a simple frightened country boy:

'*Excusez-moi!*' he repeated. '*Excusez-moi!*'

We got into the car and set off at full speed. I started laughing wildly. Rico was also laughing twisted over the steering wheel. He was laughing so much tears came to his eyes. 'Fucking hell,' I asked, 'so what actually just happened?' Rico wiped his eyes with the back of his hand: 'Who knows?' he replied, 'they must have thought I was some seriously important guy. These country boys lose all their composure the moment someone shouts at them.'

At the next checkpoint Rico limited himself to showing the

safe-conduct with a gesture of indifference. The soldier, a timid ado-lescent, turned the document round and round and finally handed it back. 'Where you guys going?' Rico didn't even look at him:

'That's our business.'

The soldier recoiled, surprised:

'Hey! No need to be rude. Go ahead, just be careful: there's gunfire at Quibala.'

Rico was euphoric. He was singing: 'Valóodia, Valóodia / Valódia fell / in defence of the Angolan people / Valóodia, Valóodia / Valódia fell / into the hands of the imperialists.' He had a rough but pleasant voice. A dazzling sun was creating mirages on the tarmac. I looked around and saw the green grasses, the vast expanse of the bush. I raised my voice to join his: 'People of Angola / everyone vigilant, / because in neo-colonialism / repression is worse / misery is a martyr / and poverty too / because neo-colonialism / has no colour.'

We were deeply involved in all this and didn't even notice that the landscape was getting denser. A little forest ran alongside the road. A curve. Rico shouts and brakes the car. Fifty metres ahead a long tree trunk was blocking the way. Two oil-drums, one on either side of the trunk, indicate that this is – or was – supposed to be a checkpoint. Off the road there was a huge sofa in good condition. The ground was littered with empty bottles.

Silence. We remained in silence. Rico took his hands from the wheel and I could see that they were shaking. 'Strange,' he said, 'if this were an ambush we'd be dead by now. They must be having their lunch. Best would be for us to move the trunk and keep going.' We got out of the car and at that moment heard a long whistle and then a mocking voice:

'Easy now, take it easy, my boys, I want you both with your hands in the air.'

The voice came from our right. We turned and didn't see anyone. Then I realised there were people behind us. I felt a blow to the back of my neck and fell to the ground. I was on my hands and knees, trying to understand what had happened, when the voice was heard again:

'Now, now, there's also no need to hit the lads. After all we don't know the whys and wherefores yet.'

The owner of the voice now appeared from behind the trees. A short, well-built man dressed in a very flowery, very tight shirt. He had a Kalasch over his shoulder and two pistols in his belt, cowboy-style. He approached swaying, gave a couple of little dance steps, stretched his hand out to me and helped me to my feet:

'Very well,' he said. 'Name, age, marital status, distinguishing features, et cetera, and so on, and so forth, and *kapuete karnundanda kapulokosso* as they say back in our Luanda.'

The soldier who had hit me went to get two beers and offered one to me. It was warm. I passed the beer to Rico. The man waited for us to finish drinking and then spoke again:

'I want to see all your cards, your ID cards and your passports, all your letters, letters of introduction, letters of notification, any notes, notices, notecards, notelets. And I want to know right now what your position is in this war.'

Rico put his hand in his pocket and showed the safe-conduct. The cowboy started to laugh:

'Well look at that, so it turns out their Excellencies are *kwachas*?' He drew one of the pistols, spun it quickly round his index finger and pointed it at Rico's head. 'I don't usually waste my time on *kwachas*!'

We looked at him in panic. Rico shouted:

'You're from the MPLA? Fuck, but we're from the "M" too! That safe-conduct is faked...'

The cowboy seemed genuinely amused:

'Of course it is. Their Excellencies are phonies and my name's Trinitá.' He stopped in front of Rico, put his face to his and bellowed: 'Shut your fucking mulatto mouth, son of a snake! You only speak when I tell you to speak.'

It was a difficult conversation. Rico tried to explain our story, but each time he said we were from the MPLA he received a blow. Eventually the cowboy sat down on the sofa, crossed his legs and looked fixedly at us:

'Do their Excellencies not know me?' he asked. 'In the "M" everyone knows me!'

He put his kalasch down on the floor, called one of the soldiers and whispered something in his ear. The soldier ran off and returned with a guitar. The cowboy took the instrument, tuned it, and began

to sing: 'Just look at Juka Kalu, / he spends the day running away /
He calls the policeman "servant" / He's really ruining things.'

Rico slapped me on the back:

'It's Santiago!' he said. 'This comrade's Commander Santiago!'

Chapter 7

In December 1961 a Portuguese second-lieutenant came to Luanda bringing a little boy of eight years old and handed him into the care of Ana de Piedade Castro de Magalhães, better known as Low-Slung Annie. The second-lieutenant told Low-Slung Annie that he had found the boy abandoned in the bush and taken pity on him because he spoke Portuguese: 'Apart from that he's smart as a whip,' he added.

Low-Slung Annie took the boy, sat him on her knee and asked his name: 'Tiago,' said the boy, 'Tiago Santiago da Ressureição André.' He had enormous eyes, round and liquid, and as he spoke he opened them even more. 'He looks like an angel,' said Annie.

The second-lieutenant smiled:

'So you'll keep him?'

The scene was being played out at the Moonlight of Roses nightclub, a renowned house of prostitutes in Marçal, between the Workers Neighbourhood and the slums. Low-Slung Annie was spread right across a big pink sofa and waving a fan. Hanging on the wall was a picture of Jesus Christ, his arms open and light streaming from his face. A fair-haired mulatta, kneeling in front of the huge lady, was painting her toenails.

Low-Slung Annie raised her eyes to the second-lieutenant:

'It's true that I do do some social work,' she said, 'and it's something I'm very proud of. But even so I don't think you understand the situation: at the Moonlight of Roses we take in girls, not boys!'

Then she pressed Tiago's head to her ample breasts and her eyes filled with tears:

'But anyway,' she said, 'this one's still an angel, and angels don't have a sex.'

That was how Tiago de Santiago entered the Moonlight of Roses. Many men envied his luck. Low-Slung Annie's goddaughters competed for his attention, going overboard with presents and treats. On Saturday afternoons they would give him money to go to the São Domingos, a cinema owned by capuchin monks, where you could watch the adventures of Django, Zorro and Sabata. Tiago would sit on the narrow wooden benches and remain in silence, his mouth open, following his horseback heroes across the dusty prairies of the American West. Around him people cheered. There were lots of people at those showings: whenever the cowboy was in danger you would hear shouts of warning: 'Careful, man, look, behind you!'; when the cowboy drew his pistol and fired his unerring shots, then there would be applause and whistles: 'Woohoo, will you look at that?! What a shot! This guy's unreal...'

The Moonlight of Roses was visited by public functionaries, by clerks and small-businessmen, people from the borders between the tarmac and the slum. With the outbreak of war a number of Portuguese soldiers began to appear and business started doing well. Low-Slung Annie put on so much weight that one day she wanted to leave the house and couldn't fit through the door. Tiago Santiago da Ressureição André retained inexhaustible memories of those glorious days. Above all he remembered the parties in the yard, with live bands, and the girls, like shining stars, dancing barefoot on the beaten-earth floor.

One of the most popular bands was The Sangazuzas, whose musicians played dressed in blue and yellow. The bass guitar fell in love with one of the girls, Eva Kissanguela, an olive-skinned girl from Malange, with eyes bright as fires in the moonlight. Tiago became his ally and confidant. It was the beginning of a beneficial friendship because the bass guitar taught him the basics of his art. At the age of sixteen Tiago was already livening up Saturday nights, singing national or Congolese folk music or the better known Afro-Cuban songs.

It was around this time that he met Santos Biker, a gloomy mulatto, who had made some money smuggling dried fish from Namibia and later established a complicated network of little bars and gaming houses in the slums of Luanda. Santos Biker lived in permanent conflict with the Portuguese tavern keepers and needed new people to enable him to grow his business. Tiago suited him because he was a popular guy, who knew everyone, and besides he had plenty of courage to spare.

Santos Biker was in the habit of chewing dark leaves, too thick to be tobacco. They said it was a herb from the North, a cruel poison used by the Zaireans in their criminal proceedings: they would give an infusion of these leaves to the accused and if he survived he was concluded to be innocent. They said Santos Biker avoided talking because when he opened his mouth his bad breath infected everything and it was so hazardous that the flowers in the rooms where he slept wilted. The girls from the Moonlight of Roses lived in permanent terror of having to go to bed with him: 'His kisses kill,' they muttered, 'and if they don't kill you they make you crazy.' Besides this he used to have nightmares: he dreamt that while he was sleeping a group of soldiers came into the room and shot him dead with machine guns. Whenever he had this dream he awoke covered in sweat and turned brutal and cruel towards the women he was sleeping with.

The dream did not make much sense, as everyone knew that Santos Biker was immune to bullets, and that he could spot a policeman, even in plain clothes, at two blocks away. It wasn't clear how he had acquired these gifts, but they said that he went everywhere with a small snake wound round his left wrist. The snake – an enchantment, or the enchanter himself? – would explain those powers.

The nationalist revolt and the arrival of the Portuguese soldiers was good for Low-Slung Annie, but extremely damaging to Santos Biker. Indeed, the tavern keepers saw the situation as a great opportunity to get rid of him, denouncing him as a terrorist. Apart from this, the constant quarrelling in the slums had people panicked: men would come back from work and shut themselves in their houses. Clandestine little bars started to disappear one after another. Many members of the network ended up arrested or went far away.

A strange war became entrenched in the tight labyrinths of Cazenga, Sambizanga and Rangel. A war of quick gunshots exchanged at nightfall, of muffled hand-to-hand fights, of treacherous stabbings in the sweet half-light of dance clubs and brothels. The name of Santos Biker was muttered with a thrill, his deeds multiplied in the mouths of the people. Few people saw him now. He only turned up at the Moonlight of Roses on the days when there was no one else there, and even then wrapped in his own shadow, ever more nocturnal, always chewing the fatal herb.

Santiago started out doing little errands and ended up as the smuggler's bodyguard and right-hand man. This he added to his music and his talents seemed to grow with him.

One night they killed Santos Biker. It happened on Good Friday. The smuggler was at the Moonlight of Roses. He had called Low-Slung Annie to one side and with a gesture told her he wanted Eva Kissanguela, the one with eyes like fire in the moonlight, with whom the bass guitar of The Sangazuzas had fallen in love. 'I'll stay all night,' he muttered, 'and obviously I'm not here, I'm never going to be here, I was never here.' He paid in advance and went up to his room alone. Santiago wandered off. When he returned, at dawn, there was a crazy commotion all over the house. Two hours earlier an army jeep had stopped in front of the house. Five soldiers burst in, ran up the stairs, made for Eva Kissanguela's room and kicked in the door. Santos Biker leapt up, but didn't even have time to reach for his gun: the first burst tore off his right hand and the second caught him in the chest, throwing him against the wall where he remained a moment, bewildered, as though unable to believe what was happening: then he sighed and fell forward.

When Santiago came in, Eva Kissanguela was crying, twisted up on the floor, while the other girls screamed at her. Low-Slung Annie was sitting on the living-room sofa, and she looked older and heavier:

'That whore,' she said, pointing with her chin at Eva Kissanguela, 'that shameless wretch betrayed us all...'

No one ever knew for sure how it had happened. What they say is that Eva Kissanguela fell in love with a Portuguese soldier, who promised her house and home, health and wealth, many children and, basically, the happy ending from a trashy magazine photo-story. The girl began to take him further and further into her confidence, and one day, inevitably, she mentioned Santos Biker. The soldier realised this was his chance to shine in front of his superiors and he set up the mousetrap.

On that wretched Holy Friday, when Santos Biker chose Eva Kissanguela, she slipped away for a moment and telephoned the soldier. Then she went to the room where the man was already waiting for her, lying naked on top of the sheets. While she was undressing she saw in the mirror Santos Biker raising his right hand to his left wrist and unclasping the little green snake like someone removing a watch. Horrified, she heard the hiss of the snake before it was put away in one of the boots. She turned slowly and looked him in the eye:

'I'll do whatever you want,' she said, 'but I'm not kissing you on the mouth.'

Santos Biker turned her over, and took her. Eva waited till the bandit was asleep. Then she freed herself carefully and knelt beside the bed. She spent a time looking at the boot where the snake was sleeping. She raised her fist, closed her eyes, and hit it with all her strength. Santos Biker moved: 'What's happening?'

'Nothing,' Eva reassured him. 'Nothing ever happens here.'

Twenty minutes later the soldiers came into the room. Santos Biker got up, thinking he was still asleep, saw the soldiers fire and allowed himself to die, thinking that he would soon awake.

Santiago inherited what remained of Santos Biker's gang, but he never abandoned music, and in 1972 recorded his first single, entitled 'Nzambi Ya Tubia'. By now he was already singing at the Kudi-Sanga-diá-Makamba gatherings, at N'Goma, in the São Paulo Social Centre and even at the Marítimo da Ilha, frequented by the *haute-bourgeoisie* of the city. He started out composing really swinging rumbas and merengues in *quimbundo*, but it was his *sembas* that made him popular. In time he developed a new style, becoming the first to sing in the language of the suburbs, mixing *quimbundo* and Portuguese, with much recourse to an exuberant slang of indeterminate origin. His amorous experiences served as his inspiration. From a certain point he invented a character whom he called Juka Kalu, and all the songs were about him. Later he began to sing of his own exploits – raids, hustles, escapes from the police – always in the name of Juka Kalu.

When the April Revolution happened Santiago was already a well-known character, especially in Luanda's slums and suburbs, but the police had managed to assemble a series of pieces of evidence to lay against him and were just about to set hands on him. They did it at the worst moment; or at the best, depending on your point of view.

The atmosphere in the city was one of extreme nervousness. The settlers were agitated at the news reaching them from the metropolis. The communists, it was whispered, were behind the military coup and were getting ready to hand Angola over to the Russians. Something had to be done.

At the same time the militants of the MPLA, who had received the news of revolution with a mixture of astonishment and euphoria, launched themselves into frantic activity, trying to win support among the students and 'the oppressed masses from the slums'. In the high schools and the universities, agitation flourished like fire through dry grass. In the slums it was a little harder, but the arrival of a group of former prisoners from the São Nicolau concentration camp changed everything. They were young intellectuals who cultivated good relations with the people, which was reinforced by their having been held for several years together with workers and countryfolk.

Santiago was arrested at the Ku-di-Sanga. He had just been performing his most recent success, 'Juka Kalu and the Taxi-Driver of Love', when a tall guy all dressed in white appeared beside him and whispered something in his ear. Santiago leaped to his feet:

'Bandits!' he shouted. 'They're arresting me!'

A hubbub broke out in the hall. Five policemen emerged from the shadows and launched themselves towards him. One of his men drew a gun but a kick disarmed him; two young black men – Santiago had never seen them before – got up to protect him and in an instant the whole hall was in commotion. The girls, both prostitutes and bourgeoises, screamed and tore at each other's hair; chairs flew through the air. 'Long live the MPLA!' shouted one of the young men, 'death to fascism and colonialism!' The tone had been set. Santiago was dragged away in a police car, followed by a crowd of people in a great hue and cry: 'Fascists! Fascists! Santiago, hero of the people!'

A week later Santiago was free again. On that same day a tall, thin young man with a long face appeared at the Moonlight of Roses and asked to speak to Santiago. Low-Slung Annie measured him up with her eyes: 'It's been a long time since we've had saints in this house,' she said. The young man laughed, but seemed to be ill at ease:

'I need to speak to him,' he murmured. 'It's very urgent. There's going to be a war starting and the people have to get organised.'

He left his name and a telephone number and went away. Three days later, Santiago received him at one of the houses he had in Cazenga. He immediately recognised him as one of the young men who had stood up to defend him. He was simply dressed, but you could tell by his bearing and speech that he was educated. He was surely something important in this MPLA. Santiago had never taken an interest in politics, but the events of the previous months had begun to trouble him. Many of the men who appeared at the Moonlight of Roses talked about the MPLA, about independence, about driving out the Portuguese. Low-Slung Annie laughed in their faces: 'Behave yourselves,' she shouted at them. 'That's the last thing we need, the blacks running things around here! What do you think this is, the Congo?!'

So Santiago received the young man in one of his houses in Cazenga; in order to impress him he posted two men at the door, armed with G-3s and dressed in black with dark glasses. The house was linked to another house, which in turn led into a third. Someone wandering through the labyrinths of the slum would never suspect. Santiago was sitting at the back of the last of the rooms, behind a heavy mahogany writing desk; he arranged to be there when the other man came in.

The conversation was long, and would continue over the days that followed. It was a conversation that would change Santiago's life. The truth was that life displeased him, but at this point no one could have known that. The young man belonged to the secret structures of the MPLA and he had been imprisoned in the São Nicolau camp. He spoke slowly and with authority, but with no trace of arrogance. He told him that the movement was fighting for the liberation of Angola, so that it would be the Angolans themselves who would decide their own destiny. He explained that the *coup d'état* in Portugal had been a result of this struggle, but that victory – though assured – might take some time: 'The thing is, international imperialism is alert and wants to neo-colonise Angola through its puppets UNITA and the UPA-FNLA.'

Blood. Fire. And feelings that Santiago knew well. He didn't like the UPA, nor Holden Roberto. He told his story and the young man was moved:

'Comrade,' he said, 'Angola needs you.'

He put his hand on his shoulder, moved closer to him and continued in a different tone of voice:

'The strategy of imperialism is to divide and rule. And unhappily it has worked. As you know, that traitor Chipenda abandoned the movement, taking with him in his madness some of our finest guerrillas. Now we really do need to count on the people. You are a hero of the people, for all these years you've fought the Portuguese colonialists and been an example to us. Now we're counting on you to fight the puppets of the FNLA.'

Santiago straightened up nervously. The young man seemed to be reading his thoughts.

'Tell me the truth,' he said. 'In São Nicolau I heard that you ambushed a troop of *tugas*. They told me that a Portuguese soldier abused a girl from the Workers Neighbourhood and you avenged the affront yourself.'

That was more or less how it had been, though the girl in question had been no maiden. She was one of Low-Slung Annie's goddaughters. Santiago had got the bastard, given him a good thrashing, stripped him down completely and drawn on his back with a penknife a phrase that was later transformed into the line from a rumba and became famous: '*Ay*, how it hurts to live!'

When the young man was leaving, Santiago accompanied him to the door. He felt himself invincible again. Now he knew the future – he knew what to do. He, Tiago de Santiago Ressureição André, was going to place a stone in the foundations of the world.

THE EUPHORIA

'It was a terrible war *[the Angolan civil war]*, in which one had to defend oneself against both the mercenaries and the snakes, both cannons and cannibals.'

Gabriel García Márquez, in *Operation Carlota*,
Mosca Azul publishers, Peru, 1977

Chapter 1

The day was just beginning to get light when a group of five soldiers from the FAPLA found Ángel Martínez, alias Pablo Vivo. Ángel saw them arrive, walking through the mist: strangely cautious phantoms. They trod on the mud as though it were glass. One of them stopped suddenly and pointed his gun. Before he fired the mercenary stopped him with a shout:

'What are you doing, *caramba*, I'm Cuban!'

It was as though he had untied an invisible thread. The tension dissipated and the soldiers began to laugh and to move normally. The one who had pointed his gun raised his hand, making the victory V-sign:

'*Compañero!*' he exclaimed. 'The fatherland or death!...'

They carried him on their shoulders up the hill. As they rose armed men began to appear. They all smiled at him and there was one who approached him and wanted to give him a hug but the soldiers who had found him kept him away with a gesture. They treated him as though he was a gift.

Ángel feared that some Cubans might appear. 'My grandmother Rosalia Hernandez,' he thought, 'didn't you tell me that my gringo accent would be my undoing?' Apart from this he wouldn't be able to get through a formal interrogation. The solution would be to faint, to pretend he was in a state of shock. Or better still, pretend to be mute. Fuck no! Not likely they'd accept mutes into the Cuban army...

When the Cubans arrived he was already in the Military Hospital. A fat, maternal nurse was seeing to his leg, assuring him that the shrapnel hadn't even reached the bone: 'Within two weeks,' she said, 'you'll be ready to take another shot.' They left him in a huge room, with some twenty other wounded men, one of whom shouted the whole time. He began with a sharp moaning and then got louder and louder until he was out of breath; then he stopped for a moment, twisting his hands and rolling his eyes, and went back to his moaning and shouting. A tall black man pointed at him and said, smiling, 'Have patience, comrade. It won't be long before I shut him up.' And in the middle of the night the lad did indeed stop screaming. The next morning they took him away.

Ángel was sleeping. He was dreaming that he was a boy and going with his father to walk the streets near the beach. His father had a little bird's head and was wearing a black tailcoat, with golden sequins. He stopped beside a ruined boat, slapped him on the shoulder and asked him, pointing his finger at a figure that was approaching: 'Is that our man?' With the second slap on the back Ángel awoke. Leaning over him was a guy in a white overall, with an amused expression on his dark face:

'*Buenos días,*' he greeted him. 'You slept like an angel.'

'*Soy Vivo!*' Ángel replied to him almost panicking, '*Pablo Vivo!*'

The doctor looked at him curiously:

'You're *vivo*? Alive? I know you're alive!' he said. 'And where are you?'

Ángel did not reply. He seemed not to have heard. But when the other man was going to repeat the question he gestured to him to come closer:

'Your wife is a goat,' he whispered in Spanish, 'she's fucking the priest.'

His eyes were shining. He opened his mouth and burst out into uproarious laughter:

'I like to eat pork with potatoes,' he shouted in a woman's voice, 'and chick peas and chorizo, and eggs, chickens, lamb, turkeys, fish and seafood.'

The doctor took a step back:

'This man isn't well,' he said. 'It would be best for us to give him a sedative. I'll come past again soon; by then it may even be possible to talk to him.'

As he left the hospital, his hands shaking, he could still hear the wounded man's shouting:

'I drink rum and beer and spirits and wine and I fornicate, even on a full stomach. I am impure! What do you want me to tell you? Completely impure!...'

Three days later Ángel ran away from the hospital. The sun was rising, causing a dazed city to appear. Ahead of him the roads opened out filled with rubbish, stray dogs emerged from the shadows and came to lick his feet, and it was all strange to him. 'I'm in the wrong film,' he thought. His leg was still hurting him. He didn't know what to do. He went up one sloping street and then another and another. Finally he came to a big square, bordered by tall buildings, and the sea opened out in front of him. He decided to walk around the bay towards the fortress. On the other side stretched a long tongue of white sand, scattered trees and houses. The word 'Panoram' could be read on a big building. The beach seemed a good place to rest, to put his ideas in order, to assemble a plan to get away from the city and join the forces of Holden Roberto.

Ángel allowed himself to remain there a good while, lying on his back, his eyelids shut, feeling the sun warm his bones. He heard voices around him but it was as though he was floating in another time. Women's laughter, footsteps, the sea rolling onto the sand.

Then something hit him in the chest. He opened his eyes and the first thing he saw was a beach-ball with the colours of the American flag. Then he saw her. She was approaching against the light, her stormy hair waving in the wind:

'Sorry,' said the young woman. She bent down to take the ball and the mercenary followed her movement with a sudden feeling of distress. 'Anyway, the beach isn't really the best place to be sleeping.'

She was laughing. She turned her body and threw the ball towards her companions:

'You're Cuban?'

Ángel didn't know how to talk to women. Fear? At that moment it was more than fear. Distress, a dark feeling. The mulatta came closer:

'Don't understand Portuguese?' she asked him. 'What's your name?'

'Pablo. Pablo Vivo,' Ángel took a deep breath and looked her in the eyes. 'And you?'

It was Paulete.

Chapter 2

We arrived in Luanda as night was falling. Santiago himself took us by jeep, driving like a lunatic. We went directly to an old English school on the Morro da Luz which the MPLA were improvising as their main jail. I should say I wasn't worried. On the contrary, I was bubbling with excitement. Rico, beside me, wouldn't stop talking. We were discussing the latest news. Santiago had heard that Holden Roberto's column had suffered a serious defeat in Quifangondo and was now retreating, in disarray, towards Zaire. The South Africans had stopped too, after taking Novo Redondo, and there were rumours that they were already retreating. Santiago laughed loud, hitting the steering wheel hard; he was sorry not to have been able to fire a single shot at the *carcamanos*.

'I never miss a shot,' he assured us. 'I give names to the bullets, each one is a dead puppet.'

On the Morro da Luz we were taken to a gymnasium filled with people. Santiago was greeted by FAPLA soldiers with great exclamations of joy. One of them, of a captain's rank, hugged him, exchanged some pieces of information about the military situation and only then seemed to notice us.

'Who are these?' he asked. 'Are they here to be shot?'

I thought he was joking, but when our eyes met I realised he wasn't. Santiago gave a laugh:

'Later!' he said. 'I think they're ours, but best to be sure. They're carrying a letter from the *kwachas*.'

Though the gymnasium was large and high-ceilinged it was stifling with so many people. They were mainly FNLA sympathisers, but there were also some Portuguese, suspected of sabotage, and an American black woman accused of belonging to the CIA. She was crying, putting her fingers through her round hairdo, and insisting that she had nothing to do with the CIA. She had come to Angola because she wanted to see Mother Africa, to take part in the revolution. Apart from this she couldn't bear one more day of the hateful rule of the whites, the capitalist system, the discrimination to which black women in the United States were doubly subjected. She seemed sincere to me, but Rico wouldn't let me approach her.

'Of course she's from the CIA,' he said to me. 'Can't you see she's disguised as Angela Davis?'

A little later they came to fetch her and take her to a room next-door. We heard her screaming for almost fifteen minutes and when she returned her shirt was torn and she had scratches on her face and neck. 'That's not right,' said Rico.

That was when I noticed a brief commotion at the door. Santiago was shoving a small, thin woman, but the expression of the two of them did not match their respective positions: she was the one who seemed to be in charge. Santiago, on the other hand, had his gaze fixed on the ground.

Chapter 3

What were the circumstances of your arrest?

Lídia: I was arrested on November 11th, that same night. It was Santiago who came to get me. It was something that was expected. A few days earlier an old comrade had telephoned me: 'They're going to arrest you,' he said to me. 'They're just waiting for independence. Then they're arresting you.' I replied:

'I'm trapped already.'

(By the revolution, by the people, by the country. Anyway, it's nonsense –)

I replied:

'You can kiss that independence of yours goodbye…'

Later it was Mário who phoned me. He was in Lisbon, at the house of Noémia de Sousa. He said almost the same thing:

'This independence, even with a muzzle on, my friend, it's going to eat our flesh and gnaw on our bones.'

(Interview with Lídia do Carmo Ferreira, Luanda, 23 May 1990)

Chapter 4

When Mário hung up, Lídia lay back out on the bed and thought of Viriato. He was dead. She remembered him as she had met him, an adolescent who looked fragile but with a determined expression, talking of things he couldn't possibly know about. After he had tuberculosis he put on weight, became slower and heavier. And yet inside, he seemed still to be the same stubborn, dreamy young man, utterly convinced that he was capable of changing the world on his own. The last letters she received from him, dated from Peking, had got her worried. In them Viriato hadn't hidden his disappointment in relation to China: 'Socialism?' he asked. 'Can this also be socialism? I only have to cover the five hundred metres that separate the tarmacked streets from the poorest neighbourhoods to be assailed by a sudden feeling of having retreated several centuries into History.'

Lídia and other friends tried to secure him a visa and permission to settle in France. The Chinese, however, were not inclined to let him leave. Viriato began to get nervous, provoking the authorities increasingly boldly. One day in a burst of rage he publicly broke a bust of Mao Tse Tung. He thought that the Chinese would expel him but instead they sent him to a little nameless village and it was there, in 1973, just a few months before the April Revolution, that Viriato died. The doctors diagnosed a myocardial coronary.

Early in the morning Lídia went out into the yard. Old Fina was still growing roses. The fighting in Quifangondo had broken a pipe and there had been no water for the last three days. 'The roses are going to die,' thought Lídia; 'fortunately we had some rain.' She caressed a rose. She closed it in her cupped hands and then opened the petals with faltering fingers. It was soft and moist and shone inside, red, in the uncertain morning light.

Lídia remembered the dancer. She had seen her for the first time in one of the few bars still serving drinks. A sombre place, set apart from the events that were shaking the city. Some of her comrades liked to meet there. They said:

'It's a place far from the world.'

The woman was hidden in the shadows but when they came in she got up onto the stage and began to dance. The image of this woman left Lídia even more unsettled. She returned to her room, sat at the desk and began to write. This much I know, and I think I know the rest. In *The Sleeping Fire** there is a poem that is almost explicit, 'State of War', which is marked as having been written on November 11th, 1975:

Her gestures like sudden birds
Her gestures like glass, and they broke
Her gestures unfurled like algae
She was the dancer and I loved her.

It was long ago and Miriam was singing
in those days we slept with our shoes on
or didn't sleep

It was the time of struggles and Miriam was singing
I was talking of the dancer, I went to a bar
of ill repute, Aldo, there were gunshots outside
and the dancer danced on the stage alone

She danced with fury and with jubilation
You see? The world was mad
and I loved her.

The lines remind you of the ones she wrote in her youth. In *The Blood of Others†*, a collection of poems published six years later, what strikes you is the fierce, devastating irony. In 1992 Lídia released *A Vast Silence‡*. Knowing what we know today it is tempting to say that there is something more than sadness in this book. There is something else, a bitter feeling of abandonment. 'Lídia do Carmo Ferreira never had any other subject but this – surrender', a critic she didn't like once wrote. Surrender? I would like to know what happened to Lídia.

* *The Sleeping Fire*, Atenas Publishing, Coimbra, 1982
† *The Blood of Others*, Atenas Publishing, Coimbra, 1988
‡ *A Vast Silence*, Crow's Voice Publishing, Luanda, 1992

Chapter 5

Ángel lived a while hidden in Paulete's home, a lovely apartment right on the waterfront. He lied to her: he told her he'd been injured in combat and was waiting to embark for Cuba. And after sleeping with her he told her that he was in love with her (that was true) and didn't want to go back to the island.

Paulete had been lucky to get that apartment. In the chaos that accompanied the mass exodus of Portuguese she met an old school-mate, the son of one of the coffee barons. The lad wasn't allowing himself to be contaminated by the nationalist euphoria, and still less by the theories of old Marx. He wanted to continue living well and he didn't care what might happen to Angola: he would go to Brazil. Paulete asked him if he couldn't rent her his house and the young man laughed: 'I'll trade it for a kiss from you,' he said.

In those days there were people trading cars and houses for things worth much less than a kiss from Paulete. At the airport nervous guys would climb onto the roof of their car and from right there would auction it off for a watch, a pen, or just a pair of shoes, anything they could carry away with them. So Paulete gave him the kiss, and received the keys.

Paulete had two girlfriends living with her: Lay and Samy. Milagre das Rosas Mattoso da Câmara (Lay) was from an old Benguela family. She had dark skin, hair that was thick but smooth which fell in curls onto her shoulders. Sabina Schwartz (Samy), also originally from Benguela, bothered men with her ash-grey eyes.

The house had one peculiarity that few people knew about: you could get through to the adjacent apartment through a hole in the closet wall. It was Paulete's idea and her handiwork. The apartment belonged to a little old lady. At least, that was what Paulete had assumed, though she had never seen her. But for the first two months after she had settled there she heard noises in the neighbouring house and in the late afternoon a disembodied hand would appear at the window. It was a sign to the pigeons who would circle down and come to rest on the thin arm, pecking at the maize that the old lady hid in the cup of her hand.

One evening Paulete noticed the unusual anxiety of the pigeons and looking out the window did not see the old lady's arm. All that night and the next morning she listened out to the noises of the building but not the vaguest suggestion of life came from the other side of the wall: no sound of running water in the pipes, no telephone voice, not even the stifled crackling of a kettle boiling.

'She's died,' said Lay. 'Best to call the police.'

'What police?' asked Samy. 'There isn't any police any more, they've all gone to the capital.'

'And that's probably what happened to her,' ventured Paulete. 'You'll see, the old lady probably slipped out.'

Then she looked at the others and began to laugh:

'Don't you think we're a little cramped in here?'

Samy didn't think so. She liked to have a lot of people around her. Perhaps that was why she was the only one against the idea of breaking through the wall and secretly occupying the next-door apartment.

'That's crazy!' she shouted. 'First of all because the old lady might be there, yes, she might. Dead, rotting, smelling bad! And besides you risk bursting a pipe or going through the wiring.'

Paulete wasn't convinced. She went to fetch a hammer, got herself into the closet in her room and began to split through the wall.

'Put the music on at top volume,' she said, 'and if some neighbour appears to complain about the noise, invite him to join the party too.'

The hole linked through to the cupboard in the other apartment. Paulete went in, her nervous hands pushing away dresses and skirts, short skirts and slips. Her entrance awoke a cloud of moths, and at the same time an old perfume was released into the air. Finally the girl managed to find the cupboard door and came out into the light.

The house was impeccable. Clean, tidy, the bed made, with sheets, covers and a lacy bedspread. Blue porcelain on the shelves, a newspaper from six months earlier open on a chair. In the dining room they found the table set, with silver cutlery and a single crystal glass. When they opened the kitchen door a thick odour made them recoil. Samy leaned on the wall and threw up right there.

'*Ayuê*, mother! It must be the old lady!' she groaned. 'Didn't I say we shouldn't come in?'

But it wasn't the old lady: lying there under a low table, sad and inglorious, there was a huge cheese, rotting.

So they occupied the house, making the other neighbours believe it was still being occupied by its old owner. It was in this apartment that Ángel Martinez – or Pablo Vivo, as you prefer – was hidden. But of course, after the first few weeks a huge number of people knew that Paulete had fallen in love with a Cuban and was keeping him in her home. 'So that he doesn't get sent back,' they said. And there were some who thought – whispered – that the Cuban had tried to desert when it came to fight, and others that he had killed an officer, and a third group that he was a leftist, like Paulete, and that they were pursuing him for an attempted uprising.

THE FEAR

'We should sing about the firing squads!'

Francisco Borja Neves in an interview with the
Jornal de Angola, 20 January 1977

Chapter 1

Lay: seventeen years old, tall, a slender body curved out at the waist. Black hair, scented and so thick that even when you separated it with your fingers you could not see the skin. I met her on the Morro da Luz, a few hours after having been arrested along with Rico.

We had seen Lídia coming in, dragged by Santiago. For me that was the moment of truth, the irreparable moment when the poison of doubt first occurred to me. I knew who Lídia was (historian and poet, founder of the MPLA, intellectual respected in Europe, etc. etc.). I also knew that she was close to Active Revolt. But arrested? 'It can't be!' I murmured. 'Is this what independence is for, after all?!'

A girl next to me laughed quietly: 'Take it easy, you'll see a lot worse yet, this independence has barely begun!' That was the first thing Lay said to me. She had been there three days, accused of connections to the student movement, the Popular Neighbourhood Commissions and by extension to the Amílcar Cabral Committees. It was her who tempted me into what would become the OCA: 'The MPLA has betrayed the people,' she declaimed, 'and it's so in thrall to the bourgeoisie and to international imperialism that there's not even any point trying to change it from within. The only solution is to create an alternative popular movement, a movement that is not ashamed to call itself communist.'

Is it worth mentioning that by the time we were released, early in the morning of November 13th, I was already opposed to the regime? As for Rico, he wanted to go join his family in Portugal.

It was also Lay who introduced me to Little Joãoquin and got him to rent me a room. In some obscure way they were distantly related. Little Joãoquin lived in the Cruzeiro neighbourhood, in a cool and spacious residence, with a large veranda running all the way around it. Dona Diamantina, his godmother, stayed in the house all day long. She hardly spoke. When it got dark she would pull two chairs out to the veranda and remain absolutely still, in a distracted silence, waiting for Little Joãoquin to arrive. He would open the gate of the garden at exactly six fifteen, give her a kiss on the hand and sit in the other chair. They would remain like that till nearly seven. Then the old lady would get up with a sigh and go and make dinner.

Little Joãoquin had inherited a watchmaker's shop from his god-father, along with the minutely detailed job of repairing watches. He was – as I think I have said before – a huge, solid man, but had magic hands and worked wonders with them: in prison I saw him cut little pieces of wood with a penknife, transforming them into exact mini-atures of trains, cars and little houses.

So when we were freed I went to live in Little Joãoquin's house. Rico spent two or three weeks in Luanda and then managed to get away to Lisbon. He phoned me to tell me that he had met my parents. He told me that my grandmother had stayed in Huambo. That didn't surprise me. She was always a very determined woman.

Chapter 2

Ángel's flight was idiotic. It's true, he wasn't very safe at Paulete's house: the gossip spread to half of Luanda – the 'LPB Luanda', the 'Literate Petit-Bourgeois Luanda', as Zorro used to call it – and the story of the Cuban proved too tasty a dish for the slanderers. But abandoning that refuge, even precarious as it was, to launch himself into a city he didn't know, always seemed to me enormous folly.

'The man's running away from Paulete,' I commented when I heard about the affair. Lay cuffed me and laughed. At the time neither she nor I knew the real intentions of Ángel, alias Pablo. Pablo Vivo.

'Paulete was eating away his soul,' Lay agreed, kissing me on the mouth, 'like I'm going to eat yours.'

Milagre das Rosas! We were in her room, naked on the enormous bed, with a mosquito net that Lay had brought from her parents' house and which there in Luanda didn't serve much purpose. 'It makes me feel peaceful,' the girl had explained. A dusky light filtered through the net and gilded her skin, sinking into her round, firm breasts, giving everything it settled on the melancholy consistency of honey.

Lay was biting my earlobes, which began to give me a tickling feeling in the roof of my mouth and then at once my blood caught fire. While I kissed her hair, and her shoulders, and her breasts, I thought of Pablo. It was strange: I thought of Pablo making love to Paulete. Today whenever I think of Ángel I remember Lay's big bed and I see the intensity of her body, floating in the amber light of the late afternoon.

Pablo couldn't get out of Luanda. By that point Holden Roberto's guerrillas had already returned to Zaire and the South African forces had retreated to the border. Savimbi had lost Huambo and had gone into the eastern bush, trying to reorganise a movement that had been completely routed. The MPLA were celebrating. In March the people filled the streets with their celebrations. Meanwhile the UNITA soldiers, a mere fifty ragged men, drank marsh

water and ate roots; they slept by day, hidden in holes, and when
night fell they advanced stumbling, imitating the song of the cicadas
and the birds to communicate between the different groups.

What happened to Ángel? They say that one of his ex-soldiers
recognised him in the street. A poor devil the Cubans had captured
easily, and who had later become an informer. They took Ángel to
São Paulo Prison and battered his body with blows. When they heard
about this, the Cubans were euphoric. To them Ángel represented
the first proof of American involvement in the Angolan war. There
it was, incarnate in a single man, a soldier of fortune and a traitor.
A few days later they caught a handful of mercenaries – under the
command of a Briton of Cypriot origin, Kostas Georgiu, known as
Kallan – and set up a trial, a noisy spectacle whose primary purpose
was to shame America.

Ángel was intelligent. Much more intelligent than all the other
mercenaries put together. He quickly understood the real purpose
of the trial and tried to subvert the rules of the game. In the very
first cross-examination he left the Popular Revolutionary Tribunal
dumbstruck:

'Yes, *camaradas*,' he said in Spanish with a thick American accent,
repeating the words of the Public Attorney, 'the North American
society in which I was raised is monstrous. It's a society where you
chase power, social position, a society of spendthrifts, in which the
weak become even weaker and the stronger become stronger. It is
a country where events unfold at a vertiginous speed and the weak
cannot bear it. People seek escape in drugs and alcohol. People are
very egocentric, they don't even think about each other.'

The Public Attorney, who was preparing himself to crush him,
launching the solid theories of Marx, Engels and Lenin at him, was
surprised, confused, wagging his finger:

'Are you saying to us that the capitalist system is monstrous?'

Ángel agreed vehemently:

'I'm the living proof of this myself, comrades. I can see that today
I have sunk to the lowest point to which a man can fall. Me, me who
came from a land of heroes, what am I today?'

He showed his manacled wrists. He shouted:

'What have I become, oh my mother, what have I become?! A

wretched prostitute, that's what I am, I'm a whore, a wretched war whore!'

In the seats reserved for the public a woman began to cry. Ángel too had his face wet with tears. He paused, cast his eyes slowly over the hall:

'So here I am now, and all that's left to me is to ask for forgiveness. I ask forgiveness of my black brothers. I beg you to forgive me, because I was blind and now I see!'

The Public Attorney was an intelligent man, too.

His father, a highlander who had arrived in Angola barefoot and made his fortune trading glass beads for leather and goats, had sent him to Coimbra to study the Law. The young Angolan frequented salons, made friends, took part in secret meetings, and on one particularly lively night – in a hookers' bar – even dared to declaim a few little protest verses. PIDE called him in to give a statement and this gave him some glory among the Portuguese left. After the April Revolution he appeared in Angola with exaggerated speeches attacking Portugal and the United States and defending popular power. His name was Rui Tavares Marques, but everyone knew him as Tovaritch Marx, or simply Tovaritch. He was, as I have said, an intelligent man. The farce with Ángel left him first momentarily surprised; then he looked at the hall full of people, saw the television crews, the nervous journalists – there were journalists of all nationalities – and understood what he had to do:

'If there were mercenaries who went to the United States to fight against the American people and if some of them were taken prisoner would they be treated in the same way you have been treated?'

Ángel seemed to have his response ready on the tip of his tongue:

'Never!' he stated. 'The United States would never set up a tribunal. The mercenaries would never make it off the battlefield.'

'What would happen to them?'

'They'd be shot!'

'Which social system is the most highly evolved? That of the United States, or Angola's?'

'I'm not a politician, but I'm starting to understand certain things. The systems are as different from one another as day from night. When I was in the Military Hospital there was a Cuban guard – a nice man, it's like I can still see him now. He was a rural man, in Cuba he'd worked with sugar cane, and that was all he knew how to do. But he offered himself as a volunteer to come fight here, not for the money, for the People's Republic of Angola. He left his family and his friends, the little house where he lived happily, to come here and fight. This made me ashamed. I felt so small' – here Ángel raised his right hand and showed his thumb and index finger – 'I felt like this thumb at the base of this index finger. I didn't know where to hide. The difference between him and me is like night and day. I came here out of greed for money. That's the system that's in force in the United States. There a man who has two shirts wants to have twenty. Here people are happy if they have just two shirts.'

At the end of the first session, Tovaritch Marx asked for the American to be brought to his office.

'The testimony you've given has impressed our people favourably,' he said. 'However we would like you to explain better the vices of the American system, the mechanisms which lead to young men like you selling their souls to the devil.'

He looked at him kindly. He smiled:

'We'll give you a pen and paper. Write down everything you remember. Show us the true face of great American democracy' – he paused, raised his narrow fingers to his long curly goatee, and stood up to accompany the prisoner to the door. He embraced him. 'If you need any help, come to me. Our people know how to forgive a man who is repentant.'

In the days that followed Ángel Martinez read out various statements. Yes, he was connected to a group of Cuban exiles. Yes, they had instructors from the CIA. When he was still an adolescent he had been bodyguard to a rich drug-dealer. Yes, the American government was involved in the international cocaine trade.

He was much applauded.

On a sultry July afternoon they lined up Kallan and another two Englishmen and an American alongside the tall white wall of the São Paulo Prison and shot them. I went by there too, a few months later. If you looked straight ahead you could see the almond trees in blossom.

Nine more mercenaries were given weighty prison terms. Ángel got thirty years.

Chapter 3

I learned a lot during that first year in Luanda. I'd enrolled in the high school and in the evenings gave adult literacy classes. Usually I'd have dinner at Paulete's house, the 'Madwomen's Barracks', as Lay used to call it. A lot of OCA meetings took place there. They were very lively meetings. Zorro, though not claiming to be one of the organisation's militants, was often there. Borja Neves too. I think they already hated one another.

I'll never forget those evenings. People would sit in a circle on the living-room floor. Lay would settle in between my legs and I'd put my arms round her waist. That's what I remember best, Lay's heat, the scent of her hair, her fingers holding mine.

Someone would roll a joint, light it, take a drag and send it around. Zorro didn't smoke, he passed the cigarette on to Paulete without stopping talking. He said that it was no longer possible to avoid the establishment of a state bourgeoisie: 'The process is being led by dispossessed slave-traders, people linked to the old Creole aristocracy. Deep down what they want is to recover the power and position of economic domination that they had in the last century. They hold up the mask of socialism, they set up alliances with the masses, whom they secretly despise, and when the time comes they push them away again back to the slums.' He defended getting closer to UNITA: 'It's the only movement with rural origins that exists in Angola, it doesn't make any sense to fight them.' This caused great outrage – Borja Neves beat the floor with his fists: 'Hey, come on now, man, easy now. UNITA are all South African racists.' His eyes shone, his beard in disarray. He spoke very loud, turned towards Paulete.

Another cause of serious discord was the imprisonment of Lídia and other MPLA dissidents. Zorro wanted to do something, to create a movement to demand the liberation of the political prisoners, to try to get closer to Active Revolt. Lay's father, Afonso Mattoso da Câmara, a republican and democrat of the old guard, linked to Active Revolt, had been obliged to leave for Lisbon, after being warned by his friends that the DISA had orders to arrest him. Many other legendary militants, like Gentil Viana, had already been detained at the São Paulo Prison. Borja Neves didn't want to know about them. His reply was aggressive:

'Those guys? They've been foreignised, they've lived their whole lives outside Angola. A spell in prison can only do them good. They'll get a deep understanding of Angola.'

He said this looking at Paulete:

'And even prison is too light a punishment for some people. Revolution demands firmness, education requires firing squads.'

Shouting:

'We should sing about the firing squads!'

Everyone knew that Paulete used to visit Lídia and Ángel in the São Paulo Prison. She would take books for her aunt and comic-strip magazines to the mercenary. She told me that once she went to the prison with Vavó Fina. The old woman, by now more than a hundred years old and almost blind, had made a huge cake to give to Lídia. One of the guards refused to deliver the cake: 'Perhaps you've got something hidden in there, I know those tricks.' The *bessangana* woman, Dona Josephine do Carmo Ferreira, aka Nga Fina Diá Makulussu, asked then if she could take the cake back. The soldier refused: 'Now it stays. It's confiscated,' he said. Then the old woman lost her patience. She took the dish, laid it down on the floor, pulled up the cloths she was wearing and urinated on it: 'It's better like that,' she said to the guard. 'Now you can eat it!'

Paulete was thinner, and quieter. Her silence infuriated Borja Neves:

'I don't understand how some people who call themselves revolutionaries even deign to talk to the reactionaries!'

She was smoking desperately. I was smoking too. I felt very light, I felt my innards levitating. I put my hand inside Lay's shirt and touched her hot breasts, her hard nipples. Lay moved closer towards me and moaned quietly in my ear. She sighed, 'This conversation gets very low *Marx* from me; when do you reckon it'll be over?'

When it was over we would be going to her big bed. Lay would get up onto the mattress and pull down the mosquito net. The light curdled, I would sit in a chair, dizzy as though I'd got too much sun. I'd see her kneeling on the bed, taking her shirt off over her head, her torso very straight. And then looking at me through the net. We would put a cassette in the cassette-player: 'The power of the people / Is the reason for this chaos.' It was a sad, melancholy bolero: 'The lackeys of imperialism want to be rid of us.' Lay would hold the back of my neck with her cold fingers. Santocas was singing, his voice full of hurt: 'Forward, people of Angola / be very vigilant, don't let yourselves be sold.' I would kiss her endless neck, I would kiss her firm breasts. 'Be very sure that the struggle continues / The people's front line is the MPLA.' Lay, her teeth biting my chest. 'The MPLA is the people, / The people is the MPLA.' My mouth on hers, Lay: 'You kiss like a little boy.' I would feel her mouth wet, her night-time belly. 'The armed forces of the people of Angola, / should be very vigilant.' Lay, anxiously: 'Come!' her nails in my back. And Santocas singing: 'We must still encourage the work of politics / Only through combative readiness can we defend our conquests.'

Chapter 4

I think it was in March. That's when the heat and the water coincide and nature is thrown into chaos by this excess of energy. The flowers burn with fever and the animals on heat. Crime rates in the suburbs go up. Stocks of sleeping pills run out at chemists' shops (suicides for love). Women weep without knowing why. Adolescents walk furiously.

It rained that night, I'm sure of that. It was already well past the curfew when the telephone rang. I went to answer it because I knew that at that time it could only be for me. It was Lay, in distress:

'You've got to come. Something terrible has happened.'

Go out at night? No one went out at night. There were the thieves, the police, and worst of all the soldiers' constant raids. Young men were hunted down like rabbits, loaded quickly into clandestine trucks and dispatched straight off to the front line. I never left the house after nightfall. But I went. I took Little Joãoquin's old bicycle and raced off, zigzagging through the shadows. I arrived wet with rain and sweat. Nervous. Lay was waiting for me at the door.

'It's Paulete…'

Paulete was in her room, lying on her bed. She was crying quietly, clinging to the pillow. Samy pulled me into a corner:

'It was Chico.'

In those days Borja Neves was giving maths lessons in the Ngola Kiluange High School. He had published a small volume of poems, *Tetembua ya Kalunga – Songs of the Revolution*, and spoke of nothing else. He'd become fat – swollen, said Lay – and he drank a lot. His passion for Paulete had transformed itself into a dangerous feeling. He telephoned her every day, went to pick her up at the Italian embassy where she worked. She received long love poems from him. Paulete treated him very badly. 'Being born white,' she'd say to him, 'it's an affliction worse than being born without legs. It's to be born without a soul.' She mocked him in front of everyone, she read his poems at OCA meetings, constantly asked him to do little things for her. She often arranged to meet him and then didn't show. Borja Neves would spend hours and hours waiting for her, chewing at his nails with anxiety and despair.

That evening he pulled up in a car by the embassy. Paulete pretended not to see him. Then he opened the door and commanded: 'Get in!' The girl had never heard him speak like this before. She got in, and Borja Neves started the car up. They went to Maianga, to his apartment. 'Strip,' the young man said. Paulete looked at him in shock:

'I will not!'

Borja Neves seemed very calm now: 'You've really got to be the last bourgeois woman I have in my life!' He took off his belt and began to beat her, till Paulete fell to the ground. Then he picked her up, took her to the bedroom and stripped her.

'He was possessed,' Paulete said, 'I don't think he could even hear me.'

He went to fetch a kitchen knife and held the blade to the girl's neck:

'Tell me you love me.'

'I love you...'

'Say you can't live without me.'

'I can't live without you.'

'Swear that you'll marry me. Swear it on your mother's good health.'

'I swear.'

As he moved he began to cry. He cried and begged forgiveness. He spent a long time with his arms around her. At last he fell asleep. Paulete grabbed her clothes and left.

I couldn't breathe:

'I'm going to kill that animal!'

I wanted to go alone to his house. At that point I really would have been capable of killing him. But Lay didn't let me leave. The following day we learned that a colleague of Borja Neves's had found him unconscious on the bedroom floor. He had tried to commit suicide by swallowing an entire bottle of sleeping pills. 'It's women that kill themselves with pills,' Samy remarked. 'Men kill themselves with a gunshot. What I think is that he didn't want to kill himself.'

Chapter 5

Chigoe Chico was immediately expelled from the OCA. I drafted the order myself: 'Comrade Francisco Borja Neves is expelled from the Angolan Communist Organisation, the Viriato da Cruz cell, on the grounds of anti-social behaviour. Comrades are encouraged to break off all relations with him.' Shortly afterwards he was arrested. The police made him pull his car over, in a routine operation, and under the seat found a box of leaflets from the organisation. That is his version. But many people believe he handed himself in. What we know for sure is that the following week four security men went to the 'Madwomen's Barracks' and took us all to São Paulo Prison: me, Paulete, Lay, Samy, Zorro and two other poor wretches, one of whom had just turned up to deliver a ham.

They put us in the wagon, a long building a bit apart from the central block. I was with Zorro in a square cell, a hot cubicle so lacking in air that the very flies suffocated and allowed themselves to be caught in your hand, dazed. In one of the corners there was a hole that served as a latrine. Early in the mornings, as soon as the sun had risen, beating at the prison walls, the latrine began to gurgle. First came a deep sigh, a kind of lament, but it later rose transforming itself to a silent laugh, a belch, then rose still further and the smell spilled out and climbed the walls and clung to your skin as though it was viscous. We stayed two nights and a day without anyone remembering we were there. To begin with I even laughed: 'We can escape through the latrine.' Hours passed and our thirst became unbearable. Then I started thinking about the latrine again. I gave Zorro a shake: 'Seriously, we really could escape through the latrine!' And the stench? I couldn't feel it any more. Only thirst. The cell walls curved over me. They burned. On the morning of the second day I lost it and hurled myself at the door hitting and kicking. A guard appeared, at a run. He opened the door, furious: 'Fucking fractionist, you think you've got servants attending you in prison? I'll smash your face in!' He pushed me hard and closed the door again. I sat on the floor and started to cry. Zorro took my hand: 'Don't cry, *bailundino*, you'll be needing your tears.' In the evening another man came – Santiago. He smiled and held out a can of water to me:

'I remember you: the little comrade from the Quibala road! So we should've had you shot after all,' – he slapped me on the back. 'Comrade Monte wants to talk to the two of you.'

Comrade Monte was a small, lean white man, his cheeks drawn and hair in disarray. When I went in he had his feet on the desk and was reading some papers: 'Hey, kid!' He looked at me as though he had just awoken that very moment. 'You want to be a communist and you don't even have the body to take a few punches!...' He lit a cigarette, holding it between his thumb and middle finger.

'Your friend Neves has been singing, he's told us everything. All I need is for you to confirm a few details.'

He showed me a sheet of paper, typewritten. It was a list of some thirty names. Some I didn't know. The others I was sure if they weren't militants they were at least very close to us.

'I don't know who they are...'

Monte held the smoke in his mouth, ran his left hand through his tangled hair. He seemed amused.

'Keep the piece of paper,' he said. 'Maybe you'll remember.'

On my way back I heard someone call my name. I turned. Lay was looking at me, laughing. I could see her teeth shine between the bars. She shouted again:

'Lilac!'

It was our colour code. Yellow: difficult situation, danger, urgent. Blue: say nothing, keep quiet. Red: someone has infiltrated us. Black: leave at once. Brown: no problem. Lilac: great, it's all gone well. We'd learned that nonsense from some manual or other on clandestine fighting but it had never been of any use to us. Lay, however, had adapted it successfully to the games of love.

Zorro was already in the cell, his face covered in blood, his lip split. 'What happened?' I asked. He shrugged: 'Nothing, *bailundino*, don't worry about it. Comrade Monte and I had a little discussion.'

Two days later Santiago knocked on the door, as he always did before coming in. 'I'm bringing a new housemate. Your little room's only small, but don't worry. United we will *fit* to the death!' He laughed thunderously. Little Joãoquin came in in his pyjamas, lowering his head so as not to hit the ceiling, hands tied behind his back. Early that morning two armed civilians had dragged him out of bed: 'They didn't even let me get dressed.' Little Joãoquin indicated his disordered pyjamas, his mud-caked slippers, with disgust. They had forced entry and in my room found the literature produced by OCA over the fifteen months of its activities. It was enough to convince them that Little Joãoquin was one of the brains of the movement. Zorro would be the other. Monte was determined to drag a confession out of them, and in Little Joãoquin's case it wasn't difficult – he agreed with everything, signed every paper they placed in front of him. Zorro, in contrast, either closed himself up in a stony silence or entertained himself by confusing his interrogators.

'Yes,' he agreed, 'the aim of OCA is to overthrow the regime. It's a bourgeois, fascist regime, inspired by the colonisers.'

'Can you tell us how many cells there are altogether?'

Zorro, heavily:

'I can't because I don't know. OCA is like a cancer. It has multiplied itself everywhere. We set up our cells in the heart of mass organisations, companies, communes. Even within the cells of the MPLA itself.'

Turning to Monte:

'Here we are, talking, and it may be that your cell in the party is already under our control. Maybe you're already one of our people yourself.'

Monte shook with fury. He began to shout, thumped the table, pointed his pistol at Zorro's head.

For me the hardest thing to bear was the heat. We spent the whole time in our underwear. We had a single mattress, an unwholesome bit of sponge so infested with bedbugs and fleas and cockroaches that it breathed like a living thing. We slept in turns, not only because we didn't all fit lying on the mattress but because we thought it was important for there always to be someone awake. 'In the silence of the night,' Zorro explained, 'it's possible to get a better idea of what's happening in the jail, to catch conversations, communicate with other prisoners.' I was mainly afraid of being bitten by rats. I imagined them climbing up out of the latrine and into my mouth as I slept. But I said nothing of this to the others.

After three weeks, when they took me to have a bath for the first time, my hair had been transformed into a fatty paste that you could shape with your hands. I opened the tap and the water gushed, first dark, red, then clean. I cupped it in my hands, I brought it up to my face and felt it pure and fresh as it must have been at the beginning of the world.

God, I was alive!

I put my head under the tap and laughed. The guard shouted something. I laughed at him and the man laughed too. Zorro and Little Joãoquin seemed just as euphoric as I was. That day we asked for a bucket and cloth and cleaned the cell, washed the clothes and the mattress. We started having baths every Tuesday. On Saturdays they would let us spend two hours in the exercise yard, under the sun.

It was there that I met Ángel again. He was stronger. He told me he spent the day working out and recommended some exercises to me. Through him I got news of Lídia, of Lay, Samy and Paulete. Ángel was very well informed. He had become friendly with one of the warders who took his letters to Paulete, brought him messages, even risked little indiscretions. I learned that Lídia, alone in a cell, spent her days writing. She wasn't too badly set up, given the circumstances, and was even able to receive visitors.

Samy should be let out soon. Her father, a German engineer, was an influential person with well-placed friends. The situation with Milagre das Rosas was the opposite: DISA wanted to negotiate the silence of old Mattoso da Câmara, in Lisbon, offering him his daughter's freedom in exchange. This might take some time. Paulete's situation was more complicated still. She spat in Monte's face during interrogations, she insulted everyone and declared herself the head of OCA.

The days locked in the cell seemed very long. Zorro and Little Joãoquin didn't talk much. Zorro had improvised a chessboard, with bottletops and cardboard, and taught us to play. Santiago, who had a lot of free time, would often turn up. Sometimes he brought his guitar, he sat down on a brick and sang. But mostly he talked, he talked a lot. He could spend hours and hours talking to himself.

He entertained himself with his own stories, amazing, appallingly violent tales in which even the most prosaic of events – things that had happened almost unnoticed – acquired the rage of myths. I think he believed them, these stories, but in some I could recognise the plots of old films. Apart from his imagination he also, as I think I have already mentioned, had a prodigious memory. He too learned to play chess and memorised entire games. As he played, Zorro tried to get him to talk about the political situation. Then what was hard was to strip the truth out from under the cloak of fantasy. One day he turned up with a new tune, a rumba called 'Long Live Proletarian Imperialism'. It seemed to be an elegy to the Cuban troops, but two lines referred to the President in a rather unorthodox way; they also suggested that Santiago knew him very intimately. Zorro was surprised:

'This song's going to get you in a fuck of a lot of trouble. What do you know of our old man's private life?'

Santiago shrugged:

'I've even seen the colour of his underpants. Does Your Excellency not know I used to be his bodyguard?'

He grimaced. He sang a little more; after a few minutes he leaned the guitar up against the wall. There was a silence.

'They stitched me up, the sons of bitches. They went and told him I was one of Nito Alves's men.'

Another silence.

'And if I was? Hell, that guy has his *matubas* in the right place!'

He laughed, and his laughter filled the cell.

'I'm one of Nito's men, yes indeed! I know the commander well, he's a friend of mine. A guy I respect, with his *matubas* in the right place.'

Santiago. His face closed up:

'They stitched me up. Left me looking after the kids. They thrashed the guys from the Central Committee. Now they want to stop the storm with their bare hands. They think they can arrest everybody. But it won't go on like this. Mark my words: something is going to happen!...'

THE FURY

'I could...!'

Inscribed in one of the walls of Cell J, the São Paulo Prison Facility,
Luanda, 1977

'I don't know everything. There were things I never wanted to know.'

Lídia Ferreira, in a letter to Mário de Andrade, written in Lisbon
on 30 April 1981

Chapter 1

Early in the morning of May 27th, 1977, I heard the crackle of shots fired, but I didn't wake up. Almost every morning there were shots fired: it could be the police pursuing criminals or soldiers entertaining themselves by startling bewildered lovers, in transit from furtive beds to the arms of their legitimate wives. I heard the shots, and in my dream it began to rain. It rained large rocks of granite, like in Huambo, and when they hit the ground they burst open and locusts emerged. The tarmac turned green, the houses turned green. It was no longer raining – now there were just locusts everywhere. I went out into the road and as I walked I heard the locusts crack under my feet. Little Joãoquin's soft voice yanked me out of my dream:

'Wake up, lad, there's something happening...'

The shots, they were getting closer and closer. All over the prison was commotion, shouts, suddenly a massive thundering could be heard, as though a wall had been knocked down. Little Joãoquin fretted:

'Could this lot be from your subversives?'

Zorro smiled:

'Who the hell knows? There are so many of them! Between Marx and Lenin there's room for more prophets that anyone could imagine.'

Perched on Zorro's shoulders I was able to peer through the 'breather', a little hole that opened through the wall, just below the roof. I could see the yard where an uncertain light was floating, people running between the shadows, weapons left lying on the ground.

'I don't know what it can be,' said Zorro, 'but it's not our people, that's for certain: intellectuals wouldn't make that much noise.'

A short while later the commotion had lessened. We heard voices approaching, and a man opened our door.

'Everyone here out!' he shouted. 'Time to separate the wheat from the chaff.'

Out on the patio there were already dozens of people. In one group far from us I could see Lídia with her arms round Paulete and Lay. Armed civilians watched the prisoners. Santiago ran past me, shouting orders. He grabbed Ángel by one arm and pushed him up against one of the walls. They brought the other mercenaries, and other young men I recognised as being from the Active Revolt.

'Are you crazy?!' I shouted to one of the civilians. 'You can't do this!'

The man looked at me with a cold hatred. God! No one had ever looked at me like that. He shouted:

'Chaff! You, over here.'

He approached me, with blows from his rifle-butt. He grabbed me by the neck and threw me against the wall. I shut my eyes. When I opened them again I saw almond trees in blossom, the sunlight cutting through the sky. Ángel was next to me. He was smiling:

'Don't be scared,' he said. 'I'm fucked, but you they're not going to hurt. Santiago's your friend and he's with them. If I understand it right, this is what they call a *coup d'état*.'

He was serious again. He turned to me, his hand on my shoulder:

'I like you,' he said. 'I'm going to tell you something.'

And that was when he told me about the diamonds. He lit a cigarette.

'I'm no politician,' he said. 'I got myself mixed up in this black men's war because of those little rocks.'

He fell silent for a moment, sucking on the cigarette. Around us everything was confusion. Nito's men dragged a hysterical Borja Neves, who cried and shouted, tearing at his beard and his hair. Ángel spoke again. He told me about how he had been hired: 'A briefcase filled with diamonds! Do you have any idea how much that's worth? I'm going to die, that's how it goes, but I want you to find that case. Get out of this country and take Lay and Paulete with you.' He told me that one of the leaders of the FNLA had hidden the briefcase in a car and left the car in the garage of a house in Damba, a town in the North.

'The case is hidden in the lining of the driver's-side door. It's an E-type Jaguar, convertible, there can't be many of them.'

I looked at him, stunned:

'Red?'

'Yes, how do you know?'

I pointed to Borja Neves.

'It might be his. They stole that car from him in Benguela.'

At that moment Santiago appeared:

'What are you doing there, comrade, do you want to die?'

He pulled me by an arm and shoved me towards the middle of the yard. Then he went back to the other prisoners, up against the prison wall.

'You lot start praying.'

A voice was heard over his, the voice of a woman.

'Stop screwing around, Santiago. We're having this revolution to put a stop to all this dying.'

She was a young pregnant woman. She approached slowly, both hands holding her belly. She seemed at once fragile and secure. You looked at her body and saw a pregnant girl. You looked at her face and saw authority. The armed men moved aside to let her pass. She came up to Santiago and slapped him. Then she turned to the prisoners:

'Anyone who wants to leave, leave,' she said. 'Anyone who wants to continue imprisoned, go back to your cells. Anyone who wants to defend the revolution, stay with us.'

She looked at Ángel.

'I saw you on television. You were meant to be shot, twice: once for being a hired killer, the other time for being a swindler. But for now you get to escape. We'll deal with you and the other mercenaries later.'

Zorro came up to me. He gestured towards Nito Alves's people:

'It's like they're already dead,' he said. 'Let's go inside, *bailundino*.'

I looked back, trying to find signs of Lay amid the confusion. But I couldn't see her.

Chapter 2

Little Joãoquin wasn't in the cell. He arrived soon afterwards dripping wet. He'd taken advantage of the chaos to have a bath. He sat on
the edge of the mattress and began cutting his toenails with an enormous pair of scissors: 'I found them outside,' he explained. The sun
was already high in the sky when Ángel came into our cell: 'Looks
like I'm alive again,' he said. 'Whatever this was, I think it's over now.'
I thought it strange that he was wandering around the prison. Ángel
shrugged. 'These blacks are crazy. They order us to our cells, but
they don't even lock the doors. The bandits have run off. All that are
left are you lot, the politicians, and us, the paid-for internationalists.'
   In the late afternoon we heard another great uproar all over the
prison. Shouts, insults, running. The door opened thunderously and
two soldiers threw the body of a man into my arms: it was Santiago, his shirt torn, his forehead open and streaming blood. Immediately afterwards they came in again, dragging Borja Neves and an
old man I had never seen before, a white man with a scrawny body
but very upright, with a little Clark Gable moustache. They locked
the door. There were seven of us in a narrow cell, all of us standing
because there was no way anyone could sit. The old man apologised
for the inconvenience, that was his word. He introduced himself:
'Arístides Lobo d'África, colonel in the Portuguese army.' I'd heard
of him: Lobo d'África – the Wolf of Africa. In the seventies he had
ordered a massacre in Cassange. He'd buried alive a group of countryfolk, men, women and children, leaving just their heads showing,
and then decapitated them all with a bulldozer.
   'This feels like a rally,' said Zorro. 'A rather poorly attended rally.'
Zorro, aiming his words at Borja Neves. 'The time for bullshit is
over now.' Zorro again, his voice lowered, trembling with rage. I
had never seen him like this before. Borja Neves tried to defend
himself. 'We're all in the same boat together, there's no point creating problems.'
   Ángel spoke for the first time:

'Zorro's right. What I'm not sure about is whether I shove the faggot down the latrine or whether I cut his nuts off.'

He raised his arm and I saw the glint of a blade. God, he had Little Joãoquin's scissors.

Santiago just groaned, delirious: 'N'gila ni kikoto ku muxima.' *I have such pain in my heart.* Little Joãoquin attempted some reconciliation: 'Please, gentlemen, enough of these fighting words, this rotten verbiage.' Imperiously:

'Let us pray!'

And he did indeed begin to chant an Ave Maria. Santiago opened his eyes and moved next to him. Colonel Arístides Lobo d'África did the same.

It was ludicrous. But Ángel really did lower his arm, and Zorro didn't speak again.

I don't know how much time passed. I think I fell asleep a few times. Did I dream? I dreamt that I had fallen into a dark well. The water was thick and hot and I fell into it, I fell endlessly, faster and faster. Then I remember the shouts. Something was shouting. I opened my eyes and I was still inside the well, in the dark water. I heard Zorro's voice: 'Murderers! It's a woman, they're torturing a woman!' Silence. And the cries again. Darkness. We could feel the fear in our fingertips. In our mouths. In our nerves. A heart beating in rhythm, slowly, slowly. I dreamed of a child who was being devoured by a pack of wolves. It was a girl and she was thrown naked onto a rock. The wolves, however, did not seem to be motivated by hatred nor by fury. They were slow and sad and they howled and they bit as though fulfilling a duty. Then the child looked at me.

It was Lay.

I dreamed that I awoke and it was raining. Hearing the rain falling we could almost feel it, beating hard on the sand of the yard, thrashing the high prison walls, spilling itself ferocious and free over the whole city. Santiago looked at me. He too seemed to be asleep:

'It can't be rain,' he said. 'It doesn't rain in May!'

It was still dark when they came to fetch Borja Neves. And then Zorro and Little Joãoquin. And then Santiago. I lay down on the mattress beside Ángel, and Lobo d'África sat on a brick. I waited for them to come and get me. When I woke up, early in the morning,

I saw the colonel, squatting on the edge of the mattress, his face between his knees. 'Why did you do that?' I asked him. He seemed to be expecting the question.

'Because we didn't have much ammunition, we didn't have katanas and it would have taken too long with the bush-knives.'

He had the shadow of sadness in his eyes.

'They were bad times,' he said. 'Unfortunately, these days are no better.'

Chapter 3

Do you want to know what I felt when they opened the door and called for me? Relief! I didn't know what could happen, but I was very tired. Fear, real fear, exhausts us. They took me to a big room with a single light hanging from the ceiling. Monte was sitting at a desk, bare-chested, with a pistol placed in front of him. He looked straight at me and I saw the deep bags under his eyes, stubble unshaved.

'Get those clothes off.'

He said this in a low voice, delicately, as though he was asking me a favour.

It was only then that I noticed Zorro. He was lying in a dark corner, arms tied behind his back. He looked like he was sleeping.

Monte spoke again:

'That's right, sonny, I'm sure you've noticed things are different now. The good life is over.'

I stood there, not knowing what to do. One of the guards who had brought me gave me a slap: 'Are you deaf? Didn't you hear the commander?' I stripped and Monte held a piece of paper out to me, the same one he had shown me the other time:

'Start saying the names of your friends out loud and what it is they do in your crappy little party.'

Zorro moved:

'Don't speak, *bailundino*!...'

Monte rested both his hands on the table. He had hair on his fingers, the thick veins throbbed:

'Start singing, kid, I haven't got much time.'

From that position I couldn't see Zorro. But I could feel his eyes on my back.

'Word of honour I don't know them. I'm not from Luanda.'

Monte seemed to relax. He picked up the pistol and began to play with it.

'I don't think you've realised yet,' he said. 'This is really serious now.'

Raising the barrel of the gun:

'Them up there, they've given us a free hand to do what we want. We'll get rid of you, of everyone. Fractionists, leftists, racists or tribalists. Everyone! Don't think I enjoy it, but someone's got to do it.'

He pointed at Zorro:

'See your leader? I want you to be my witness, you'll see how I loosen his tongue.'

Then he looked at me:

'Your girlfriend is very pretty. We spent the night playing with her. Then we handed her over to the mercenaries. Imagine nine guys at once, I don't think even the *Kama Sutra* describes anything like it.'

I felt sick. I wanted it to end quickly. I took the sheet of paper and gave him the names, told him who had the copying machine, who helped us, what they did and where the other comrades were. Monte asked questions, alert, his faced tilted towards me. He didn't take notes. When I came to an end he leaned back in his chair and smiled.

'See, that wasn't so hard. It doesn't cost much to be a traitor.'

He turned to Zorro:

'I've already got half the story, now you tell me the other half.'

My friend raised his head:

'Why don't you go to your country – you're Portuguese, aren't you? Weren't five centuries of exploitation enough for you? What's the difference between you and Lobo d'África anyway?'

If he had wanted to annoy Monte, he'd hit the bullseye. When I think about this today I feel sorry for Zorro. Heroism is just a kind of stupidity, perhaps the most dangerous kind. Monte leaped to his feet and kicked him in the face: 'The *nguelelo*!' he shouted to the guards. The two men forced Zorro to his knees and placed a sort of tourniquet to his head, with two sticks and a piece of rope. Monte grabbed him by the hair, pulling his neck back while at the same time tightening the contraption. Zorro screamed:

'Mother! Oh, mother!'

I covered my face with my hands, and I was back in a well, in the dark water, thick and dark as mud. I wanted to get out. God, when I was a child I used to invent dreams. Lying on my side I'd see the shadows dancing on my bedroom wall and I'd give them names. I would turn and see my grandmother in the other bed, a massive bulk, and the moonlight filtering through the slits in the blinds. I'd invent dreams, ghosts, but when the fear became unbearable I would get out of bed and wake up my grandmother.

Monte was shouting. He beat Zorro's back and head with his fists. He wept:

'Talk, for fuck's sake, why don't you talk, you want me to kill you?'

He wept! With his left foot he held Zorro's neck and with the other began to stamp on his head. One of the guards took him by the arm: 'Let be, comrade, the boy can't take any more.'

Chapter 4

'Where I come from there are no walls. All I remember is the light. And the sea. Or perhaps, the sound of the sea. I remember it was night-time and there was a passageway. They said to me, "Come!" There was a body, and I went in.

'I walked with my head lowered. My poor head, my body. (My body?) I walked inside the night, hearing the sea. They said to me, "He who sleeps, walks." They said to me that sleep is the closest place to death.

'I dreamt of landscapes where I had never been. Someone said to me: "Sleep." Someone whispered slow words into my ears. I don't know where they came from. At night I arrived in a strange body. I looked at myself in the mirror and saw myself: the other woman. I looked around and recognised the places from my dream. Then they said to me, "Sleep."

'When I awoke you all appeared. You asked me questions. You wanted to know where I had come from. And I said, "Where I come from there are no walls." That's what I said. The woman laughed and I saw she didn't have any teeth. Then I told you about the light. And about the night, and the passageway of the night: "There was a body, and I went in."

'The woman was no longer laughing. She watched me, very alert, almost afraid. You did the same. That one over there wanted to know my name. I said to him, "I've had many." It was hard for me to get used to the noise and the walls. That may have been the hardest part.'

(Fragment of an unpublished text by Lídia, in the possession of Paulete Ferreira. It is dated July 1977.)

Chapter 5

Zorro spent a month unable to move his hands. They had tied his arms with such violence that the ropes had torn the flesh and cut off his circulation. Little Joãoquin fed him, washed him, helped him with the most basic things. He also spent hours massaging his arms and I think that was what saved him. The *nguelelo* had left deep scars in his head and he had wounds all over his body. But he seemed more determined than ever.

We spent eight months in that cell, only going out to bathe. They didn't let us take any sun, or receive any visitors, and the only news we received of what was happening out there came through the guards. For those eight months, long, silent months, Zorro only spoke to me once or twice and only in monosyllables. Most of the time he behaved as though I didn't exist.

In spite of everything we were lucky. We, the ones from the OCA Case. With Nito Alves's men there was no pity. They died in their thousands. On some misty mornings, tired mornings, dull like an old mirror, I watched through the breather as trucks passed laden with dead bodies. The stench was so bad that the guards covered their noses with bits of cotton soaked in perfume. Some of them went crazy. Even the latrine no longer smelled of shit, but of blood. We fell asleep to the screaming of the people being tortured, and we woke up when their screaming stopped.

Chapter 6

In January 1978 they moved us to a common cell, Cell J, where some fifty people were already being held. I remember how in the first few days it felt vast to me. It was in the middle of the night. They pointed me to a blanket in the bathroom and I lay down and fell asleep. I woke up early in the morning with the feeling that I was in an open field, a raw light gnawing at my eyes. Someone was singing a terribly sad ballad:

> I flee away
> I flee
> This is the day
> Jesus
> I flee
>
> I fly...

I got up and moved towards him. The man was sitting in the gloom, in one of the corners of the cell, his head lowered, pretending to play a guitar as he sang. I tapped him on the shoulder with my fingertips.

'Santiago?'

He raised his head.

'That's a voice I recognise,' he said, 'you're the little comrade from the Quibala road.'

He laughed. His laugh was still the same.

'You're shocked, aren't you? They tell me I look like the ghost with no face.'

I don't even know what he looked like. They'd torn out his eyes, his nose and his ears.

'I'm so sorry. Why didn't they kill you?'

I fell silent, horrified at my own question. But the wretch laughed again.

'You think they didn't?'

Santiago could have hidden in the slums. No one would have been able to get him out of Cazenga, Rangel, or even Marçal. He had many friends there, blood brothers. Men who were loyal, women who prayed for him, who lit candles for him on altars. He could have fled into the bush, and then to Congo or Zaire, that was what others had done.

'Why didn't you run away?'

Santiago, laughing:

'Flee, my friend? I'm Tiago de Santiago!'

Who tore out his eyes? Santiago didn't know for sure. Monte was one of them, but he wasn't alone. First they took him to a small room and sat him in front of a table. Four or five people were looking at him. Santiago was confused, they'd beaten him before throwing him into our cell, and again on the way to his interrogation. A fat bloke started asking him questions. Borja Neves was there too, and Monte and a mulatta woman without teeth. 'All growling, apart from the fat man. A nice guy, that fat man.'

Tavares Marques:

'Shall we talk?'

He wanted to know what had led Santiago to ally himself with the fractionists, if he knew that they were in the pay of imperialism and fighting against the interests of Angola. Santiago looked at him and saw him smile, in his white suit, white shoes, a glass of wine in his hand. 'Water,' he asked. Tavares Marques made a gesture and a soldier brought him a cup. Santiago straightened himself up in the chair and drank slowly, feeling the taste of blood in his mouth:

'Fractionists,' he said, 'that's all of us. The difference is that we're a fraction of the people.'

He spat on the floor.

'The difference,' he continued, 'is that we're the children of the people, and you're the settlers' bastards.'

Tavares Marques looked at him with a melancholy smile.

'Maybe,' he agreed. 'And yet it was us who made this country.'

He turned to Monte:

'Too bad, there can be no quarter given with these guys. I'm handing the man over to you.'

They beat him until he passed out, then they put his head into a bucket of dirty water and when he opened his eyes they beat him again. At last someone showed him a blade. The world went dark, a place without light and without time. Days may have passed, or just a few hours. Santiago can't say exactly. He heard a shrill voice:

'Know who I am?'

Santiago knew. He couldn't see him, but it was as though he saw him. The body in a dark suit, the thick-framed glasses, the sad smile.

'I'm very sorry to find you in this state.'

Silence. It was cold and damp. The sound of water dripping from the roof. This wasn't São Paulo Prison.

'You don't want to talk to me?'

Where was he? It was like he was underground.

'Am I dead?'

The other man laughed. A short burst.

'Not yet. I liked you, you know that? I could have given you everything. But I don't forgive traitors. See what you are now? A rag, you matter less than a thrown-away newspaper!'

Santiago lifted his face:

'They can kill us, but they don't dishonour us!'

Another burst of laughter. Bitter. Now the voice dragged a little.

'This isn't a film, Santiago. This is life. We make our way through here stumbling, arm in arm with ghosts. But it's us who die, it's us who hurt. Honour? Can you eat your honour? Do you feed other people with your honour? And the country, Santiago, you think a country is built on honour? A country is built on blood! We feed our people with the hunger of others, we buy our lives with other people's lives.'

He fell silent. He seemed very tired.

'I'm not even going to kill you, Santiago. You don't even deserve to die...'

Chapter 7

Were you mistreated during your imprisonment?

Lídia: No. If that's what you want to know, I was never mistreated physically.

But you were subject to interrogations?

Lídia: Yes, of course. Monte interrogated me various times. Always alone. In general two soldiers would come to fetch me from my cell and take me to his office, a big room with a dresser full of books. On one of the walls, behind the desk, there was a portrait of Agostinho Neto. On the facing wall I expected to find Marx or Lenin, but no, he had hung a photograph of Vladimir Nabokov...

Nabokov?

Lídia: Isn't that strange? One day I asked him what the photograph was for and he laughed. (I tell them it's Engels and they believe me. Have you noticed no one knows what Engels looks like?) Also attached to the wall he had a display case with a collection of butterflies. Monte liked to show me the butterflies. They weren't really interrogations. I think he needed to talk to someone who could understand him.

What did you talk about?

Lídia: Almost always about literature. Monte said the future of Angolan literature would happen through the recreation of the Portuguese language, what Luandino Vieira was doing. Yes, I thought, it was one way. But I also thought (I still think) that Luandino created that style to escape the stigma of his race. He was born white and Portuguese and he wanted to be Angolan. Changing race wasn't possible, but he could change the race of the language. That was what he did.

(To quote Luandino, 'The skin is only the wrapping for the soul.') Have you noticed how the best Angolan writers are white or *mestizos*, the best South African writers are Boers, the best writers in the world are Jews? There's an urgency to what they write. They suffer, they are sick. They write because they need to know who they are.

(Interview with Lídia do Carmo Ferreira, Luanda, 23 May 1990)

Chapter 8

I have confused memories of the first days I spent in Cell J. I was a little dazed. I walked in very small steps and was startled when other prisoners made more expansive gestures. The cell seemed vast to me, excessively bright and noisy. To begin with I was forced to sleep in the bathroom because there wasn't space in the cell to stretch out a blanket, but even this seemed a luxury to me. There were a lot of us. The people all talked at the same time and I didn't understand what they were saying.

I took slow baths, till the skin on my fingers became yellow and spongy. I sat on my bunk and stayed in silence, trying to escape from there in my thoughts. Mainly I didn't want to think about Lay. I tried to reconstruct trips. The train, you remember, sis? We were little and the trip seemed to know no destinations, the days following one another to identical horizons. Sometimes the train would stop at dusk and from our hiding place behind the windows we could watch the arrival of the slow herds of antelopes. They came fearfully to lick the humidity from the cold iron of the rails. We would leave with the dawn and once again it was the white extent of the savannah, the train creaking, panting, the ground burning. I also liked thinking about rain. I was naked, outside our house, watching the rain arrive. A twisting wind lifted the dust of the paths. It ran free and dirty and the sky was suddenly lower. The *quitandeira* trader-women felt the air with their tongues. They laughed, and everything was mysterious to me. Then the rain fell, illuminated, and birds emerged in the waters. They appeared in flocks, beating their white wings. They flew in with the rain on their wings. In the distance you could hear religious chanting. The air carried the harsh smell of life in secret ferment.

And Lay? Someone told me she'd been released with Samy. A few days later Zorro came to me, put his hand on my shoulder:

'Have courage, *bailundino*. The little girl wasn't able to resist.'

She killed herself. I don't know where, I don't know how it happened. I never wanted to know.

I walked the cell as though asleep. No one paid me much heed. There were others worse off. Borja Neves, for example, had tried to kill himself again. No sooner had he been moved to our cell than Zorro called together all the prisoners connected to the OCA. 'This man's an infiltrator,' he said, 'he doesn't stay here.' That night, just as Chigoe Chico was receiving his plate, Zorro fell clumsily onto him. 'Sorry,' he said, 'I tripped.' The next day, at lunch, the scene was repeated, and again at dinner. This lasted two weeks. Borja Neves was thin and pale as a Christ. He trembled whenever anyone approached him.

One morning I awoke to see a line of tiny black ants. I followed the ants to the bathroom and found Borja Neves lying on his back. The ants went into his nose, and came out of his right ear. I called one of the guards, thinking he was dead. But he wasn't. They took him to the infirmary and soon afterwards he was released. But we still used to see him, every once in a while, during the interrogations. He stood next to Monte and lowered his eyes if he had to speak to us. He blew his nose and ants would come out.

I recuperated slowly. Sitting in my corner I watched Little Joãoquin make guitars out of oil cans and pieces of wood. I watched how Zorro, who had been elected 'cell chief', organised the lives of the prisoners. He himself taught me mathematics and accounting. A young doctor, also from our case, led a seminar on first aid. There was also a tractor-driver, accused of belonging to the FNLA, who gave *quicongo* classes. But the biggest hit was the astronomy course. The teacher was Simon du Plessis, a Boer lieutenant, captured in South Quanza during the South African military invasion. He painted the constellations on the ceiling of the cell, using a phosphorescent paint he had made himself from the preserving oil of the Russian fish they gave us for lunch. At night, when the lights went out, we could see the universe shining above us.

I began to teach Angolan literature. By this point we had managed to establish good relations with some of the guards, the so-called 'conductors', and they acted as go-betweens, taking and bringing messages to and from the prisoners in the other cells. Ángel, who in the meantime had become a cook, also walked freely round the prison and never refused us a favour. That was how I came to start corresponding with Lídia. I asked her opinion on some aspects of my classes and I sent her poems. Lídia always avoided passing comment on my lamentable lyric activities, but in compensation she managed to get manuscripts to us with long dissertations on the Angolan nationalist movement of the nineteenth century, *négritude*, Brazilian and German literature, which she knew well, among several other general subjects. Little Joãoquin read Lídia's papers out loud, a task he undertook with rigour and a strange solemnity. He would wait for everyone to be quiet, and only then raise his fine priest's voice. Everyone listened to him.

Chapter 9

Then Zorro invented 'television'. It was a wooden box with a glass front. I recall the image of Colonel Aristides Lobo d'África, sitting very upright, the box resting on his knees. The silence was absolute. In front of him were sixty men, among them stonemasons, electricians, artless and luckless thieves, public functionaries, students, doctors and lawyers. Almost all of them Angolan, but also a Zairean, two South Africans, three Portuguese, an Italian. They were sitting on the floor, on their respective bunks, on benches or on bricks. They listened to him in absolute silence. With the box resting on his knees he spoke about Mozart. Most of those men had never even seen a piano. Lobo d'África spoke of *The Magic Flute*, his fingers running along the edge of the box as he hummed the first notes, moved, his eyes shining behind the sheet of glass. He spoke of Chopin's nocturnes and his voice turned hoarse and dusky. The men in front of him listened to him, their muscles tense.

I was named director of information services of the 'television'. It was fun: at first we were still trying to reproduce reality, or what we believed reality to be. We constructed a news bulletin based on pieces of news brought to us by the guards, by relatives or friends who visited us or taken from the rare newspapers and magazines we managed to get hold of. Bit by bit we began to invent brief news stories, and then other more significant ones, entangling the other prisoners in a universe of fiction. We announced news of a revolt in the Soviet Union, the end of the Eastern Bloc and the fall of the Berlin Wall.

Fidel Castro suffered two attempts on his life...

In the United States a group of Indians kidnapped the president...

The Angolan government is internationally isolated...

Mandela was liberated. *Apartheid* is coming to an end...

Jonas Savimbi, having lost the support of South Africa, agrees to negotiate with the government. The problem is, there no longer is a government...

An Italian journalist photographed the Pope in a disco for homosexuals...

– Some of the prisoners protested indignantly and on the next bulletin we issued a denial of this news story.

Our Lady of Fátima appeared to a group of Dominican shepherds dancing a merengue atop a banana tree.

– Another denial.

Agostinho Neto won the Nobel Prize for Literature and during the official ceremony denied the existence of political prisoners in Angola.

– This item, illustrated with a photo of the president, raised boos and whistles: 'This story isn't true,' confirmed a man from Lubango who had been arrested accused of eating cats. We called on Zorro to comment on the event. He appeared in the television, damp hair pulled back, a white bow and a cigar, and made a passionate defence of the poetic work of Agostinho Neto. 'I still don't believe it,' said the man who ate cats. 'They don't give the Nobel to black men.' He was a thin mulatto, the grandson of Madeirans, who in colonial times had earned his living going from village to village with a little projector, a large sheet and a collection of Charlie Chaplin films. He'd stop in the little towns which cinema had not yet reached and set up the machine and the sheet, being careful to arrange a row of chairs for the dignitaries of the town. 'The whites stayed on this side,' he explained, 'and on the other side of the screen, sitting on the ground, would be the blacks. They would come in their hundreds, bringing me chickens and goat kids. They would dance when the film came to an end.' If we drew his attention to the racist nature of what he had said he was given to get angry. 'I'm not a racist!' he would say, vehemently, 'but I'm not colour-blind either.'

– Extraterrestrials have landed in Brazil. Contrary to what had been supposed, they do not speak English...

– Fidel Castro suffers another attempt on his life...

Twice a week the guards opened up the cell and we went out to the yard to play football. They were hotly contested matches, which immediately led to endless discussion. There were also draughts and chess championships. I ended up organising literary contests. Birthdays were an excuse for big parties.

In secret we made wine. Alcides, a veterinary student from Bié, managed to obtain an excellent white wine from a base of sugar, bread and water. I myself experimented with a few drinks made from tinned fruit. Rice spirits were the easiest. And apart from this they had the great virtue of not giving off an unpleasant smell.

Almost every month the guards raided the cells and took away the wine flagons, the guitars, the flat-irons, the electric coffee-makers and all the instruments we had made. So we decided to dig a hiding place, a space about forty centimetres deep and a metre long. The hard thing was to hide the earth. This worked for some time until one of the searches when a flagon exploded. And then another of them, and another. The explosions, though muffled, provoked panic among the guards. One of them shot at the bunk that hid the hole, lightly wounding Colonel Lobo d'África. When they realised what had happened they became mad with rage. They lined us up and beat us with the butts of their rifles. They destroyed everything.

In September 1979 Lídia was put on a plane to Belgrade. Officially she was going for treatment, as she suffered from a stomach ulcer. The Yugoslav ambassador went to see her off at the airport and handed her a small volume: 'My daughter is waiting for you,' he said in such a way that the DISA men accompanying her should hear him. 'Do me the favour of giving her this parcel, it's a gift.' In Belgrade as well as the ambassador's daughter she was awaited by a tall government representative, a man she had known when she was in exile in Germany, an old friend of Alberto Rosengarten. The man embraced her, moved: 'Welcome to freedom!' He smiled: 'The Angolan authorities have asked us to keep watch over you, but as you know this is a free country. In two hours you have a flight to Lisbon. If you want to stay, you stay, if you want to go, you go.'

In prison we didn't learn that Lídia was in Lisbon till Christmas Eve. We held a big party. It was not long after the night of the explosions. We managed to prepare some white wine, but we didn't have instruments. Even so, The Kimbandas of Rhythm, a group of which Santiago was the vocalist and bass-guitarist and soloist, played and sang all night long. Santiago was better than ever, not just singing but also simulating guitar solos. Xico N'Dau, a South African from the ANC, arrested on the orders of the leadership of his movement

(I never found out why) performed jazz and blues numbers: 'Black Africa's always a victim, / 'Cause there are two superpowers in this world…'

On the first day of 1980 a captain came into our cell looking for Santiago. The old bandit asked me to help him put on his boots. 'It's not worth it,' the officer said to me, 'where he's going he doesn't need boots.'

THE END

'Coming back from the Fire, returning, / little by little / and as in fragments / first the torso / the head, then the fingers / that feel out the air / in turn. / In panic / Then the hair, my lovely hair / of my youth / Returning from the Fire and for moments / lucid / such short moments. And returning to the Fire.'

Lídia Ferreira, in *A Vast Silence*, Crow's Voice Publishing, Luanda, 1992

Chapter 1

When I was a child I took a bird out of a little cage. The bird didn't fly. It stayed, circling, circling, terrified by the size of the wide world and the enormous responsibility of having to fend for itself. When they released me I felt like that. I wandered the streets aimlessly. I also found it hard to recognise things and people. That city no longer belonged to my organism, it was a prosthesis.

Once they took me to a party. I found the clothes strange, the trousers with pleats and without a crease, narrow at the heel. The boys had their hair short and sharp sideburns close to their ears. The women all seemed to me to be beautiful, but stupid, of a solid, frank, fundamental stupidity that infected other people. I didn't know how to dance, I didn't know the songs or even the singers. People looked at me sidelong – that's what I thought, perhaps they didn't even notice me – and avoided talking about the political situation. Even our old comrades were changed. One of them said to me, 'Look – what happened, happened. They were mistakes of youth, that's the way it goes, you've got to forget all that now and start a new life. Pretend nothing happened.' He was an FAPLA major. He died at Mavinga.

I went to Huambo to visit my grandmother. I found her in the yard looking after the vegetable garden. She turned, slowly: 'What are you doing here, are you done with the revolution?' She was as I'd left her. The house too. Elias Justino, the old cook, told me that a few months earlier he had awoken to the sound of voices. Looking out of the window he'd been able to make out figures in the yard. He went to call my grandmother. 'Prepare yourself, ma'm, we're going to die!' The old woman turned on all the lights and opened the door in her nightdress. 'Get away from here!' she shouted at the group of men who were creeping around in the yard, 'You're ruining my roses.' They were UNITA commandos. The leader got up and begged much forgiveness, they'd thought the house was occupied by Cubans. Elias laughed to recall the episode. 'Madam's a lion!' he said to me.

'Your parents were right.' The old lady muttered this while she did her knitting. I couldn't see her face. I saw her head lowered, her white hair held high up in a plait. 'They were right for the wrong reasons. Leave here, boy. This country has no destiny.'

'And my grandmother?'

She raised her clear eyes:

'I'm like the grass, I don't bear any fruit, I don't give any shade. And in this country that's a good thing. No one notices us!'

Chapter 2

I met Lídia in the Tropical Garden, by the Monastery of St Jerome. She had never seen me before. I had seen her for the first time on the Morro da Luz, on independence night, and caught a fleeting glimpse of her on the morning of May 27th, 1977. Now she was sitting on a bench. Behind her were red roses and a bougainvillea which exploded into a dusky wonder. I shook her hand, not knowing what to say. Lídia smiled, amused: 'You wouldn't think we'd met before.'

She was fifty-three years old. A beautiful woman. She was lecturing in African History at the Classical University in Lisbon. 'With a certain amount of distaste,' she confided to me, shaking back her hair. 'Not many students are students by vocation.' I asked after Paulete. She smiled again: 'Just the same.' Paulete continues to scandalise Luanda. She was living with a Swedish engineer but turned up all over the place arm in arm with an important member of the party. She'd written herself to her aunt to explain the affair: 'One completes the other, one without the other is something that makes no sense, like a cigarette without nicotine, coffee without caffeine. Platonic love.' In the same letter she wrote that Zorro was now living with Samy and that they were both studying economics.

Ángel had fled to Namibia with Simon du Plessis and Colonel Lobo d'África. The mercenary, who had walked around the whole jail as though he ran the place, and was a kind of unofficial cook, had swiped a number of bottles of Largactil from the infirmary – this drug was used to sedate lunatics – and he had used it in the food. With the guards neutralised, he had freed Lobo d'África and Simon du Plessis. The rest was easy: they waited for the arrival of a military lorry which used to deliver fresh groceries, and they escaped, taking the driver with them. It's said that they had waiting for them somewhere on the coast a boat from the South African navy. In Windhoek they gave a press conference denouncing the brutality with which the Angolan government treated its prisoners. Ángel said he wanted to stay in Namibia. Colonel Lobo d'África expressed his desire to return speedily to Portugal.

Little Joãoquin had resumed the work he'd always done: 'As long as there's time, there will be watches,' he said to Paulete. Old Fina died in her sleep and the Ingombotas mansion was occupied by a high-ranking functionary of the Presidential Palace.

Borja Neves was running the cultural supplement of the *Jornal de Angola*: 'He drinks more than he breathes,' wrote Paulete, 'and he's as swollen as a pufferfish.' But in spite of this – or perhaps because of this – he had lately published a new book, an immense novel, more than a thousand pages long. *The Prophet of the Cranes*, the story of an obscure crane-operator, semi-literate, who invents rumours. As they are propelled by the people as legitimate facts, these end up transforming reality; in this way the gossipmonger is able to overthrow UNITA, South Africa and the United States of America and makes Angola a peaceful and prosperous, multi-racial and anti-racist country. Lídia had already read the book and she liked it: 'It's an extravagant utopia that enriches our literature.' It seemed to me to be rubbish multiplied by a thousand pages, the work of a drunk who finding himself unable to organise reality according to his own desires chooses to set up around himself a vast and laborious fictional universe (we had done the same in prison with 'television').

Lídia had also published a new book, her second, following *Antique Stones*, which had been published in 1961 in Lisbon, with the seal of the HSE, the House of Students of the Empire. It was *The Fire that Sleeps*, which nobody noticed. In Angola the intellectuals ignored her. In Portugal the Africa-friendly critics – most of them her former colleagues and comrades in the struggle of the fifties – passed her by without recognising her. Lídia pretended to accept this: 'Never to have existed is more practical than dying.'

In 1988 I returned to Angola. It was a stormy visit. I was part of a delegation of young exiles, invited to visit the country through an initiative of the party's youth organisation. It was part of a political offensive launched by the government with the aim of keeping Lisbon's important Angolan community outside UNITA's orbit. But things went badly, apparently because someone or some structure within the apparatus of the State didn't want them to go well. There was a series of incidents, and in Lubango one of the girls from the group was raped. They sent us back quickly and amid much scandal to Lisbon, but in the airport I met Paulete. She had come to introduce me to her twin daughters. Twins, but not identical. One was very dark, with tough, untameable hair like her mother's. The other blonde, with light eyes: 'They're products of my internationalist belly,' she said laughing, and I noticed for the first time her black gums, her teeth solid and gleaming. The people in Luanda had seemed to me to be tired and sad as at the end of a party. Not her.

When I arrived in Lisbon I was asked for an op-ed on Angola. A week after the article appeared I received a postcard signed by Aristides Lobo d'África. He wanted me to go and visit him. He sold parrots and other exotic birds in a shopping centre: 'I have a business partnership with Ángel Martinez,' he explained; 'he gets hold of the birds from Africa. I sell them here and we split the profits. It's a good business.' He was a nice old man. It was as though he'd done nothing else in his life but sell parrots.

Chapter 3

I returned to Angola several times after 1988. I happened to be in Luanda when Jonas Savimbi entered the city, and in September 1992 I went to cover the elections for a Lisbon daily paper.

Zorro was moved when he saw people waiting their turn in endless queues, burning in silence under the fury of the sun. We were in a remote town in South Quanza and those people were wearing their best Sunday clothes.

Me: 'They think they're at Mass!' That was how it was everywhere, in the cities or in the most distant villages. Zorro went very serious. He said:

'They're voting against the war.'

He and some other old OCA companions had started up a small party. Paulete: 'At least we'll discover the exact number of people who buy books in Angola.' She didn't believe in anything. What she wanted was to dance in the new bars that had been set up on the sands of the Island. To have fun with her friends in the clubs which were doing reasonably good business all over the city.

'Democracy? The same people who're talking about democracy now, two months ago they were defending the conquests of social-ism. I know them well. I've slept with all of them.'

Despite this she insisted on voting.

'It's a racial vote, pal, I voted for the "M"!' A pause, just long enough for a complicit smile. 'They're sons of bitches, but they're *our* sons of bitches!'

A lot of people thought that way. Lídia, who had agreed to stand as an independent deputy on the list for Zorro's party, thought Jonas Savimbi was dancing to the MPLA's tune:

'Savimbi has been blinded by his obsession with race. When the smallest bit of good sense would have told him that UNITA should attempt an alliance with the Creole group, he went off onto speeches of loathing against the city. And now even the people who've always been against the regime are going to vote MPLA to prevent a UNITA victory.'

I too was afraid of UNITA. One day Zorro asked me to go with him to visit a colonel from the FALA, the UNITA army. 'You remember an old servant of Borja Neves's, a guy called Calandula, who joined the MPLA and disappeared during the occupation of Benguela?' I did know him.

'Well then.' Zorro opened his arms, amazed. 'Seems he was kidnapped by UNITA, and later joined them. Now they call him Sudden Death and he's a colonel.'

André Calandula, Colonel Sudden Death, received us in his room in one of Luanda's hotels. He embraced Zorro warmly. He asked after Borja Neves and wanted to know how Paulete was. In spite of his dark, well-tailored suit, he was just the sort of man it is easy to imagine leading guerrilla groups. He asked short, incisive questions and made notes in a school exercise-book. He seemed genuinely interested to know Zorro's opinions on the political process.

Halfway through the conversation he asked permission to turn on the television. The face of a UNITA dissident appeared on the screen. 'I used to know him well,' said Sudden Death, 'he was my friend. Unhappily he sold himself to the MPLA.' The dissident was attacking Jonas Savimbi. He was accusing the UNITA leader of ordering the killing of internal opponents. He said those terrible things with conviction, his eyes shining: 'I now want to address my friend Sudden Death, alias André Calandula, my old friend.' I became nervous, Zorro too. Sudden Death just shrugged: 'It's not a problem,' he said, 'he's playing his part.' The dissident raised a finger: 'André, my friend, could it be that you believe that there are women who fly at night? I know you don't believe it! But when Savimbi ordered you to arrest Teresa Catalaio you went to fetch her and you pushed her onto the bonfire yourself.' Another pause – this man was a fine actor. I couldn't take my eyes off the screen. 'André, my friend, I know you're listening to me. What I want to say to you, is that the time for fear is over. The time is over when we were forced to commit horrors. You have been through the "technical hut" too. Why don't you go to the beach? Are you afraid to show your back with its whip-marks?! The time of the whip is over, André. The time of the bonfire is over. Join us and we will be rid of that time once and for all.' Sudden Death turned off the set. There was an uncomfortable silence.

Zorro: 'It's hard for me to ask you this right now. But it's important for us to know what truth there is in all those stories going
around about UNITA. Stories of sorcery, witch-burning, all of that.'

Sudden Death looked at him at length:

'The truth, bro? Truth is, that's just what Africa's like. You live
here in Luanda, you listen to American music, at Christmas you eat
salt-cod from Portugal, you go to the beach on Sundays and you
think that's Africa. The real Africa is in the slums, it's in the bush.
And that is just what that Africa's like, so don't come to us with your
lectures.'

He was feverish, euphoric:

'This city is rotten. The mulattos have taken over everything.'

Zorro: 'I'm a mulatto too.'

'You're a mulatto too? I know, bro, yes, you're a mulatto too, but it's
as if you were black. We want to return Angola to the African world.
We're fighting for the dignity of the black population of Angola.
With elections or without them we will take power. The leaders of
the MPLA are weak, they spend their days drinking and fornicating.
In three days we will take Luanda, we will take over Angola.'

Chapter 4

One night we woke up to the sudden spectacle of the end of the world. The whole city seemed to be exploding. Many people appeared in the streets in their underpants, guns in their hands. The roaring shook the buildings. The brilliance was such that it was possible to read even with the curtains drawn, the blinds closed. Some men I saw were laughing. A neighbour called to me: 'You people still don't have guns? Come and choose.' He showed us a room filled with pistols, rifles, machine guns. God, I swear there were even howitzers, grenade-throwers. Little Joãoquin looked at it all with an expression of intense horror. He shook his big ox's head slowly:

'There are more weapons here than there are people to kill!'

And then came that month of November. November is when the rainy season starts. God, it had been years, how many years since it had rained in the city?

I'd been to visit Lídia, who was living in Paulete's apartment, and I didn't leave. The shots seemed to be coming from everywhere. Zorro phoned: 'A group of men came to kill me, but the neighbours told them I'd already run away.' He lowered his voice: 'I don't want Samy to know. I put a valium in her soup and now she's asleep.'

I phoned Little Joãoquin. His voice came with an echo as though he was speaking from inside a well. 'We're barricaded in the corridor,' he said, 'a howitzer shell came in though the living-room window.'

The television was showing images of war. Kids with red ribbons tied round their foreheads, Walkmans in their ears, munitions belts crossed against their chests. They brandished guns in the air and danced in front of the cameras. In one of those images there was a man I thought I recognised: Monte, a nasty little beard creeping up his neck towards his cheekbones. Shortly before the elections I had met him on the street. He came up to me and embraced me: 'Don't you recognise me?' He embraced me again: 'I hope there are no hard feelings, OK? Let sleeping dogs lie.' He took out a piece of paper and wrote down a number. 'That's my telephone number,' he said. 'I'm in Kinaxixe now, give me a call and we'll arrange a big *funje* dinner, my wife's a fucking amazing cook.' I said yes, and the following Saturday, with the night already fallen over Luanda, there I was in Kinaxixe. He was on the fifth floor of a ruined building that seemed ready to sink into a lake of putrid waters. The staircase had no banister and occasionally there were steps missing. Someone had arranged lit candles every few flights and the wax dripped onto the floor. The light danced, making the walls come closer, move further, and come closer again. I thought, 'This building lives and breathes.' Something dark ran past, struck my legs hard and disappeared into the void behind me. In Monte's house there was light. The heavy purr of the generator made the floor shudder, but Monte didn't seem troubled by this. 'People get used to anything,' he said, leading me to the kitchen. His wife was a very short woman with wide hips and an enormous bosom. But the skin on her face was smooth and glowing, and she was almost beautiful when she smiled. She was called Marilinda and she worked as a secretary in a state enterprise. In the living room two adolescents ate in silence: 'Those are my sons,' said Monte. After dinner he wanted me to see his collection of butterflies, carefully kept in shoeboxes, and I got the impression that this was what he lived for. 'I have incredibly rare specimens,' he assured me.

The television showed images of the streets again, and this time I was sure I saw Monte. The reporter approached him and held out the microphone; Monte passed the gun to his left hand and took it:

'Here we are!' he said. 'We, the people. To defend the will of the people, the conquests of the people, liberty, the free market. Today Luanda is the front line of democracy in Africa...'

He seemed very tired, deep bags under his eyes, greying hair in disarray. The reporter asked him how the situation was. Monte moved his lips, showing his rat's teeth, and I didn't know whether that was a smile:

'It's very well now!...'

Lídia didn't want to watch television. For those three days she closed herself in her room, writing. Later I read what she wrote. Terrible things. When the shots stopped I went out with her. We went on foot to the end of the Island, pretending that we couldn't see the city ruined by the latest confrontations. The madness prowled around us, stretched out to us with its long spider's legs. The smell reminded me of May 27th. The same fury, the same vertigo. It gathered on the street corners, crawled along the ground, climbed up your legs, your body.

There was no one on the beach. We sat on the sand and watched the wreckage that the tide had brought in. Lídia said, 'The chaos is prodigious!' She said, 'It's been years since it's rained.' It was true. It had been many years since it had rained in the city. In the dry season there was a whiter light. Sometimes the sky went dark and the sea grew anxiously in the bay, but the clouds passed and it never rained. The beach was full of little dead monsters. The crabs had all died inside their transparent armours. White fish looked at us with big watery eyes. Lídia grabbed my hand: 'What country is this?' In the distance shots could still be heard.

I wanted to get her out of that state.

'Hope is like a fire that sleeps,' I said to her, quoting one of her poems. 'We stifle it and we think it is dead, but it just sleeps.'

Lídia didn't even smile.

'Now I know more than I did then,' she said, 'now I know that exactly the same thing happens to despair.'

She raised her hand to her hair and tied it with a ribbon.

'Don't take me too seriously. Old people's hearts are a bitter mineral.'

The launch of her last book, *A Vast Silence*, was set for the following week. I asked her if the date still stood. Lídia made a vague gesture. We stayed a long time listening to the sea. Then I stood up and went away.

Chapter 5

'I awoke blind, the night dark. A small noise woke me. A low sound,
a brushing of tiny bodies moving under the bed, in the floorboards,
climbing up the cupboards and up the walls. I got up and I felt them
alive, under my feet. They were there in their dozens. They climbed
up my poor old woman's body, smelling me with their long anten-
nae. I got several of them with both my hands and put them in my
mouth, and bit them and swallowed them, like I'd bitten and swallowed the roses before.'

(...)

'We are in ruins, like these houses. I'm talking about how we are
on the inside: on our knees. Eaten away by leprosy, slime, a vast
tiredness. For some people it's hatred that sustains them. For others
it's not even this: they wait. At least for the fire to come and clean
our bones. Even our souls. I walk these streets and what I see are
corpses. They are all dead. One of them passes me. I say to him:

"You are dead."

And he laughs. His skin is stretched across his bones.

We go into the Biker together. We sit at the same table.

I ask for a coffee, he a soup. It seems we used to be friends. He
tells me about that time, but I don't remember. I'd like it to be true:
that we had a past. The soft light of the late afternoon crosses the
room and settles on the billiard tables. In one corner are the old
men. They have been there since independence. They play dominos
and drink in silence. My companion gestures towards them with his
chin. He asks me:

"Are they dead too?"

They have been dead for some time. They play dominos and they
drink their lukewarm whisky and avoid catching each other's eye.'

(...)

'The old men said it's dangerous to confront the light of the dusk.
They said with a start, "It sets clothes alight." There was one man

whose hair burned. They also talk of carbonised houses. Trees in flames. "The blood," they repeat, "devoured the horizons."

(…)

'My heart is full of ants / and of a nameless horror. Will I return? Must I return with you to the acid lands? Between the shadows and the water what was left of us?

Life was more lovely in March. / The rain bringing the termites; fevers, and between the mud, / and the slime / pieces of armed men (the war I never had room for).

In the mud there were tiny creatures, things without any use, including flowers.

What was left of me in these places? Who was I? I was never anybody's. Nothing anywhere awaits me.

My heart is full of tiredness. It sleeps in the mud between the flowers. I died and nobody knew anything.'

(Fragments of an unpublished text by Lídia do Carmo Ferreira, in the possession of Paulete Ferreira. It is undated.)

Chapter 6

Lídia didn't turn up on the day of her launch. We waited for her – some thirty people – but she didn't turn up. Paulete shrugged. 'Well,' she said, 'that's not going to stop us from drinking.' And she started serving whisky. Borja Neves was there too. He insisted on reciting one of Lídia's poems: 'The Little Animals, Silent and Pale'. His voice was hoarse, gnawed away by alcohol. Then he took me by the arm and dragged me to a corner: 'Know who I saw today? Commander Santiago!' I told him it couldn't be:

'Santiago was shot!'

Borja Neves rested his lost eyes on me.

'You're right,' he said. 'Maybe that's why I thought he looked so rough.'

He started telling me about his new novel. A man travelled in his dreams to a distant planet. Every night, when he fell asleep, he saw himself arriving at the planet where an old man was waiting to talk to him. 'I've already written two volumes,' he told me. At that point his wife came to fetch him. She was a very black, very fat lady, with an expressionless face. Lídia called her *Musa paradisiaca*, the scientific name for the banana tree. 'We're going,' she said. 'You've already had too much.' Borja Neves shook her off roughly. He embraced me: 'You remember my old Jaguar?' He laughed till tears came to his eyes. He choked and started to cough. He turned very red, even redder, almost purple. His wife grabbed him to stop him falling. He pushed her away again. He wiped away his tears with the back of his hand. 'I found it for sale at the Roque Santeiro market and bought it for a hundred thousand *quanzas*. Completely broken up.'

'Can I see it?'

Borja Neves laughed again.

'See it? I gave it a burial, kid. A proper funeral. This war hadn't yet started up again. I took it to Caotinha and launched it into the sea.'

He embraced me again. He said to me, his mouth close to my ear:

'It was the last thing that was left of me.'

I went back to Little Joãoquin's house. It had been months since there'd been a drop in the pipes, but Dona Diamantina always arranged for me to have a tub filled with green water. In the corner little mushrooms were growing. I stripped off, put on some rubber sandals and poured a bucket over my head, holding my breath. I'd heard it said that some people had contracted cholera just because they hadn't closed their mouth while taking a bath. Sadly I noticed thin stalactites hanging from the ceiling. Suddenly the house seemed to me to be on the verge of ruin.

I went out into the street distressed. Where could Lídia be? I decided to go by Paulete's house. She received me wrapped in a towel, water dripping from her hair.

'I don't know what's become of her!' she said to me, before I'd even opened my mouth. 'She's disappeared, flown away, who knows! This relation of mine has witchcraft...'

'And the girls?'

Paulete leaned on the wall. She unrolled the towel and let it drop.

'I've sent them to Lisbon,' she said. 'Haven't I done well?'

Naked she seemed larger. Her body glowed, but not like it was reflecting the light, it was as though the light came from within. I said to her, 'I think you're burning!' She laughed. She continued to laugh as she removed my clothes. She covered my neck, my arms, my torso with sandalwood oil. She opened a little glass bottle and took out a small pellet of *gindungo* pepper. She rubbed it on her gums.

'They say my kisses burn.'

They burned.

God, where could Lídia be?

Chapter 7

Borja Neves was right. A few days later, I saw Santiago myself and spoke to him. It was in Kinaxixe. The sun was melting the tarmac. The smell of dead bodies was a thing at once solid and diffuse. It could be felt on your fingers like mist. I made my way, concentrating, head down, in part because of the smell and in part so as not to trip over the rubbish, the bodies mixed up with the rubbish. I heard a squealing of tyres and jumped to avoid an old scooter running into me. I shouted:

'Santiago!'

It was him, mirrored glasses attached to his head with sticky-tape. He was driving the scooter. Sitting behind him was an old man with no arms, white beard in disarray, eyes red and glowing like hot coals. Santiago turned his monster's head towards me.

'Speak again.'

'The bastard blind man! My grandmother does say you can never get rid of the bad ones.'

Santiago gave one of his famous roars of laughter:

'You, here!'

He got off the scooter and embraced me. He slapped me hard on the back. Finally he detached himself and gesturing to the old man introduced him:

'This is Antoine Ninganessa!'

And added, as though guessing at my emotion:

'The man himself, the Prophet!'

Antoine Ninganessa gave a little bow, impassive, and I thought he seemed quite whole even without arms. Santiago began to tell me about his life:

'I've gone into business with the prophet.'

In truth it was several businesses, not all of them very clear. On the one hand they had founded a sect, the Church of Christ the Black Redeemer. On Friday afternoons they would come together to pray, sing and dance. On Saturday they would do miracles:

'Great miracles,' Ninganessa assured me, his voice serious. 'Things of great wonder and inspiration.'

They also set about organising funeral ceremonies and burials:

'We have the party and we take care of the burial,' said Santiago. 'You know, death's hard these days; you can't get so much as a little basket, let alone a decent casket. So instead of selling our casket, we rent it.'

They had a single coffin, beautiful, painted in pink and gold (Santiago: 'It's so lovely we've even given it a name: the Passion Bus'). They'd put the dead person inside, bury him, and that same night they'd go back to the cemetery.

'What we do by day we undo by night. We dig up the Passion Bus, take out the dead man and strip him.'

'You steal from the dead?'

'Steal?' This was Ninganessa, offended. 'Don't you know the word of the Lord? "As he came forth of his mother's womb, naked shall he return to go as he came. And this also is a sore evil, that in all points as he came, so shall he go."'

Another profitable business was selling blocks of ice at the Roque Santeiro market. Santiago had managed to get his people inside the morgue, and that's where they produced the ice: 'They're the only industrial freezers that still work in Luanda,' he sighed, getting back onto the scooter. As they moved away, penetrating right into the smell of the dead, I could still hear Ninganessa directing the other: 'Straight ahead, now turn right…'

Chapter 8

It was increasingly dangerous to go out onto the street. One evening I witnessed a lynching. First an albino on a bicycle passed me, cycling like a thing possessed. Behind him, crewing an ice cream van, came two police officers. While one drove, the other, crouched on the box of ice creams, his head and arms out, shot a little automatic weapon. He shot various bursts, but without hitting the target. Then the bicycle struck a rock, rose up like a bird, the albino spun in the air and fell hard. The policemen jumped on him.

'Cut his head off,' said the one who had been driving.

The other hesitated:

'Here?!'

At that moment a little woman appeared waving a fistful of dollars. 'I'll pay a hundred!' she shouted. The policemen exchanged a quick glance: 'One-fifty!' The woman separated the notes, smoothed them out with her fingers and handed them over. The albino began to cry. 'Don't do this, ma, for pity's sake, I have nine children!' It didn't do him any good. The woman pulled out a katana and cut off his head with two vigorous strokes. Then she put it away in a plastic bag and left.

I went to Paulete's house and told her what I'd seen. She shrugged:

'It's like that all over the city,' she explained. 'Someone started a rumour that an albino's brain produces a juice that will cure AIDS.'

It was already possible to buy this juice in Roque Santeiro, served in little bottles. The television ran a report on the subject. One albino, interviewed in his home, protested in panic: 'I'm not albino, I'm really white!' And he raised his hand to his hair, painted black and straightened, parted in the centre: 'You see? I really am white!' A doctor in the studio confirmed that there was no scientific basis to justify the rumour: 'Albinos' brains are in every respect the same as ours,' he stated.

Paulete gave me a smile. She'd made herself up as though for a party: 'The albinos – fuck 'em,' she said. 'I was waiting for you.' She hid her laughter behind her hands:

'I love you!'

I did not love her. I wanted to get out of there, out of that house, of that city which no longer belonged to me.

Chapter 9

I found Little Joãoquin sitting on the veranda, hand in hand with Dona Diamantina. The dusk was intense and sad.

One question had been troubling me for some days:

'And now what?'

Little Joãoquin gave an expansive gesture, taking in the house, its walls eaten away by bullets. The city irremediably rotting. The buildings with their entrails devastated. The dogs eating the dead. Men eating the dogs, and the excrement of the dogs. The lunatics with their bodies covered in tar. The wounded with an eye missing. The soldiers in panic in the middle of the debris. And beyond, the deserted villages, the burned plantations, the restless crowds of fugitives. And further beyond still, nature thrown into chaos, the horizons devoured by fire.

He said:

'This country's dead!'

Lisbon/Luanda
26 September 1994

REFERENCES

The two quotations from Senghor (from 'Governor Éboué', p.45, and from 'Joal', p.50–51) are taken from Léopold Sédar Senghor, *The Collected Poetry*, translated by Melvin Dixon. Published by the University Press of Virginia, 1991.

The quotation from Guillén on p.53 is taken from Nicolás Guillén, *The Great Zoo and Other Poems*, translated by Robert Marquez. Published by Monthly Review, 1973.

GLOSSARY OF ACRONYMS

Following the country's independence from Portugal in 1975, Angola was the setting for a long civil war that pitted the governing MPLA against (among others) the rebel UNITA movement and the FNLA faction. (Pre-1975 these three groups had fought alongside one another for the common goal of independence.) The civil war only came to an end in 2002.

MPLA (Movimento Popular de Libertação de Angola) – The Popular Movement for the Liberation of Angola. Led by Viriato da Cruz, and subsequently Agostinho Neto (the first post-independence president) until 1979.

    EPLA (Exército Popular para a Libertação de Angola) – The Popular Army for the Liberation of Angola, the main armed wing of the MPLA until 1974. Replaced by FAPLA.

    FAPLA (Forças Armadas Populares de Libertação de Angola) – The Popular Armed Forces for the Liberation of Angola, the armed wing of the MPLA from 1974 (replacing EPLA).

    DISA (Direção de Informação e Segurança de Angola) – The Angolan Information and Security Directorate; which later became the Ministério da Informação e Segurança de Estado, the State Security and Information Ministry (MINSE).

UNITA (União Nacional para a Independência Total de Angola) – The National Union for the Total Independence of Angola. The main anti-MPLA rebel movement after independence, led by Jonas Savimbi. UNITA party members are sometimes referred to as *kwachas*.

    FALA (Forças Armadas para a Libertação de Angola) – The Armed Forces for the Liberation of Angola – the UNITA army.

FNLA (Frente Nacional de Libertação de Angola) – The National Front for the Liberation of Angola, originally a militant organisation, subsequently a political party, which fought for independence and subsequently against the MPLA. Led by Holden Roberto.

UPA (União das Populações de Angola) – The Union of the Angolan Peoples, an older group that subsequently evolved into the FNLA.

ELNA (Exército de Libertação Nacional de Angola) – The Angolan National Liberation Army, the armed wing of the FNLA.

OCA (Organização Comunista de Angola) – The Angolan Communist Organisation, an extreme left movement opposing the MPLA.

PIDE (Polícia Internacional e de Defesa do Estado) – The International and State Defence Police, the security services of Salazar's Portugal.

ESTAÇÃO DAS CHUVAS

TRANSLATOR'S DIARY

In September 2008, when my work on this translation was just about to get under-
way, James Smith agreed to host a 'Translator's Diary' on the excellent Booktrust
Translated Fiction website that he edits (www.translatedfiction.org.uk).

The aim of the blog was to allow readers to follow the process of translating a
novel, José Eduardo Agualusa's *Estação das Chuvas*, from the first draft of the first
page right through to the complete polished and edited version ready to go into
production many months later. Some of the posts would deal with specific linguistic issues (and would invite comments and suggestions from readers), others
with more logistical ones. It would attempt to draw its readers' attention to the
complications of translation and its delights, the choices it demands, to the varied
role of the translator that extends beyond just translating, to general problems
and to problems that are specific to this pair of languages or this particular text.

The blog was well received by readers around the world (many of them translators), who sent in questions and comments, and who suggested ways of getting
round problems I had presented; so following this pleasing response it has now
been reproduced here, as an appendix to the translation it describes.

What follows, then, is the full text of my translation blog, just exactly as it
appeared on the Booktrust site. Because it was (as blogs are) originally intended
to be read at the pace at which it was written, a post at a time, there will be the
occasional repetition, and little infelicities of other kinds (a few sentences which,
frankly, I could have written a lot better if I'd had the time…); but it has nonetheless been left just as it appeared online, undoctored, to give you an honest sense of
precisely how the translation process worked, and how the blog itself worked, too.
When there was nothing much to report, the posts on the blog said so; and those
posts are included too, lest you be given a false impression that it all went smoothly
and nothing went wrong and no one was ever kept waiting or missed a deadline
(or an airplane). No, this is the thing itself, unedited and unvarnished, which I
hope is a virtue in itself. And I hope this makes up for any little inconveniences
that this approach may bring, and that readers might therefore forgive them…

My thanks to James Smith for generously hosting the blog on his great site for
this past half-year and more; and also as ever to José Eduardo, always so generous
to this translator, for apparently not thinking this blog (and its publication in this
volume) an imposition too far.

D.H.

Post 1

What this blog is for

Translation – like most kinds of writing, like most kinds of artistic creation – tends not to expose itself to an audience till it has reached its finished form. A reader is encouraged to read a finished book – which may be a third, fifth, or fiftieth draft, which has been worked and re-worked, corrected, questioned, edited, polished and proofed – and to disregard the imperfect stages that have preceded this final one. You are requested kindly to keep well away from the rehearsal room until the performers and production team have their show ready for public viewing, if you please.

In this blog I hope to examine the translation process, working through a novel from my own first launching into a first draft, right up to publication. It's not a blog about the life of a translator – musings about translation generally, reports of events I've attended or readings I've given, people I've met at launch parties, books I've read – but intimately about a single piece of translation work, which I hope will bring you closer to the experience, to the pleasures it brings and the questions it raises.

I am just about to embark on the translation of *Estação das Chuvas* by José Eduardo Agualusa, a wonderful Angolan novelist I've been privileged to work with a few times before. This book – our fourth together – presents a search for the story of Angolan poet Lídia do Carmo Ferreira; but it's also the story of many other people who spin into and out of her life and the narrator's; and each has his own rich back-story told, and each engages with the setting – the state of their country through the second half of the twentieth century.

It looks back at Lídia's childhood, back through her family's history, through narrative but interspersed with passages from interviews with Lídia later in life, carrying through to her unexplained failure to appear at the launch of her last book... It opens on the night of Angola's independence in 1975 – a day of celebration which would also mark the beginning of a two-decade civil war...

So over the coming weeks I will be using this blog to record my work on this book, posting as I go. I'll be exploring challenges particular to this book and this writer, his voice and language and the world he evokes, presenting specific problems as they arise, and perhaps asking you to help with creative ways of solving some of them too.

Our publishers Arcadia Books, José Eduardo and I have only just agreed on which of his many fine books to tackle next – trying to balance our judgements of the relative books' qualities with the demands of particular accessibility and appeal to English-language readers (it's about Angolan politics, among other things – will it be too unfamiliar?). Not to mention the question of how well this piece of writing will work in English. So far I have read *Estação das Chuvas* just once – but this was some years ago, and only rapidly, and today I remember little of it, and nothing at all of how the story develops and ends. And so far I've translated the first couple of pages as a sample for Arcadia, again a few years back.

Here's that opening:

That night Lídia dreamt of the sea. It was a deep sea, dark and full of slow creatures that seemed to be made of that same sad light you see at dusk. Lídia didn't know where she was, but she knew that they were jellyfish. As she awoke she could still make them out moving across the walls, and it was then that she remembered her grandmother, Dona Josephine do Carmo Ferreira, aka Nga Fina Diá Makulussu, a famous interpreter of dreams. According to the old lady, to dream about the sea was to dream about death.

She opened her eyes and saw the great pendulum clock hanging on the wall. It was twenty minutes past midnight. Angola was already independent. She thought about this, and wondered at her being there, lying in that bed, in the old house of the Ingombotas. What was she doing in that country? A useless question, that tormented her every day.

But at that moment it had another meaning: what was she doing there?

She was lucid and felt nothing, neither the bitterness of the defeated nor the euphoria of the victors (it was both at once that night). 'It's the night of praying mantis,' she thought. And she saw herself, newborn, with a large praying mantis resting on her chest.

When she was small, old Jacinto had talked to her about it: 'Not long after you were born your mother looked over at you and saw a huge praying mantis on your chest.' Much later, grandmother Fina had retold the episode. She had said to her, 'Life will swallow you up.'

Grandmother Fina had turned 105 that month, but remained a practical, solid woman, just as she had always been. Lídia believed in everything she said, including her premonitions. She considered waking her grandmother to tell her of the dream, but she didn't move. She had no strength. She inhaled the quicombo-perfumed air deeply, and felt lighter. A distant, round rumbling drifted to her ears; she couldn't separate the different sounds but knew that they were gunshots, explosions, cries of pain, of fury, of delight. Almost all were sounds of rage, but there must have been some groans of love too, the barking of dogs, the deep sound of beating hearts. Lídia thought about Viriato de Cruz, she thought about death, she thought that beyond her closed bedroom windows life was carrying on. She sat up in bed, stretched her hand out and took from her nightstand a little black-covered notebook, one of those long notebooks that grocers use to pencil down the day's accounts.

'Life is happening out there,' she wrote. She crossed the line out and wrote again: 'Out there life was happening / In all its brutal splendour.'

Then she put a circle round the two lines and added the date: '11 November, 1975'.

It's a start… For a translator it's a gentle start, a nice, straightforward opening, I think. And engaging and intriguing enough, I hope, to hook people in for page two. More to come…

Post 2

Anticipating general problems

Before I get into detail on the text of my *Estação das Chuvas* translation, I thought it might be worth sharing a few concerns I have as
I set out, attempting to forestall a few general problems I anticipate
coming across in these months' work. (Though it's salutary to note
that the most complicated problems arising never turn out to be the
ones I've managed to anticipate…)

Having done a few of Agualusa's books before, I know that one
issue that will undoubtedly arise is how to deal with cultural par-
ticularities of the Angolan setting, a setting we have to assume unfamiliar to most Anglophone readers. What to do with the shorthand
references to local dishes, for example – these books are full of such
things – and whether to gloss them extensively, to footnote them (to
be avoided at all costs, surely?), or simply to retain the words in the
original and assume that even if people don't know them it doesn't
always matter.

For example, to say 'He served himself a plate of *funge*…' or to
explain what exactly *funge* is at the risk of interrupting the flow? In
the opening passage I quoted last week, there's the word *quicombo* –
should I explain what it is (which might be awkward), or leave it in
the original and assume that this adds something useful colourfully
tonally even while the precise meaning or reference might not be all
that important.

There are plot and contextual issues of this kind, too; much of
Agualusa's writing is not only embedded in the physical and cultural
Angolan setting (local birds, recipes, rivers, music), but also in its
history and politics, with references dropped to names of people,
organisations, political parties or significant events with which my
readers will not – I'm assuming – be conversant.

This book in particular works within a very particular modern political context, and depends on knowing and understanding certain things about how systems operate and who is who – that's potentially a trouble to be solved if we possibly can, if the reading experience is going to be comparably rich to that of an Angolan reader. In that same opening passage, then, most readers of this blog would have no way of knowing whether Lídia do Carmo Ferreira is or was a real person appropriated by the author for his fiction, or his creation; and you never know, that might be significant.

(Just while I think about it, I should mention too in the interest of full disclosure that one of the difficulties I anticipate for this translation is the writing of a blog about it. Like most people I know who do this kind of work, I find I do a lot of it by instinct and without examining what I do; having to think about what's happening in the process, and finding a way of articulating it, may prove to be really hard… Interesting, though, or so I tell myself…)

So… There will be linguistic snags, too – and while I can't predict what exactly they'll be I know they'll be there and can guess at least at the *types* of problems Agualusa will have created for me and his other translators to sweat over. He is a writer who likes to play with his words, who likes little verbal games, who likes poems and song lyrics; this book, like all his books, will be well sprinkled with this sort of thing, and each one will require a new and creative solution if something of the effect is to be retained in my necessarily imperfect version.

And there are more macro-scale linguistic issues too, broad questions of tone, of cadence, of how the sentences read in English, how the whole thing will be made to feel like a piece of writing in English – and yet still attached to its former self in Portuguese – and not some odd hybrid… Getting that quite right is always tricky (and particularly hard to define and describe), always a worry and potentially a problem. On the whole I find Agualusa's sentences sit very well in English, but is that because I'm venturing too far away from the original cadences, and creating a piece of English writing no longer properly moored to its original?

(I remember one sentence in my first Agualusa book – *Creole* – which seemed so very right, seemed to sit so well in English, and it wasn't till after publication that I realised it was because I'd inadvertently let myself roam too freely away from Agualusa's sentence and more or less hijacked a sentence from *My Fair Lady* to fill the gap...)

Though a difficult question to answer clearly, it's one of paramount importance: does it all sound just right, and how does one know? What to look for?

So to begin at the beginning, does that first passage quoted last week work as smoothly as it should? There's only one way to find out.

More on Friday.

Post 3

To footnote or not to footnote...

Putting a bit more flesh on the bones of my last post now:

The first is the question about how you know when something is right, when after a little playing around with alternatives you know you've got it. For me, there's only one way to measure that, and that's by reading it aloud.

Last night I read from my translations of Agualusa's work at a great live literature event called Plum, hosted by Natasha Soobramanien and Luke Williamson at the Whitechapel Art Gallery in London, and took the opportunity to read not only passages from the three published books, but also the opening to *Estação das Chuvas*, the piece I included in my first post. I don't think I've read from a translation-in-progress before, and for all my concern it sounded good, I think, quite fluent – Agualusa is such a pleasure to read aloud! – and all the rhythms felt very natural.

That night Lídia dreamt of the sea. It was a deep sea, dark and full of slow creatures that seemed to be made of that same sad light you see at dusk. Lídia didn't know where she was, but she knew that they were jellyfish. As she awoke she could still make them out moving across the walls, and it was then that she remembered her grandmother, Dona Josephine do Carmo Ferreira, aka Nga Fina Diá Makulussu, a famous interpreter of dreams. According to the old lady, to dream about the sea was to dream about death.

Then I came home and read the same passage aloud in Portuguese. (Which I would never do in public, as my accent is horrible...) And it sounded totally different. Smoother, humming, it felt as though it were all m's and n's and l's. And indeed, look at this first line – even if you know no Portuguese, just look at the letters that constitute it: *Naquela noite Lídia sonhou com o mar.*

I wonder if I've done what I'm always afraid of doing, produced something that reads well but at the cost of forgetting some of its kinship to the original?

I'll worry about that later.

I mentioned in my last post too the issue of local specific words/things that my readers won't know, and I gave the example of *quicombo* – this exotic something that in that first extract was perfuming the air in Lídia's room as the novel opens.

The alternatives would be to find a closeish translation (it's a kind of wood, so a reasonable alternative – a scented wood – sandalwood? rosewood? It's neither of these, quite…); to retain *quicombo* in the Portuguese and maybe italicise it so it's obviously foreign and assume it doesn't much matter if no one knows (my usual inclination); or to footnote it – 'A wood with which beds used to be made because it was believed that its intense scent repelled insects.'

That last solution seems the least appealing – a very distracting thing to a reader. But… rather curiously, there's a footnote, with just that text, in the original edition too. This makes things more complicated.

I'm working from a Brazilian edition of the book, so was the footnote added to help non-Angolan Portuguese-language readers deal with a very local word? Or do these appear in every edition of the book, for the original reader (whoever that is) too? In other words, is it a footnote from Agualusa, part of his writing of the novel, or something added by a trying-to-be-helpful foreign publisher?

If Brazilian readers need footnotes, should we assume that English-language ones must surely need them too? Or is there a distinction to be drawn between readers in Brazil who speak the language and therefore assume to be able to understand everything and so need the odd bit of help, and those of us who are culturally and linguistically much further away who might expect a little bit of exotic mystery to the details of what they're reading, and therefore could just get away with an unannotated 'quicombo', and assume it's something interesting and heavily perfumed and local and that's all they need to know to give them the colour of the scene?

Hmm. I'll write to ask Agualusa about how this works in the edition of this book read in Angola. (It's such a luxury having an obliging author at the other end of e-mail...) And will return to this issue when I have an answer.

How this is resolved will also depend on how things pan out later, because flicking forward in this edition I can see lots of footnotes to come. It may be something that makes sense as a stylistic part of the book. A lot of the questions I ask now won't be answered till much later in the book, when I get a sense of what is regular stylistically and what it anomalous – this applies to vocabulary, to tone, to questions of local particularity – everything, really. There's a little bit of groping in the dark about the start of this process, hoping that nothing I do is going to be proved thoroughly inappropriate as things progress...

And talking about things progressing, I really have to start chapter two...

No Largo Primeiro de Maio, o Presidente falava à multidão.
On Primeiro de Maio Square, the President was talking to the crowd.

Talking, or speaking? Primeiro de Maio Square, or First of May Square? Anyone?

More next week.

PS Thanks to everyone who's e-mailed in response to the first couple of posts, and glad you're finding it interesting. We don't currently have a regular comments facility set up, but I'll try and respond to questions you raise as I go.

Post 4

Agualusa's literary DNA

Other work has meant I haven't made much progress this week,
but a couple of observations from the few pages I've done. Both are
obvious, commonsense, but they're worth having in mind…

First, then, is to report how smug I felt working on pages 31 and
32. The vocabulary on these pages included the following words:

- *casuarinas*
- *funge*
- *nespereira*
- *gindungo*

They are, respectively, a kind of shrub (the same word can be used
in English); a dish common in Angola that is made with manioc
paste (to which I referred a couple of posts ago); the tree on which
medlar-fruit grow; and a spicy kind of chilli berry.

Now, my vocabulary in Portuguese is actually not all that exten-
sive (shameful to say), but these are all words I knew without having
to look them up. Because they're all words I've come across repeat-
edly in my work on earlier Agualusa novels. They're words that are
all very much a part of Agualusa's world; they're words employed in
standard Portuguese and yet which may never be heard in Lisbon or
Rio – words with particular local freight, that are part of the furni-
ture of one particular place, but not another.

They're a clear indication, then, of that particular local-ness
of writing (which makes the task of someone with Brazilian Portuguese translating an Angolan novel difficult, but translating his
fourth Angolan novel rather easier…).

But also of the distinctiveness of the linguistic tools any individual writer uses. Over the page a beautiful woman with a long gazelle

neck is described – a long gazelle neck is the most Agualusa-like of phrases. (There's a woman with one in *Creole* too, as it happens.) These little things are like literary fingerprints – Agualusa only writes like Agualusa, and that's something no one else can do quite the same. He has words he particularly likes and others he doesn't, he has rhythms that are uniquely his own, he has ways of describing that aren't like Doris Lessing describes things or Thomas Hardy describes things or Jerome K. Jerome describes things.

(Btw, when I was with him in a workshop this summer I mentioned a particular word which I felt I kept finding deployed in his books, which kept coming up again and again, and having mentioned it I think made him self-conscious about it… So I'll not repeat it as I know he's reading this blog… Clearly the insistent and beady attentions of a translator can be most destructive to the flowing of un-self-conscious prose…)

My job, then, is to find an equivalent language in English – an equivalent set of linguistic habits, heartbeats, eccentricities, flavours – to match the uniqueness of Agualusa's literary DNA. I don't think about that consciously while I do it, of course, but finding peculiar old friends like *funge* and *nespereira* in this new book is a good reminder.

A note too on the voice of this particular book, or I should perhaps say 'voices'. Because different bits of the book are told in different ways – sometimes third-person narrative, sometimes the transcript of an interview with the main character, etc. – so one thing I'll have to keep an eye on is that the subtle differences in language between the two are respected in the translation – the newspaper articles have to sound like articles, the political speeches have to sound like speeches, the interview transcripts like real dialogue, and so on.

As with so many of these things, it's not something readers notice until it goes wrong.

If a character picks up a newspaper and reads the headline 'Retail slump set to continue, warns PM', it just sounds right, it sounds like a newspaper headline, and the register isn't something you even think about. (There's a joke to be made here about 'just doesn't register', but I'm ignoring it.)

Whereas if a character picks up a newspaper and reads a headline which says, 'Anyway, so Gord said basically he reckons people're not gonna be doin' lots of shopping for a while yet, which I'm sure you'll agree is pretty crap news for all of us, really, see?' you'd wonder how a bit of second-rate dialogue suddenly crept into a sentence about a newspaper headline.

Yes, this is an unrealistically extreme example, obviously, but the cheap effect I hope makes the point – while it's much more subtle in reality, there is a very distinct right and wrong register, and in a book that switches very quickly between modes it's worth being reminded of the functions of each in the English. Just something to keep an ear out for as we go...

(Likewise the main character will need – each character will need – a speaking voice, a voice of her own, just as she has in the original. I'm sure I'll discuss this before too long.)

Post 5

Tackling the first draft

Just a little example of working process, if you're interested.

I don't know how most translators work, but I'm someone who never works slowly and methodically from the beginning of the book to the end, getting it right as I go. I prefer to hurtle through, basically translating at the speed at which I can type, and leaving notes to myself, queries, vocabulary problems etc. marked down along the way, but not letting myself be tripped up by them as I go (I find getting the rhythm right is much easier like this, even if I don't know all the words or what I'm doing...) And then I go back over the whole thing and slowly fill in the gaps: look up in the dictionary those words I didn't know (usually sitting IN UPPER CASE, accusingly, waiting to be attended to); find the right English word for the ones I do know in Portuguese but haven't quite yet pinned down satisfactorily in my version; solve those tricky problems of wordplay and other things that require more attention than I can give them on the fly.

So my first draft always looks something like this:

(It's the very brief second chapter of the second section of the book.)

Chapter 2

Did you have many friends as a kid?
Lídia – Artur was my first friend. There was also [I also had?] a dog [cão], a gigantic PERDIGUEIRO, who was a bit crazy, which my grandfather named after the Portuguese governor of the day, Eduardo Ferreira Viana. We had another dog [cachorro], but he was old and avoided children. He was called Salazar.

When was the first time you left Luanda?
Lídia – The first trip I remember taking was to Canhoca, a stop
[apeadeiro] on the Malange railroad. My grandfather went to visit
a friend and took me with him. The train scared me. It seemed very
large, tumultuous*, smoky. We occupied a compartment in the first
class carriage, and I was at the window [had the window seat?]. It
was early in the morning [madrugada], the air was wet and smelled
of ripe fruit. I looked out and saw the quitandeiras* selling large
green oranges. A blue-suited [-uniformed?] man unrolled a BAN-
DEIROLA and went past us, trotting towards the locomotive. He
was shouting: PARTIIIIIIIIIIIIIIIIIDA.

(Interview with Lídia do Carmo Ferreira, Luanda, May 23rd 1990.)

That took about five minutes, and no mental effort at all – but it also
produced nothing worth reading, and the real work is yet to come.
At the end of the book, the sprint completed, I'll have hundreds of
pages of queried, asterisked, hesitant mess, and the fun begins…
    For example…

- Should 'kid' in the first line be 'child' instead? More likely
  interviewer word?
- 'apeadeiro' isn't the usual word – is the neutral 'stop' quite
  right?
- Should I be distinguishing between the two dog references? A
  different Portuguese word for 'dog' is used for each.
- Salazar – should I assume everyone will know who Salazar
  was (who gave his name to the dog) in the way that everyone
  in Portugal or Angola would certainly know? It's not a very
  funny line if you don't…
- 'perdigueiro' – I think it's a pointer or something like it (a
  'perdigão' is a partridge), but look up in dictionary to be sure.
- 'quitandeiras' gets a footnote in my edition – 'Vendedeiras
  ambulantes' (walking/travelling saleswomen) but footnote
  policy is still to be resolved in the English… I'm tempted just
  to keep the Portuguese word – in italics – and leave it like
  that; a reader's guess here is likely to be right.

- 'tumultuous' – I don't like this word. Can think of something that sounds better if I try.
- 'bandeirola' – a 'bandeira' is a flag, so some sort of little flag, for signalling, I guess? (I'm sure there's a word in English – umm…) Dictionary again.
- 'Partida' is 'departure'. Should he really be shouting 'Depaaaaaaaaaaarture'? 'Depaaaaaaaaaaarting'? But in English wouldn't it be something like 'All abooooard'?

And so on, and on.

I've had a lot of people e-mailing in with questions and comments in the past couple of weeks (thank you!), so I'll use my next post to go through and try and answer some of those.

Post 6

Answering your questions

Other work has prevented me from making much translation progress to report on this week, so I'll take the opportunity instead to respond to some of the comments and questions you've been emailing me.

First, then, in response to some of the particular questions I raised:

The question of how to deal with untranslatable local words seems to have struck a chord; the responses seem to be guided by what you prefer as readers – and that's certainly my own measure, I avoid footnotes as a translator because they annoy me as a reader. So 'No marking in the text', says Alex Z, suggesting instead endnotes; while Anne, also a translator, suggests an option I hadn't thought of – a glossary. She doesn't mind footnotes, but the glossary gets her vote (and she gets annoyed when there are words in a book that require explanation and no glossary offered).

That opening line from Chapter 2 also brought up some preferences – First of May Square, said Sara, rather than Primeiro de Maio, which is the solution I'm leaning towards too. Rather than 'speaking to the crowd' or 'talking to the crowd', Alex offered 'addressing the crowd', which I think is just right.

('Speaking' is clearly an acceptable alternative – speaking to a crowd sounds right; whereas talking to a crowd is plainly wrong. Anyone venture an explanation why? I'm sure I can't, except that I just know one is right and one isn't…)

Matt of the armchair reader blog asked a few interesting general questions, which I'll take one by one:

1) How closely do you communicate with the author?
Very closely – we're in touch frequently, fortunately. I would find it hard to do this if I couldn't use him a lot. Agualusa is very patient with my persistent questions, which is a great help; and he also has a very good understanding of what translation entails, so he's not unrealistically precious about the integrity of every word of his original, which is an even greater help...

2) There are two poles – capturing literal accuracy and capturing the feel of the original – do you agree? Do you feel this is more or less true regarding contemporary translations of prose?
I think that's true in theory, but in practice – when we're talking about books that are sold in bookshops, just fiction, sold on an equal footing with books originally in English – I don't know many translators who will compromise on the readability of the work in the interests of literal accuracy. I think for me the most important thing is not fidelity of word by relentless word, but fidelity of the reading experience. If the original has a joke you're supposed to laugh at, sometimes you just have to change the joke a bit to make it still funny in English – keeping some of the details may be good where possible, but keeping the laugh itself is important too.

3) What inspired you to become a translator? I saw that you're also working on non-fiction works of your own – do you consider that or translating to be your main priority?
I've translated for a very long time, just technical or academic things, and with no aspirations to be a literary translator. It never occurred to me that I could do it, to be honest. And then a friend at Arcadia Books asked if I'd translate a book by Agualusa for them – I'd read the book and loved it, so said yes. Then, of course, wondered why I'd been so foolish to say yes, and what hubris to think I could get away with it.

Yes, I have a few different hats – I write a fair bit, I edit reference books, I translate – and sometimes (to mix hat/star metaphors) one or other is ascendant. It's sometimes because of particular things that catch my interest, sometimes because of the jobs that happen to be offered to me (at the moment I'm suddenly being offered quite a lot of translation work, relatively less writing work, for example), but I'm fortunate enough to be in a position where I can just look at each project as it's offered to me and decide whether or not I like the sound of it, and that usually leaves me with a good mix of things, which is how I prefer it. I'm not sure I could do any one of these all the time.

4) Translators typically receive less credit than the original authors of the work – how do you feel about that? Many publishers seem to go out of their way to hide the fact that the work has been translated – do you think this is more a response to a public distrust of translation or a contributing factor to the lack of awareness of the importance of translation?

Hmm, I'm going to leave this one. This is a big question – basically, what's wrong with the publishing-translations world, which deserves more than a paragraph or two. I might do a post just on this at some point, I think – I do think you're absolutely right to point out the problem, and the reasons you suggest are I'm sure at least part of the explanation.

But to answer quickly the first question you mention – I think it's right that original authors receive more credit. I think they do the harder job, the bigger job, and I think even after translation the book is still more theirs than mine. That said, the translator should of course always receive a decent credit, as our role is far from insignificant!

On to Claudio (who translates Isak Dinesen and others into Portuguese), who asked whether it would be possible to include the Portuguese original alongside the translations that appear on the site. Yes, I'll certainly try to quote the original when I'm talking about specific bits of text when it's just odd lines or phrases, but I won't often be looking at very big chunks of the original text on this blog simply because I'm assuming most visitors aren't Portuguese readers. But if you are a Portuguese reader I'd urge you to get hold of the original and read the whole thing anyway, as it's a marvellous book...

In the 'further reading' category, Sara recommended a look at Umberto Eco's *Mouse or Rat*, which I agree is fascinating, and certainly worth reading if you don't know it. And Chris Hughes has drawn my attention to a translation wiki, which looks like a great project to enable access to amazing writing – have a look at their work on Brazilian writer Artur Azevedo here: www.librilang.org

Now, to Joey Rubin and ZD Smith and others who asked about getting an RSS feed or some way of knowing when a new post has gone up, the answer is I think someone is working on this, but I'll let you know when I know what's happening… [that's right. Ed.]

And finally a special mention to Roland whose comment included the word 'sonorities', which I think is lovely and I'll have to use for something too very soon if I can.

Thanks for these messages, and all the others. Will respond to any others as they appear.

Will leave you with the words of Alex Z, translator from the Czech, who ended his comment 'translation is impossible. And yet it must be done.' Brilliant. Will quote that a lot.

More next week – have a good weekend.

PS Just one further little observation; most of the comments seem to be coming from people who are themselves translators. I don't know if that's because it's only translators reading the blog or only translators choosing to share their opinions on things. If there are nontranslators out there, I'd love to hear from you with your thoughts too!

Post 7

A conundrum

Apologies for the silence this past couple of weeks. Have been working mainly on other books (writing short biographies of two English poets at the moment) and travelling, so have had to neglect Agualusa. Normal service will be resumed next week.

Meantime, a little something for you to worry about:

Those who eat at the table with the Flemish people are going to feel fear in their hearts. But we're not! Antoine Ninganessa is walking alongside us – we're not afraid of oppression.

OK. Except that while that's a simple and pretty literal translation of the words I've just come to on page 91, it's rather more complicated than that. They're meant to be the lyrics of a song.

Here's the context for you:

There were some men who were carrying little round stones and they said these stones were bewitched and when you threw them at the Portuguese they'd explode as though they were bombs. There were also some who carried old [canhangulos – some kind of weapon – anybody?] *and other katanas or long sticks. They were singing: 'Those who eat at the table with the Flemish people / They are going to feel fear in their hearts. / But we're not! / Antoine Ninganessa is walking alongside us / We're not afraid of oppression.'*

In the Portuguese it looks like this:

'Aqueles que comem à mesa com os Flamengos / Esses vão sentir

*o medo no coração / Mas nós não! / Antoine Ninganessa marcha
ao nosso lado / Nós não tememos a opressão.'*

(Incidentally there's a footnote to the Flemish bit, saying it refers to Zaire, formerly the Belgian Congo.)

As you can see, lines two, three and five all rhyme in the Portuguese; and for something chanted like this by a crowd it would be a shame to lose that rhyme in English (and would sound odd without it). So we need a version in English which keeps that sort of chanty rhyme and rhythm, and of course the sense.

All I've got at the moment is the following:

'He who eats at Flemish tables / Struck with fear his heart should be. / But not we! / For with Ninganessa near us / We need fear no tyranny!'

But, well, it's not good enough…

Any offers?

PS Next week a bigger bit of text, some responses to the things discussed in previous posts, and a really tricky pun…

Post 8

Finding a voice

Dialogue can be difficult. That much is obvious, I suppose. The difficulty lies not only in making the way the characters talk sound plausible, but also making them sound distinctive one from another, making them recognisable, characterful.

We all have words we like more or less than others when we speak (I referred in a previous post to a writer's pet vocabulary too); we might naturally speak more or less formally, with older or newer words – in English we might tend towards the Anglo-Saxon or the Latinate; we probably contract our words when speaking aloud – 'don't' for 'do not', 'isn't' for 'is not', and so on. Our language is precisely of its time, and of our background, and it's local too.

And there's the question of accent, of course, which is conveyed in written dialogue, too. Again, are the words contracted because of the way they're spoken? Are we in London and dropping our aitches? Are words elided or each one enunciated (and spelled out) in full?

Think about what different things you get from

'Good evening, Mr Bond.'
and
'Evenin' Mr Bond.' ('We've a-bin hexpectin' you...')

Or

'Well, hello. How are you?'
and
'Well, 'allo. 'ow are ya?'

(Incidentally I remember noticing that certain characters in children's books tended to say not Hello or Hallo, but 'Hullo', which was somehow instantly friendlier…)

Mercifully *Estação das Chuvas* has very little in the way of dialogue; but there's one voice that's important to get absolutely right, which is that of Lídia herself. As you may remember from the bit of text I was working on for my fifth post, there are various points in the book where the story is filled out by transcripts of interviews with Lídia, so we do 'hear' her speaking rather a lot. So the task is to identify what sort of voice she has in Portuguese (formal or colloquial, high or low register, standardised spelling or reflecting some particular accent, fluent or broken up, long sentences and well-paced or hesitant, etc.) and replicating that in English somehow.

The passage I'll show you now is one of those interviews, which is Chapter Eight of the fourth little section of the book. As I go I'll underline a few of the words I'm going to comment on afterwards. Here it is:

How did the world react to the 15th of March?

The revolt of March 15th and the <u>subsequent</u> revolt of the Portuguese launched Angola into <u>the heart</u> of the world's attention. The UPA, <u>notwithstanding their receipt</u> of American support, managed to arouse sympathies in certain sectors of the revolutionary left, forcing the MPLA to <u>radicalize</u> their position. In interviews and statements to the American press, Holden Roberto denounced them as a group of communists ENFEUDADO [Anyone have a good word for being in a feudal relationship? Enfiefed? Anyone?] *to Moscow. At the same time, realising that the UPA would never be able to assert themselves nationally and internationally as long as they were tied to the old ideals of restoring the Kingdom of Congo, having been present at its creation, Roberto tried to establish alliances with other groups and individuals of different ethnic <u>origin; and</u> this was how the National Front for the Liberation of Angola, the FNLA, was born. In hallway discussions the directors of the FNLA characterised them as the children of the colonisers, <u>mulattos</u> and whites, who wanted to usurp power from their parents. It was the best definition <u>I've</u> heard of the MPLA to this day.*

Maybe it is a good definition. But it's worth remembering that in the United States or in Latin America it was also the children of the colonisers who brought about independence.

That's true, but they were careful to eliminate the Indians first. Whatever the case, the FNLA sought to _emphasize_ our petit-bourgeois origins, insinuating that not one of us had links to the rural masses and that we _weren't_ capable for this reason of structuring a movement of armed action against Portuguese domination. Frantz Fanon, who at the time was held in very high regard by the European left, owing to his support for Algerian independentists, was one of the first personalities to defend this position.

How was it that the MPLA reacted to these kinds of accusation?

In 1962 the Portuguese Communist Party managed – with Soviet support – to liberate Agostinho Neto and he was elected _President_ of the MPLA at National Conference, now in Kinshasa where the leadership of the movement had been _transferred_. It was clearly a manoeuvre to silence the UPA's insinuations. Neto was black, he was the son of a protestant pastor and had great popular support from Catete, the area he was from. Beside this, his imprisonment in 1960 had made him a hero of international recognition. In Paris there was even a petition demanding the Portuguese government to _free_ him. Sartre signed it, for example.

At that point there was still nobody disputing Agostinho Neto's leadership?

Nobody! Except, of course, for Viriato da Cruz. Viriato never accepted the decision of National Conference. He was mad with rage: 'This man's an autocrat!', he shouted in the middle of a meeting, pointing his finger at Neto. He was completely alone. Mário de Andrade and all our _companions_ from Conakry remained silent. Some stood up to denounce him as an opportunist or a radical. And I, I hardly knew what was going on, I got on a plane and flew to Kinshasa in an attempt to reconcile the two positions. I _didn't_ succeed at all. Viriato

thought we were against him because he was a mestizo, and Neto, with
that bovine obstinacy of his, refused to have his name at the top of a
list on which Viriato's name appeared.

(Interview with Lídia do Carmo Ferreira, Luanda, 23rd May 1990)

Lídia chooses her words carefully (being a very good journalist),
and we have to do the same on her behalf. There are no obvious
pronunciation markers (so I don't feel the need to drop aitches etc.)
Her language is rarely flowery-formal, but it doesn't lapse into infor-
mality, either. The 'subsequent revolt' is a bit richer than the Portuguese (which is closer to a simple 'later'); and 'the heart of the
world's attention' is too much, too – there's nothing more flowering
than 'the centre of...' in the original. Oh, and for the same reason
'notwithstanding their receipt...' has just got to go.

'Independentists' is a pretty remarkable word, but it's pretty conspicuous in Portuguese too, I think, so I'd keep it even if it's a bit
weightier than we might expect from its surroundings.

Now, while Lídia's not casual, I'd still elide certain very common
words to make her sound like a natural speaker as she does in Portuguese – ***That's** true, I **didn't** succeed, best definition **I've** heard*; but
I'm tempted to change 'we weren't capable' to 'we were not capable'
just because of where the emphasis falls in the sentence. (On the
other hand the whole of that sentence could use some rearranging
in English, so we'll see.)

'Mulatto' and 'Mestizo' are more straightforward words to Lídia
than to us – can we keep them or should we find some other equivalent that would sound less foreign in English speech, which might
require some paraphrasing?

I wonder if there's something subliminal we're encouraged to read
into Lídia (or the way she speaks) about the fact that I've spelled
emphasize and radicalize the American way?

And that I've capitalised (or capitalized) the word 'President'?

In Portuguese Agostinho Neto is 'liberado', but is a straightforward Anglo-Saxon 'freed' a less conspicuous – and more natural –
word here than 'liberated'? Likewise the leadership of the movement
had been 'transferido', which would be simpler in English as 'moved'

(again, Anglo-Saxon rather than Latinate) but for the fact that 'the movement had been moved...' sounds daft...

And these two sound quite different too, I think: 'Except, of course, for Viriato da Cruz.' 'Except, of course, Viriato da Cruz.'

The semi-colon after 'origin' in the first answer is mine – I've repunctuated that because the big sentence felt unwieldy in English. But I wonder whether that changes the sense we get of the flow of her speech?

And what about 'companions' – do we know enough about Lídia to judge whether she'd call them 'comrades', perhaps?

I could go on and on...

I should acknowledge, incidentally, that while I'm drawing attention to lots of little details, I think you do as a translator (just as you do as a writer) come to know a character's voice very well as you go along, and are soon knowing how s/he would express something more or less by instinct without having to rationalise all these word-by-word decisions.

OK, a couple of communist jokes in my next post. They're funny. In Portuguese, at least.

Post 9

Two communist puns

Puns. These are the sorts of thing that make me send Agualusa resentful e-mails at four in the morning.

(As he's someone who loves language, they're just the sorts of thing that make dealing with a writer like him something of a hazard.)

There's no point trying to deal with wordplay literally in a translation, of course, so the hope is to find something which retains the effect, and retains the important components of the joke, even if the precise meaning of the joke itself must be a little different.

I'm going to give you a couple I'm dealing with in this book.

The first chapter of part five ends with this little bit of dialogue – I'll part-translate it, and give it to you in mixed Engl-Portuguese first...

*'You're a reactionary,' she said. 'A **filho da puta**.'*
*'Much worse,' Zorro muttered. 'A **filho da luta**'*

'Filho da puta' is literally 'son of the whore' – and it's used just as we'd use 'son of a bitch'.

'Filho da luta' means 'son of the fight/struggle'. They're almost identical – and rhyming in Portuguese. It's a good line.

Whereas

'You're a reactionary,' she said. 'A son of a bitch.'
'Much worse,' Zorro muttered. 'A son of the struggle.'

is – to put it politely – not very funny and not very clever. Suggestions?

And here's another, possibly harder still.

A couple are listening to some people talking at great length about matters communist. After a time she leans over and whispers in his ear...

'*This conversation is going **de Mao a pior**...*'

Which literally means, it's going from Mao to worse. But the only reason it's funny (and if you don't speak Portuguese you just have to trust me, it is funny) is because in Portuguese mal (bad) sounds an awful lot like Mao (Mao). So it's very, very close in sound to being 'going from bad to worse', except that it's niftily a joke about long-winded communists too.

Again, in English 'This conversation is going from Mao to worse' is not funny. It's just odd.

I've got one possible solution to this one, which is about half-adequate, but I won't tell you now as it will I think distort how you think about it. I'll e-mail it to James at Booktrust for safe-keeping and will tell you later, but meantime, any suggestions for how to replicate the effect in English?

Post 10

Advocating for the book

I want to leave the text for a moment, if I may...

There's an aspect of the translator's job that I've not mentioned before, but which (especially I think in an English-speaking country) is a significant one.

Very often the translator is tasked not only with translating the book, but also with being, in a sense, its local advocate. Publishers not-infrequently buy books for translation without having been able to read the original – they may have read a bit in sample translation, will have commissioned a reader's report or two, received encouragement from an agent, may have read another book by the author or read this book translated into a more accessible third language, or whatever – but that is often all. No publishing house will have every potentially-translatable language well spoken among its staff.

And so it is with Agualusa, where Arcadia doesn't have a Portuguese speaker on staff and so the translator's job expands somewhat to be the book's expert representative in other non-translation matters.

I mention this now, because one thing that occupied me last night was thinking about the jacket for the book, which is being worked on as I write. I'm delighted that we have a great designer doing it – James Nunn, who's created such beautiful, striking images for our previous Agualusa books – but with neither Jim nor Arcadia able to read the book itself at this stage they rely on someone (in this case, me) who has to offer guidance on the jacket. Often at this point the translator is the one person in the equation in a position to do this.

So... What is the tone? (How do you actually *describe* the tone of a book?) What sort of colours? What does the main protagonist look like? Important themes, particularly striking images we might play with, recurring metaphors. Is the rain in the title an important image running through the book? And so on…

It's an interesting exercise (especially for someone with as little visual intelligence as I have) and makes you consider the book in a very different and quite particular way. One thing I felt quite strongly, for instance, is that while Lidia was the key protagonist and of course crucial to the story and should *in some way* be represented in the cover image, at the same time I knew I wouldn't be comfortable with too clear, too precise an image of her – because, yes, the book is about her, but it's also about her absence, about the search for her, and she's so often just out of shot, or out of focus, or seen from afar.

And I knew that to me it felt like the sort of book with a dark cover (politics, violence, urban settings, rain) rather than the lovely African sun burnishes we've had for our previous books. I may be quite wrong, and I find it hard to explain *why* I felt I had some idea of what would characterise an appropriate cover and what would not, but an interesting exercise.

So James is working on something now and I'm very much looking forward to it – I hope my e-mailed thoughts to him were useful, and I also hope he disregards many of them since actually he knows far better than I what would work – but as the book's representative in the UK (at least until we have a translation the publishers can read for themselves) it's good to have input.

And there's not much time – even though the book isn't published till the summer, the cover design has to be done soon – it has to go to the sales team, it may go into catalogues or other promotional material (it'll be up on Amazon long before publication date), and the book itself will I guess have to be ready to go to press towards the middle of March…

And talking about the schedule, just to let you know some plans: I'm hoping to have the first pass done in the middle of December (this is rather later than I'd hoped but my hard drive has just died and I have to re-do all the bits that couldn't be recovered and I don't want to talk about it…); and then have a month to fill in gaps, check things over, look words up and iron out things that sound funny. In mid-Jan I hope to have something I'm pleased with, and hopefully will then (this is the fun bit) go and spend a couple of days with Agualusa in Lisbon to talk it through ready for delivery at the end of January. That, at least, is the plan... (Ha ha.)

PS Apologies for the delay in answering some of your comments – I'm going to have to ask James S to re-send them to me as they've vanished (computer... hard-drive... grrr...) but I'll get to them soon. And a whole post about the word 'people' will follow before too long, too.

Post 11

Pe? Peo? Peopl?

I mentioned the other day that I was going to post on the word 'people'. I've come across a problem I don't remember having encountered before. It's not, though, a problem of semantics, but of spelling and the way the word is constructed compared to how it's pronounced.

So... there's a scene in the novel that ends with the following paragraph (as I've done in the past, I'll leave the few troublesome words untranslated for now):

> *A few months later, a group calling themselves the Rosengarten Committee detonated a bomb close to the American embassy, in Brasilia. On the broken wall a sentence could be read, in large red letters: 'Rosengarten did not die! He lives* no coração do po...' *That was where the sentence was cut off by the explosion.*

The graffiti line in full would have been *no coração do povo*, meaning 'in the heart of the people'. Although the word 'povo' is cut in half by the explosion, it's quite clear what 'po...' is referring to.

And now look at the English:

'Rosengarten did not die! He lives in the heart of the pe...'
(Huh?)
The heart of the peo? The peop?

The problem for me here, you see, is that because the word 'people' is so peculiarly spelled, if you break off early you're left with a part of a word which doesn't in fact sound like the first half of the word we know as 'people' (since we do 'hear' words as we read, I think), or indeed of anything. As you read the possibilities you hear 'the heart of the peh' (a short vowel as in pen/pep/pet), or 'the heart of the pea-oh', or 'the heart of the pea-opp', not 'the heart of the peep', which is what we need to be in the reader's head for it to be obvious what the graffiti is saying.

If the word were properly spelled 'peeple' (which would be nice and tidy) then 'He lives in the heart of the peep...' would suggest the right thing. But I'm not sure pe/peo/peop do. I suppose it could be 'the heart of the peopl...' but just trimming a letter off the end doesn't have quite the same effect, I think, as slashing the word right down the middle.

Another alternative would be to restructure the phrase, to something like: 'He lives in the people's hearts'.

But (yes, you guessed it) that doesn't work in English either. Because 'hearts' is spelled unhelpfully too.

'He lives in the people's he...'? 'Or the people's hea...'?

(This could be trying to suggest 'head' just as easily, and again the sound is wrong. You hear 'hee' or 'heh' but certainly not 'har' from either of these.)

He lives in the people's hear...?

No. Still wrong.
Hmm.

PS Looking at it again, I don't much like 'could be *read* in large *red* letters', either, by the way. Though spelled differently they sound the same, and if you do hear words in your head as you read it's jarring. Another little thing on the list to solve...

Post 12

More comments ... and replies

After a little hiatus – for which, my apologies – I just wanted to respond to some of the e-mails you've been sending in.

First of all, some interesting suggestions for particular problems I asked about...

So, Filho da puta / Filho da luta *first, then.*

Alex had a couple of interesting ways out of it, one of which would be to keep the rhyme with 'son of a bitch' with something albeit a little more obscure, but then if necessary just explaining it; so have the response be something like:

'Much worse,' Zorro muttered. 'A son of the ditch – I'm with the workers.'

Roland pointed out how straightforward this would be in French – *fils de lutte* – which is certainly something I've come across before, with Portuguese quirks that I can see exactly how to translate into French or Spanish but which simply can't operate the same way in English.

My friend Carmo e-mailed from Portugal with another suggestion, which was the same I'd found myself, and I think is the one I'm going to go with. She suggested that instead of changing 'filho da puta' as one would naturally do from the literal 'son of a whore' to the more common equivalent 'son of a bitch', we instead keep it literal, which allows us to do this:

'You're a reactionary,' she said. 'A son of a whore.'
'Much worse,' Zorro muttered. 'A son of a war...'

Pretty good, no?

The 'de Mao em pior' seems to have been trickier. What I have to do is find another pun – inevitably it has to be a totally different one – that combines the elements of

a) Communist icon
b) Something bad and getting worse

And though I haven't quite got the exact wording, the idea is to do something along the lines of 'Personally I give this conversation extremely low Marx' – or similar. As I say, the wording's not quite right, but using 'Marx' for 'marks' is the best I've got so far.

(One remaining problem with that, of course, is that the pun arises in dialogue and in my English version there's no way of the listener knowing it's a joke because 'Marx' and 'marks' sound identical – whereas in Portuguese 'Mao' and 'mal' are very similar but not identical – but that's yet to be solved. Yikes…)

[Btw, a very interesting e-mail from Paul Wilson drew my attention to another pun made on just the same phrase; he cited a friend who commented that getting ready for dinner in Germany might involve going from *Bad* to *Wurst*…]

Next, for *pe/peo/peop*, Sara suggested a couple of useful changes:

By making 'heart' into 'hearts' she cleverly suggests that the final noun will also be a plural; and she cut the final word after the very first letter – which hadn't occurred to me – which intercepts it before the funny phonetics start, and allows you to read 'p—' as just the letter ('puh') or as 'pee…' and still understand how it might be the beginning of 'people'. So:

> On the broken wall someone had scrawled, in large red letters,
> "Rosengarten did not die! He lives on in the hearts of our p—"

I think '*the* p—' still rather than '*our* p—', but this is the best solution yet, I think. She also added the 'scrawled' so as to avoid read/red, which is pretty neat too. Too far from the original, or not?

And while we're on these solutions to particular problems, we had some suggestions for the anti-Belgian chant, too; here's Alex's:

Those who with the Flemish sup
Their hearts will fill with fear
Not we!
While Ninganessa is with us
We fear no tyranny!

Thanks for these, and your other suggestions – sorry not to be able to quote everyone's...

In other messages...

The discussion about italics / footnotes / glossaries etc. continued. 'Like you, I hate footnotes,' wrote Mahmud, a translator writing from Bangladesh; and I'm definitely with him on that; but leaning towards a glossary (both Anne and Jeremy liked this idea), having recently reviewed a translated book that used a glossary in this way and worked very well, I thought.

And the Primeiro de Maio Square (Celina's preferred option) / May the First Square (as Jacqueline suggested) question continued to raise comments, including quite adamant ones (I'm glad I'm not the only person in the world to take this seriously...) from my friend Kit who made the sensible point that the First of May doesn't mean anything specifically significant to English-language readers, unless it's given as May-Day; so we could use May-Day Square, but only if the celebration that we know as May-Day (international workers etc.) is indeed the same thing the square was named for in Angola. (In other words, if a country has a street named '23rd April Street' because that happens to be their independence day, translating it to 23rd of April Street is meaningless, and Independence Day Street might be reasonable, and St George's Day Street is incongruous nonsense.) From which I suppose we either stick with the Portuguese or we go with May-Day Square if indeed it's referring to the same May-Day we all know. So... Anyone know anything about Angolan national holidays? I think it's off to Wikipedia for me...

Finally, thanks to Celina for answering some of the queries I raised in my fifth post (in which I sped through the first draft and left doubts in the Portuguese – Isabel also had a thought about this, distinguishing 'dog' and 'mutt'); she also asked an interesting question, which is 'you've mentioned that you translate spontaneously, based on instinct so how is writing this blog affecting that process?' And now having acknowledged that interesting question I'm not going to answer it because I don't know the answer, but I'll think about it and might come back to it.

And I'll also come back later to a question from Matthew about alliteration – this relates, I think, to something I mentioned in my third post relating to the repeated consonants in the novel's opening sentence, and which probably deserves more attention in a forthcoming post.

PS Thanks also to Jeremy for bringing my attention to a brilliant VQR interview with García Márquez – which you'll find here: http://www.vqronline.org/webexclusive/2005/06/24/marquez-journey-back/ – and in particular to a fascinating discussion of idiom (in this case, to do with recognising a particular sausage) towards the end.

PPS Matthew, who asked the alliteration question, also asked this, which is much easier to answer: 'Do you ever feel that the richness and beauty of the original language is so great that the task before you is well nigh impossible?' The answer, of course, is 'Yep, absolutely, all the time, every day, how could I not?' After all, I know Agualusa is a far better writer than I am a translator, and I know without even pausing to think about it that my versions of his books will be less good than his books. And yet I rely on the possibility that they could still be pretty good… Yes, absolutely, keeping it just the same, losing nothing, is, indeed, impossible, I'm sure of that; but I'm sure too that creating something else that's worth creating is not! If I didn't believe at least that much, there would be no point in doing this job. But yes, it is sometimes pretty difficult, though! (Though my engineer friend Paul, on reading the blog, did point out that dealing with weld details is harder, so I should be grateful.)

Post 13

A little break

This blog is going to go quiet for a few weeks now. I'm going away for three weeks, and though I'll be working on the book while I'm away I don't know how easily I'll be online – and in any case, I don't think I'll have a lot to report. This fortnight or so is the least interesting part of the work, I think. My plan for while I'm away is to finish up the full first draft, and do the first less-interesting bit of filling in the gaps (by which I mean looking things up in a dictionary).

But then it gets more interesting. Because when I'm back on January 8th, having done the dictionary checks etc., I'll suddenly have something complete and fairly presentable – not polished by any means, but something readable (albeit still with particular issues to be resolved). I'll post a chunk of that for you to read and comment on as soon as it's done. (And will have all sorts of new problems that will doubtless have arisen by then, too...)

After a bit of polishing and problem-solving, my aim is to have something I'm pleased with by the middle of January, ready to send to the author then; and I hope to go to Lisbon and talk through it with him around the 23rd/24th. Then, if he's happy with it, there'll be just a few last bits of ironing and off to the publishers for their feedback at the end of January or start of February. But more about all that as it happens...

These six weeks or so, especially the polishing phase during the first half of January, while not the most labour-intensive period, are where the big qualitative shift happens. Right now the most advanced bits I've got still look like that passage I showed you in my post of October 20th; so looking over the rubbish I've got so far it's hard to believe it'll be worth reading by this time next month, but that's how it goes... (Well, that's how it's worked in the past, so here's hoping.)

So – more from me in the first week of 2009. Check back here around the 7th or 8th and there should be a bit of a book waiting for you to read… Have a good couple of holiday weeks meantime.

D.

Post 14

Book 2 of the novel

Hello –

And Happy New Year. Sorry to be a few days later than planned resuming this blog. It has taken rather longer than expected to make the progress I wanted to make over the New Year break (hardly a surprise). But I'm getting there.

I still haven't worked out what to do with my definite articles in the section heads. I have doubts about the register of some sort-of-taboo language. And there are bits that are much less pleasing to read than other bits, as yet. But yes, definitely getting there.

So – this is where we are now:

I've been going through that very rough sprinted version of the whole book, gradually filling in gaps – where there were awkward/ unknown words I had left in the Portuguese, problems I didn't deal with as I rushed through, etc. There was lots of looking stuff up in The Big Dictionary, quite a lot of Wikipedia trawling too.

And alongside the filling-in-gaps, there's also the process of watching the original chaos become less start-stop, more a coherent piece of prose with a rhythm and tone of its own. That's exciting. So the more the gaps get filled in, the more I can just do a proper edit – read through like a reader would, querying things that don't quite work, inverting phrases where the rhythm is wrong, and so forth. Ironing it out a little better with each pass. That bit's fun...

It's far from finished, of course, but I'm attaching a piece of where-it-is-now to give you an idea. This particular little section required – apart from lots of dictionary work – also learning to distinguish between flea species; and debating specific vocabulary for bird-trapping; identifying lots of trees and plants (and btw, is it 'surinam cherry' as in my dictionary, or 'Surinam cherry' as in Wikipedia?);

attempting to develop for myself some basic understanding of the layout of the different bits of the city of Luanda; and working out precisely what kind of dance a 'maxixe' is and why on earth being Brazilian it might be sung in Spanish. And I've still not managed to resolve some very nice wordplay in a poem, but there's time yet. (Well, a bit…)

If you've been reading this blog from the start you'll notice there are footnotes (hmm…); and you'll notice too that one part of this passage (Chapter 2) is something you've seen in an earlier, messier, more hesitant incarnation some time back.

OK. What this is, then, is Book Two of the novel (it's made up of eight 'Books'). Book One ended with the young Lídia being brought into town to live with her grandfather, Jacinto do Carmo Ferreira, and Book Two picks right up from that.

The passage is still full of queries – things I don't understand or don't know what to do with or where I've done something I don't think I like – but apart from these countless little trip-ups I hope it's still readable, and I hope you enjoy it.

This weekend (perhaps, perhaps…) a slightly better version will go to JEA for him to look over for accuracy and to help resolve some queries. Friday of next week I'm spending the day with him in Amsterdam (not Lisbon this time, but Amsterdam's pretty nice too…) to go through it and finalise some answers/choices.

Then I have about a week to tinker with it all, with how it *sounds* especially, to iron out things that I don't like, and on the 31st to the publisher it goes, right on schedule.

(Meanwhile, in the real world…)

PS For anyone reading this who has some Portuguese, I hope to be able to post the original of this passage for you to look at them side by side if you want to. It's not as simple as you might think, though, so please be patient and I'll try and get that up for you as soon as I can…

23 January 2009

Post 15

Breaking my duck

It's never happened before.

I travel a lot, really a lot, and have done all my life (viz. thirty-five years and counting), and I have never, ever missed a flight. Once I left my passport at home and still had time to go back and collect it and made it onto the plane. Once a friend and I dozed off in a departure lounge in Istanbul and had to be paged for final-call boarding. That one was pretty close. But I have never, ever missed a flight.

Well, so much for that.

I'm writing this on the train down from Luton Airport (you know, the one where the Amsterdam planes leave from), to head back for an unscheduled, unexpectedly free day back home in Brighton. A combination of certain confusion regarding the departure time, and also leaving later than planned, and also some roadworks, and also – and especially – a critical wrong turning off the A1, meant that we arrived at Luton three minutes after check-in closed. And that was that.

You notice I said 'we', because there was someone else with me, who was driving, and whose fault it was (except the roadworks, I'll have to find someone else to blame for those). And having told him that I would now have to humiliate him on the blog, I've since relented and won't reveal his identity here after all. (I think he feels bad enough already.) I'll only say that for anyone who knows him you'll have no trouble guessing.

Anyway. Heading home now, and not spending the afternoon with José Eduardo in Amsterdam to go through textual queries after all – we'll have to do that by e-mail, which is straightforward enough, if, clearly, less fun. I'm sorry not to be seeing him. But when he comes over in a few weeks (we're doing an event together at the Bath Lit Festival) I'll invite him to a lovely dinner somewhere nice by way of apology; my delinquent driver this morning, usefully guilt-struck, reimbursed me for my missed flight, so I have some dedicated funds now. Every cloud etc.

A post that is actually about translation will follow shortly.

PS Talking about translation (oh, and why not?) it occurs to me that if the contents of this blog were ever (inexplicably) to be translated into some other language, the pained translator would find him/herself sighing particularly deeply at the title of this post. Any offers for 'Breaking my duck', in any other language at all? It's a nasty one, that...

PPS Btw, if it weren't six in the morning and I were cleverer, I'd be coming up with an opening paragraph which turned around some nice conceit about a broken duck being the reason it's impossible to fly, but it is, and I'm not, so I shan't. And won't give it any more thought. I do sort of have a life, you know...

Post 16

While we wait...

Just another holding note to say I've not disappeared from the face of the earth or just forgotten about the blog (or just missed another plane) but I'm waiting for some answers/comments/reaction from Agualusa to the text I sent him and won't be able to make much progress till I've heard back from him.

(I do still have to finish and send him the final section of the text, and will do that this week.)

In the meantime, thanks for the comments that have been coming in. Some ingenious solutions to things I'd raised (including one involving a bit of sexual slang I had to look up on urbandictionary.com – oh, the things I'm learning...).

Paul Verhaeghen – winner of last year's *Independent* Foreign Fiction Prize for *Omega Minor* (which he both wrote and translated, rather impressively) – wrote from the US with something new for 'filho da puta/luta'; his solution was 'son of a bitch / son of a gun'. And while he then said he thought actually it might be too subtle, I wonder whether there might not be something clever we can do with that 'son of a gun'. For example, if *she* were to call him a 'son of a gun' (which is common enough to be reasonable), and he were to correct her with – not just a son of a gun, a son of the war; or not a son of a gun but of *the* gun; or something. Hmm, interesting...

Shane Newberry (a translator from Japanese to English) wrote from Australia with several suggestions for 'De Mao em pior', pointing out that it's a shame to lose the specifically 'Mao' element (which we do with my Marx solution, and I agree it's a pity). One suggestion I liked would involve a reference to the Mao content of the conversation making malcontents of its listeners. Will see what I can do with that...

Other correspondents in recent weeks have included Giorgio de Marchis, whom I've not met but who is José Eduardo's Italian translator – who is set to translate *My Father's Wives* this summer. (There are a few nice little traps he's going to have deal with, but it'll be a pleasure, I'm sure.) He pointed out the importance of not simply having your answers ready before you embark on a translation, but of being always attuned to the questions raised by the text as you go along.

Since I'm writing anyway, a couple of things in the book I still have to resolve that might be worth mentioning –

First is that I have to translate the epigraphs to the chapters. Which is a little different from translating anything else because they're all quotations and in some case quotations from real people (e.g. Agostinho Neto, Gabriel García Márquez). In other words they're things that may already exist in English – may have been published somewhere or other in English already – so this is slightly more a research job than a translation job. (In the past Agualusa has quoted things that were actually originally in English – Martin Luther King in *Book of Chameleons*, say, or Breyten Breytenbach in *My Father's Wives* – and rather than translating his Portuguese translation of MLK back into English it's been a question of tracking down the original quote to use as it first appeared.) And another question raised by these (see, Giorgio, I *am* paying attention) is what to do with the epigraphs that aren't given in Portuguese – there's one in Spanish, one in French – should I leave those as they are and assume all my readers can understand? Or just treat them as though they were all in Portuguese and translate them all into English?

The other big thing still pending resolution is the question of the book's section headings. Each section has a noun heading: Poetry, Exile, Fear, Euphoria. Now, in Portuguese all these words have definite articles – only because they have to (as in French, say, you would call a chapter La Peur or L'Exil or La Poésie), whereas in English you don't need the article. Poetry, Exile, Fear, are much better. But there are some headings that *do* require the definite article in English – the first chapter is O Princípio and the last is O Fim, and there's A Busca, and O Dia Eterno in between – which are better as The Beginning,

The End, The Search, The Eternal Day than Beginning, End, Search, Eternal Day. So I can either compromise and use definite articles for all of them (so half don't sound quite right – 'The Poetry', 'The Euphoria') or use definite articles for none of them (so the *other* half don't sound quite right – 'Beginning', 'Search') or do what's best in each case but then lose the nice pattern that runs through them all in Portuguese. O Principio, A Poesia, A Busca, O Exilio, O Medo, A Fúria, O Fim, etc. become The Beginning, Poetry, The Search, Exile, Fear, Fury, The End. I don't like any of the solutions right now but will just have to choose, I guess.

More when I've heard back from JEA.

26 February 2009

Post 17

Still nothing...

Still nothing...

But a couple of other matters to report meantime.

The first is to tell you that I'm in Salzburg, where I've been spending the week at the Schloss Leopoldskron (beautiful snow-covered lakeside palace...) with a group of people from around the world all of whom are interested in promoting literature in translation. Writers and translators, publishers and funders, associations and press and others besides. I can't list all the interesting people I was delighted to meet, but just to give you an idea of the range, the contingent coming in from the UK included Antonia Byatt and Kate Griffin from the Arts Council, *Independent* literary editor Boyd Tonkin, translator Shaun Whiteside who chairs the Translators Association, Caroline McCormick who's the executive director of International PEN, writer Marina Warner, and Amanda Hopkinson, Director of the British Centre for Literary Translation. That's pretty good company. And then there are all the other countries...

Apart from the inevitable grumbles about how much we get paid (which is what happens when you put several translators in a room together – and, predictably, rather amplified when there are publishers and funders within earshot too...) there were all sorts of interesting discussions about strategies and individual initiatives for encouraging the publishing and reading of translated literature, predominantly in the English-speaking world (where there are particular problems) but more broadly too. The mixture of background – both in terms of the parts of the world the seminar fellowship came from, but also in professional terms (not just those of us here as translators but also people involved in all sorts of other parts of the translation chain – the promoters, booksellers, editors, etc.) led to some good recommendations and – I think – to a sense that good things will come out of this.

Certainly the seminar itself was very valuable – five days with lots of people thinking interestingly at each other – but the follow-up is where the change will happen, of course. The publication of a report with recommendations, the birth of projects that were born from discussions here, from the network that was built, great-sounding projects in one part of the world being replicated in others, etc.

(I'm pleased to say there were many people there I didn't know who'd been following this blog, and saw it – and the contributions from those of you who have been reading it and writing in – as a really good way to bring together people interested in the subject, and to interest new people in it too.)

The translation seminar was also the perfect place to be for the announcement of the longlist for the Independent Foreign Fiction Prize (a prize cited several times this week as a good example of a really effective promotional initiative), and I'm delighted to say that my last book with Agualusa, *My Father's Wives*, is on it! It's my favourite of his books, and I think his best, too – the most ambitious and I think utterly beautiful and rich and surprising, but it's less easy and less obvious than *The Book of Chameleons* so it's especially lovely to have it recognised.

It's lovely too, after a few days of discussing the promotion and business of translated literature, to be reminded of the work. Translators seem to spend an awful lot of time being advocates for translation (which is right and proper and often – as this week – extremely stimulating and enjoyable); but the translation is, of course, the thing.

The translation-advocate role of a translator is inevitable – and in certain respects it's a role only a translator can fill (though this week I felt I was acting not only as translator and advocate but also as agent, keenly selling Agualusa on to other countries – will be e-mailing his real agent with an update shortly...). But it's about producing quality translated work foremost, of course – so the *Indy* longlisting is a very welcome recognition of that for which I'm most grateful.

And while I wait for more on *Rainy Season*, I'll leave you with what I think is my favourite paragraph from the just-longlisted *My*

Father's Wives, as a little taster in case you don't know it. Read it aloud if you can...

[To set the scene: Bartolomeu (who narrates this section) has told us earlier in the novel about the death of his father, killed during the recent war. Now he and his friends are driving through the desert, and they stop in a middle-of-nowhere café for a bite to eat. When they get into conversation with the old café-owner it becomes clear that this was the man who killed his father. Bartolomeu, shaken, goes outside to compose himself. The older man – who has just realised what is going on – comes out to ask for Bartolomeu's forgiveness, and offers him his hand...]

I took his hand, a broad, bony hand, a little calloused. I noticed his face properly now. He had light eyes, hazelnut-coloured, clean and sincere, with little wrinkles at the corners. Deep bags under his eyes. I remembered an old turtle from my childhood. He went by the name of Leonardo because he really liked listening to Leonard Cohen. Sometimes he'd disappear for weeks. But to bring him back all you had to do was put on the record of the Canadian singer – at the first lines of 'Famous Blue Raincoat' – 'It's four in the morning, the end of December, / I'm writing you now just to see if you're better ...'– *Leonardo would emerge from some unknown abyss somewhere, still dragging behind him the torpor of a long sleep, he would get up onto his tiptoes next to one of the columns, he'd stretch out his neck, and for brief moments would seem to be completely happy. Then he would go back to being sad again. A sadness like the sadness of the deserts. This man in front of me now, he looked like Leonardo looked, the turtle, when the music came to an end.*

I love it. More soon.

Post 18

Consulting the oracle

Some progress to report!

On Saturday night I drove up to Bath, where Agualusa and I had an event to do at the literature festival there the following day. And took advantage of our being together to force him to do some text work…

We spent probably about three hours (maybe a little more) on Sunday morning and evening, working through various queries – some large and general, some small questions of regional vocabulary – covering about the first three-quarters of the book. (The rest will have to be mopped up by e-mail, as it got late and we got too bleary-eyed to be useful at the end of a very long day…)

At the event JEA had talked about how hard it sometimes is to answer questions about his own work – why he chose to use word x rather than word y – so under those circumstances he was very tolerant of my dozens and dozens of requests for him to explain himself, to tell me what a line is meant to mean, what he's trying to do here or what he's suggesting there…

I won't go through everything we talked about, but will mention just three points we discussed which all raise the same general question.

1) In Portuguese the noun 'tarde' can mean 'afternoon' anytime or earlyish 'evening'. So when you have a neutral sentence opener like 'One TARDE he went out to meet Antonio…' should it be an English afternoon or evening?

Sometimes it's obvious from the context – in one case someone's eyes are burning in the darkness, so if it's dark then we can probably assume it's more 'evening' than 'afternoon'; but more usually there's no contextual clue like this. So I asked JEA, each time the word occurred, to tell me which he meant – to describe the sort of time of day he had in his imagination writing the scene, so I could (of necessity) be a little more specific in English than he had to be in Portuguese.

2) A character called Francisco – Xico, for short – is at a meeting where his comrades are each choosing nicknames; he tries to think of a suitable *quimbundo* word (he doesn't want them to think he's Portuguese), but can't think of anything that will work. He ends up blurting out the first word he thinks of – *bitacaia* – and hence becomes known, unfortunately, as 'Xico Bitacaia'. I say unfortunately, because a 'bitacaia' isn't something attractive or heroic, it's a particularly unpleasant sort of insect – *pulex penetrans* – that burrows under the skin in a most irritating sort of way. (Its English name – I had to look this one up – is the 'chigoe flea'. Anyone know this?)

I asked JEA if he had any objection to my changing the contracted form used for Francisco from 'Xico' to 'Chico', which is essentially the same but would be more recognisable to English-language readers. It also has the very pleasing side effect that our character is now lumbered with the nickname Chigoe Chico. Nice, no?

3) And I had some annoying chicken trouble to solve. There's a nice little sequence discussing angels (good), demons (bad), and chickens (neither, but also have wings); and how you don't always know whether somebody is an angel or a demon or just a chicken... (Trust me, it makes more sense in the book.)

The problem is, of course, that there are associations to calling someone a 'chicken' in English that there aren't in Portuguese – it's hard to describe someone a complete chicken without suggesting a cowardice that isn't anything to do with what we're trying to convey. So I wanted to change chicken for another bird (keeping the wings is important). So a pigeon, perhaps? JEA suggested a dove, but that too has particular unhelpful associations. We settled on 'parrot', because the 'talking' association makes sense in this context. But here's my question:

Would I have dared to make this change of bird myself without

JEA's agreement? It may seem a small change but it does alter the image – and it also loses a connection to other chicken images in the book (we talked at our event about the recurrence of chickens in his work…) – so it's not insubstantial. It would seem quite presumptuous to make this replacement unilaterally, I think.

And would I have changed Xico to Chico – Xico Bitacaia to Chigoe Chico – without JEA's approval?

And what would I have done with all the 'tarde' scene-settings if I couldn't check with the author just what he had in his head?

I've usually been in the fortunate position of having an author to consult – an author who is living, and obliging, and on e-mail – which both helps to clarify unclear things but also allows me to be freer with the things I change (it does seem paradoxical that the fact that the author is looking over my shoulder – and indeed, reading this blog – means that I can be *less* faithful to his original, rather than feeling I have to be more so); but what do I do, in comparable instances, when I'm working on a book by someone no longer alive, or who doesn't want to help? There'll be a whole new set of problems then…

But for now I'll continue to take advantage of my good fortune and get JEA to respond by e-mail to my queries for the remaining quarter of the book. And then it *must* go to the publishers as it's really very late. We publish in May!

PS We spent some of our time in Bath with James Nunn who's designing the jacket for the book (and has done the lovely jackets for the last couple, too); we talked about the current drafts, which are nice-looking but haven't yet quite got to the point where they perfectly capture the book. I'm e-mailing him a draft of the book tonight for him to have a read and see what else he comes up with – when we have something we're all happy with I'll ask him if I can put it up on here for you to look at too.

Post 19

So very close...

Final stretch almost done now. Over the last week or so I've extracted answers to all my final queries from JEA, who has been very busy but kindly found the time to help a lot, as he always does. He explained things that I hadn't been able to get my head round; he gave his blessing to little bits where I wanted to make a change, usually just adding a little explanatory phrase within the text to help non-Angolan readers with context; and we went back and forth on a few things that weren't absolutely obvious, such as (with apologies to the squeamish among you) which verb would best suit the action of a bulldozer on a lot of human heads.

(Incidentally, my questions for JEA are usually of a basic linguistic nature – help me, I don't understand this word... – rather than a matter of questioning him on the accuracy of his own work, but this isn't the case for all translators, especially those with better Portuguese than mine and more expertise in other useful subjects. He's just received what sounded like a very involved query from his German translator, working on *My Father's Wives*, who thought the symptoms of a very specific car breakdown scene were not consistent with his detailed knowledge of how cars work in the real world. My questions are never that clever.)

I've also now been through and resolved all the outstanding queries I had for myself – usually where I knew the meaning of the Portuguese but hadn't worked out how to recreate it in English; for example, where there was a play on words in the original without an obvious equivalent in the English, so it just needed some time sitting down and wrangling into a solution...There are now solutions to all of these problems, some of which I'm very proud of, some of which are basically adequate and will just have to do (and if I have a *eureka* moment in the coming weeks I can always amend at proof stage...).

I've removed the last of the footnotes and dragged the information, where necessary, into the body of the text. (The footnotes in my edition were apparently unique to the Brazilian version and weren't in the original Portuguese, so there's no reason to keep them, which I'm pleased about.) The only footnotes remaining now are those that are, as it were, bibliographic, where there's a quote from one of Lídia's poems, or from someone else, and the footnote is there simply to give the reference.

I've also worked out which 1948 American film one of the characters is considering going to see. The titles in English and Portuguese don't quite correspond, so this involved a little detective work…

And I've been to the British Library to check out a few quotes from Senghor so they're reproduced in their standard English translation.

And other little bits of all kinds. The very final three things I've resolved (to give you some idea) are the naming of one of the characters, the confused tangle of political acronyms, and some adjectival issues concerning breasts:

1) Character name: There's a character in the book who's properly called Ana de Piedade Castro de Magalhães but referred to always as 'Anita Voa-Baixinho': 'Anita' as the diminutive for Ana, and 'Voa-Baixinho' meaning sort of 'Flying Low'.

This one is now my only remaining query-to-myself in the whole book: at the moment she's nicknamed 'Low-Slung Anita' (I like 'low-slung', suggesting she's rather sagging, past her best), but I still wonder if she shouldn't be 'Low-Slung Annie' instead? To me, 'Low-Slung Annie' sounds like she should be a tired old madam in a brothel, perhaps in a western or something. And indeed, this character of ours *is* an aging madam in a brothel, and though calling her Annie sounds a bit American it seems (as a diminutive of Ana) quite legitimate to me. I think that's the last query answered, actually. Low-Slung Annie. I'll know for sure if it works when I read it through.

2) Acronyms. There are lots of them. For political parties, for militia groups, armies, security services, etc. So I've just put together a little glossary – a three-line explanation of how the main ones relate to one another (MPLA and UNITA fight alongside one another for

Angola's independence; then after independence they begin to fight each other instead, in a civil war, with the MPLA in government and UNITA the rebels) and a brief explanation of each acronym. It's less intrusive than footnotes, but it's an important kindness to readers who could otherwise be enormously confused when they're supposed to remember which is which of the FAPLA, EPLA, FALA, MPLA, FNLA etc.

3) Breasts. On two occasions female characters are described as having 'altos' breasts. This 'altos' means the breasts are 'high', the idea being just the opposite of the sagging, low-slung Anita, in other words. My problem is that having unthinkingly used the adjective 'high' in my first draft, when subsequently reading through I had visions of a character whose 'high breasts' are high in the sense of being 'high up', unusually placed, in some anatomical anomaly, perhaps just below the chin...

So I clearly need another adjective. 'Raised' and 'lifted' both sound as though they've been lifted artificially. And before you suggest it, 'pert' is a ludicrous word. The closest I've got is something like 'firm', which is obviously not really an equivalent word – being about consistency/solidity rather than outside appearance – but at least conveys the right kind of breasts to a reader. The English-language version has, in other words visually equivalent breasts to the original, even if they aren't linguistically/adjectivally equivalent. Translation is a weird job.

So, all done.

Well, all done except for the most important stage of all.

Tomorrow when I wake up I'm going to read the English book, from start to finish. Some bits I'll read aloud, probably. Unless there's something that really troubles me I expect not to make any reference to the Portuguese original; I assume that that source-target relationship is strong now; so what's left is the question of being sure that what we have is a good, smooth piece of English writing. So I'll read it end to end – just as I would anything written in English – and mark any little tweaks, polishing as I go; and then all being well it will be on its way over to the publishers by the end of the day.

Will report back. Fingers crossed.

Post 20

Done!

It's 2:21 a.m., on Monday, March 30th. And it's all done. I've read it through. It's pretty good, I think – I hope.

There wasn't too much to do to it today, largely just tiny bits of re-punctuating for rhythm, changing the odd word that sounded not quite right, just fiddling here and there. One or two little tweaks per page, more or less. (Below you can download a pdf of one chapter with the final day's little polishes marked, if you're interested in seeing it. I've chosen one of the chapters that was most changed, but even this had no more than a handful of little cosmetic things…)

This final stage is so pleasurable – so satisfying to be able to read through from beginning to end, and to see how things all fit together, just as you would when reading a book for the first time with some momentum – especially a book that's a little tricky as this one is, with quite a few characters and lots of complicated political factions etc. It all just sort of makes sense when you read it like this, in a way that it simply doesn't when you're sitting looking at one single page for hours (especially when that page has question marks and queries and competing-possibilities all over it), and when last time you read the preceding chapter may have been two months ago and so you can't really remember it too well… So the whole time you're just sort of trusting that it will work as a unified thing, and it's a relief when it does…

So… I've just e-mailed the full manuscript to the publishers, Arcadia, and we'll wait and see what happens next. Arcadia's great editor, Angeline, will be the first person to read it, and she'll probably come back to me with some queries; Angeline is also the person who'll be doing the light copy-edit on it in the coming weeks to get it ready for typesetting. And then proof-reading, and then – at last – to press!

I'll keep you posted.

Post 21

Ash Thursday

Well, this is a nice treat. A sample jacket design for the book has just dropped into my inbox, and I think it's stunning. I'm so pleased with it!

(As you can imagine, it can be a bit grim working lovingly for weeks/months/years on a book only to learn that it's going to be presented to the world under a design you hate...)

Of course, the final decision is for the publishers to take – in consultation with JEA too, and he won't have seen it yet – but I very much hope we can go with this or something very like it.

After we met up in Bath the other day I sent James, the designer, the full manuscript of the book, and having now read it he has created this image. I'm so glad he was able to read the whole thing before we had to finalise the design; this isn't an image he could have come up with if he hadn't read the whole lot – it's not a moment of the book that's narratively important enough to make it into any synopsis or brief we could have given him, but nonetheless it's an incredibly powerful image, and one of the things I think will stick in readers' minds.

The fragment that prompted the image is Chapter 7 of 'Exile' (Book 4), a one-paragraph chapter, which currently reads as follows:

Blind airplanes bombarded the forests of the North for almost six weeks. In his desperate flight to Zaire, Tiago de Santiago da Ressureição André saw the villages devastated by the fury of the Portuguese, the rivers and forests devoured by napalm fire. Close to Nova Caipemba, he told me, they found a wood made entirely of unvarying ash, and within it a few huts also of ash, and inside the huts, mats and water jars; and a variety of utensils, all of ash. Fixed to the smallest branches of the trees were hundreds of little birds, also of dead ash, with their happy songs of rain crystallised at the tips of their beaks. The bombs of the Portuguese had frozen the passage of time over the wood, enclosing that anxious instant in a bell-jar of ashes. When a moment – a moment that everyone felt was never ending – had passed, someone raised his arm and with the tips of his fingers touched the fragile ash structure. Then the whole wood began to collapse, with a slow whisper of light rain, and with it the birds and the huts and the domestic utensils, and soon there was nothing around them but a broad plain of unchanging ash.

And here, in the pdf below, is James's suggested jacket. I hope you like it as much as I do. The colours, the tone, the fragile outlines, all seem to me to suit the book perfectly – and quite apart from that I think it's just very striking to look at. Do hope the others agree with me …

Post 22

The edit

In the week since I delivered the translation to Arcadia, it has had its first and most substantial edit; following this, it has now just been returned to me with queries. But the edit process for a translation is different from the edit process for an original-language text, though. This is essentially because one crucial stage is entirely missing.

You see, if I had written a novel I would be sending it in first-draft form to the publisher now, and my editor – probably the person who had commissioned it – would be in a position to make some pretty substantial comments. Chapter 17 isn't very interesting. You should expand the character of the lion-tamer. The ending with the failing parachute is very funny, but that whole section doesn't really link together yet. Consider cutting the dining-room scene (not funny); and maybe add a little to the dog-walking sequence in chapter 21, which is quite good but could be expanded a bit so it's not so lost between the much stronger hen-party and the Bible-salesmen vignettes. And have you thought the heroine should perhaps be a man instead? Or the whole thing might be narrated by Monty's fish?

. And then, when I had dutifully rewritten according to the editor's suggestions – or bravely argued that what I've done is better – only *then* would we get down to the copyedit, the line-by-line edit-and-polish.

With a translation it's different. The text – which has already been edited and published in other languages – may be a *translator's* first draft but is still considered fundamentally a stable thing, not a negotiable one (the plot / characters / sequence / dialogue / scenes / themes / paragraphs are fixed now just as they are, as they were at first publication, and neither the new publisher nor the translator can / should do anything about that). So the first sight the publishers get of the translation it goes straight into the line-by-line edit.

So that's what's been happening. Angeline has been through the text this week, reading it to see if it makes sense, to see if it sounds good, standardising things to the publisher's norms (single or double quotes, UK or US spelling, etc.), correcting things that are just wrong (any typos that have slipped through my own reading, spelling mistakes…), and raising with me any queries that come up during this polishing-up process. In one case I'm deferring to the author to solve a query I can't answer myself (I've just e-mailed JEA tonight to ask him – *aseptic* or *ascetic*?), but otherwise he has no part to play in this process. Indeed, unless he particularly wants to look at proofs, he has nothing to do but wait for the finished copy to turn up through his letterbox.

I've only had the briefest of scans over the main edited text itself, but Angeline has said she thought it read well and seems to have amended only with a very light touch (which I appreciate, obviously).

And once that light-touch edit was done, there were a total of twenty-something queries left for me to answer. They range from pointing out little things that sound odd (a word repeated within a couple of lines, perhaps) that I simply hadn't noticed; to suggesting slight improvements (this word is OK, but maybe that word would be better?; in this case relating to that pesky breast adjective again); to a question along the lines of 'Just checking, did you really mean this?'; to a slightly more dubious 'Something seems not quite right here…' when I've inexplicably missed some words out entirely…

Angeline is the book's first reader, so if a line isn't clear to her (it's not clear whom the locusts are fighting, exactly…) that's a good enough reason to consider changing it. More often than not her suggestions to rewrite involve tiny changes that make a dispropor- tionately big difference (add a comma here, change 'could' to 'must' there) and then it's easy enough for me to see that what she's sug- gesting is clearly an improvement. Occasionally I'll defend what I've done, usually justifying it by returning to the original (yes, I know it's a bit odd, but the comma's definitely correct here – it's definitely meant to be 'dark, red' rather than 'dark red').

Anyway, all extremely straightforward. Responding to all the queries took perhaps half an hour. And that's it – Angeline will incorporate the answers, including the one I expect from JEA tomorrow, and we may then exchange thoughts on a couple of things not quite resolved (there's a word I've used that doesn't actually exist, and she – quite unreasonably – wants me to stick to *real* words, and we may go another round over that one); but that's it – off to the typesetters it will go next week. Next stage, proofreading.

PS Thanks to the person who e-mailed me to say how much he loved the jacket design; I won't mention his name here because I want to be able to say (without getting anyone into trouble) that he also commented that the jacket design of his own new book (he's a translator) is *much* less attractive, and that even after some struggles with his publishers to change it. (He sent a couple of versions and I quite agree.) I think Agualusa and I both know how lucky we are. And I'm very glad you like it too.

Post 23

Rounding up

Now that things are coming to an end (sob...), I thought I ought to allow myself a post with a few musings about the blog itself (solipsistic, *moi*?).

I've avoided going back and re-reading my posts as I've gone along, to try and avoid it being too self-referential and to encourage it to be as closely as possible a true reflection of the translation work that was actually happening. (Even at the risk of asking questions I've never got round to answering, etc.) But I have no doubt that – in certain respects at least – the translation process has been affected by the blog. The thing itself redefined by the very fact of its being observed, as it were.

I don't mean that the translation text is massively different to what I would have produced unwatched – I suspect I would have ended up with mostly the same words. But the process of getting there has been changed in two ways, I think.

The first is just a logistical one – the timing has been affected. I might on a usual book rush through a translation in a matter of a few intensely busy weeks, and then do nothing on it for several months while I worked on something else, and then come back to it ages later for a polish, and then again nothing till proofs months after that. This time the process has been evened out, with a much more regular drip-drip attention, with some sort of progress most weeks, and only relatively brief periods of neglect; and even on a week without much progress to report I've thought about it at least enough to produce a post on something – to answer your e-mails, or to make some general points, or whatever. The shape of the work has been affected by the fact that, frankly, I thought if I did nothing for three months it'd be hard to expect anyone following this blog not to give up on it pretty quickly.

And the second change is to do with my awareness of what I'm doing. I think I said quite early on that most of the time I spend translating I'm not particularly deliberate, not particularly consciously aware of what I'm doing, of the choices I'm making, and so on. It has been odd obliging myself to change this habit – both making myself identify the issues as they arise (and not just go with the usual momentum and simply work straight through them without stopping to think consciously) and also making myself consider how this choice/problem might be articulated (especially to readers who may or not be Portuguese speakers, or indeed who may or not be professional translators themselves). It turns out that describing a process that happens in your head is difficult. I probably shouldn't be surprised by that.

So as I've said, I've not done much re-reading of old posts, so I don't know to what extent my attempts to describe the issues that have come up, the choices I've been obliged to make, have in fact been successful – whether they've evoked something that resembles my real experience of this wonderful job, or whether it's been largely baffling to anyone who isn't a translator, a Portuguese speaker, or ideally both.

When I set out on this blog I hoped it might get people thinking about what the process of translating a novel might consist of, and so ideally it might encourage readers to think about process whenever reading translations. It may or not have done that. I will be reading through all the past twenty-two posts this week and see what I think.

But casting my mind back now, I rather hope the blog has had another effect, too, which is to celebrate the quality of the original writing – every time I've raised some problem, whether obvious or subtle, in producing an English word or phrase, it is invariably a reflection of the sophistication, ambition and precision of what the original novel is doing. I don't know if I've said this before in the blog, but I admire Agualusa's writing hugely, and I do hope that this enthusiasm has come across in previous posts – and I hope it's helped to encourage some new readers to try him out too.

I'm always reluctant to read over my old writing – specially something like this which has been written pretty spur-of-the-moment and unedited – but I really do want to read over the whole sequence of posts now. The main reason is that Arcadia and I have talked about whether we might publish the whole of this blog as a sort of appendix to the book. It's an interesting idea, I think – a sort of Translator's Diary, which you'd read having read the translation itself. If we do it, I think it would only work if it is just as it's appeared here on the site, not edited or adapted or polished – a record of the translation process (and the blogging process too, I guess) that reflects all the start-stop of the process, the repetitions, the unproductive morning when I missed my plane, the problems whose solutions I was honestly never quite satisfied with, and of course the contributions from those of you kind enough to write in with comments, questions and suggestions.

So I'll read it all through this week, as I say, and if it seems to make some approximate sense, it will go into the book.

[Obviously you may already be reading this in the book, in which case you'll know what we decided, and you can give a wry smile as you appreciate the real meta-something nature of this whole section. (Meta-*what* – anyone?)]

Anyway, we're nearly there. The draft is complete, my doubts have been resolved, the editor's queries answered, the text should also be set now ready for proofing, and a great jacket designed and agreed. We will probably proofread this week, and then off to the printers. I'll let you know when that's happened, when my work on this book is finally done!

And just a mention: my only other related task this week is to start reading JEA's just-completed new novel which he has e-mailed me (it's out in Portuguese next month, I think) and about which he's very enthusiastic; if it's as good as it sounds my next step is to write a report about it to suggest to Arcadia that we get started on that one next, now that *Rainy Season* (Arcadia's Agualusa book 4) is about to be put to bed. It's called *Barroco Tropical*. So – for our book 5, in 2010 – how's *Tropical Baroque* as a title?

Post 24

The Last Post

First of all, a quick thanks for the latest round of comments – this time including a couple of translators from French (one working on a book about 'revolution and rebellion', which sounds fun...) and an expert in lipsynch translation (how hard must that be?), a children's books enthusiast and someone who I think was trying to sell me something. An e-mail from a friend who thought the cover design good but not commercial ('needs more depth, or more colour, and better type to be commercial'). And Jess who made the connection between our old friend the 'chigoe flea' and what was called a 'chigger' in the southern US. (According to Jess's mum it is extremely itchy indeed.)

I've read over the proofs this weekend, making mainly tiny changes and a few layout suggestions, but really had very little to do – they're looking good. I did have to re-italicise a few things that had lost their formatting, and I rephrased a couple of lines I somehow didn't quite like the sound of. And I also spotted the place where somehow by accident the 'two oildrums' had been transformed into 'two praying-mantiss', which conjured up a very distressing image indeed. But that was the worst of it – and it's now back with Arcadia for tinkering with and sending to press.

Reading the proofs also gave me the chance to read over the whole blog, about which I had rather mixed feelings. There are several moments when I said something like 'I'll deal with that in a later post' and then never did; and there's a fair bit of repetition (how many times did I start a post with 'Working on other things this week so not much to report...'?), but I'm hoping that that wasn't too noticeable for those of you reading it week by week rather than in a single burst. (Apologies, then, to anyone reading it in the book...) Most interesting for me was rereading the questions and opinions from those of you good enough to write in, so thank you again for those. It's made this normally solitary process unusually collegial, and I've enjoyed that aspect of it very much indeed.

So... presses will roll shortly, then the books will be on the shelves, with those communist puns sorted and all those poems and song lyrics more-or-less-sorted, and a few still outstanding niggling doubts I'm just trying to ignore, and plenty of the finally-christened Low-Slung Annie (I do like how that sounds, actually), and those disappointingly inconsistent chapter heads, and the parrots and the chickens and the broken ducks, at least three pairs of firm breasts, the sons of a war and the hearts of the p–, a place that is possibly called Mayday Square, and various tones and compromises and voices and jokes, all under that lovely jacket design. Very pleasing.

And so here we are. Thanks again to James S for his constant hospitality on this site, as we've made our erratic journey over these past seven months. And to those of you who've made it this far, thank you for the company along the way.